Ice Ice Baby

CARLY ROBYN

Ice Ice Baby

Published by Blue Dog Press

Cover Art by Melucia Art

This is a work of fiction. Names, characters, places, and incidents are products of the author's imagination or are used fictitiously. Any resemblance to actual events, locales, organizations, or persons, living or dead, is entirely coincidental.

No part of this book may be reproduced in any form or by any electronic or mechanical means, including information storage and retrieval systems, without written permission from the author, except for the use of brief quotations in a book review.

ISBN: 979-8-9890722-0-0

*For every reader who's ever fallen a little too hard for a fictional man.
And for anyone still waiting for the real thing. You're not behind.
You're just on a different chapter.*

playlist

Heartbreak Hotel | Abigail Barlow
You Put A Spell On Me | Austin Giorgio
Before You Leave Me | Alex Warren
The First Time | Damiano David
Give Your Heart a Break | Demi Lovato
Power Over Me | Dermot Kennedy
Love Of My Life | Harry Styles
Only Love Can Hurt Like This | Paloma Faith
Love Me Not | Raven Lean
Wildest Dreams | Taylor Swift
Something Just Like This | The Chainsmokers
Happy Together | The Turtles
Ice Ice Baby | Vanilla Ice

author's note

Ice Ice Baby is written in a light and humorous style but does include explicit language, references to the death of a sibling (past, off-page), and absent parents. It's a slow-burn, open-door romance that portrays sexual content and is meant for readers 18+. Please take note!

The focus of this work is on the fictional characters and events within the NHL world, and deviations from the current schedule are intentional for storytelling purposes.

"I LOOK MASSIVE IN THIS PHOTO." Logan frowns. "And not in a sexy lumberjack way. Seriously, out of all our team shots, they had to choose this one?"

I roll my eyes to the heavens. The blown-up team photo isn't the most flattering, but then again, no one looks good after playing three grueling periods in a championship game. In it, I've got blood streaking down my chin—thanks to an elbow to the face—Cameron practically sparkles with sweat, Jake's beard is giving full caveman energy, and yes, Logan, buried in his pads and gear, could easily pass for Bigfoot's long-lost cousin.

But it's hockey. What does he expect?

Jake, our best right-winger and one of my closest friends, eyes Logan, then assesses the photo again, as if he's giving the comment real thought.

I silently beg him to keep his mouth shut. The last thing anyone needs is Logan's vanity acting up any more than it usually does. While the rest of our team travels with a duffel or a small carry-on, he rolls up with a full-size suitcase filled with skincare products and essential oils. He takes bubble baths after post-game ice baths.

"You look fine," I reassure him. "Same as always."

He squints at me. "So you think I always look large and in charge?"

I bite back a scoff. *Lord, give me strength.*

"Pads and protective gear make every hockey player look bulky." Jake's tone is placating, though he turns away and rolls his eyes. "You don't have an ounce of fat on you, dude. Relax."

"How do you know that?" Logan asks, chin lifted and jaw clenched. "Have you been checking me out in the locker room?"

"Don't be a perv," Cameron fires back.

Before Logan can fire off a comeback, Jake clasps his shoulder. "Why don't we go make our rounds, gentleman? Booze and schmooze?"

Cameron scans the crowd, his forest-green eyes narrowed, like he's bracing for a natural disaster—ever the antisocial grump—while Logan hops in place like a squirrel who's just discovered espresso.

I place a hand on each of their backs and give a firm shove. "Let's go."

We make our way through the room, weaving between clusters of Boston's elite, our sponsors, and a sprinkling of friends and family. Here and there, I greet familiar faces, my professional persona flicking to life on its own as I talk about the upcoming season, my words practically scripted. *Our defense is looking sharp. Strategy's solid. The new offensive line should give us more flexibility in transition.*

We've been schmoozing for less than an hour when someone brings him up.

"Your brother would be proud of you."

I force a tight smile at the sponsor I'm chatting with. His

expression is kind, but there's a softness behind it, a look akin to pity that makes my chest tighten. "Mm-hmm."

"It's wild that your parents raised two hockey legends," he continues, as if he has any right to speak about my twin. "Nate was one of the best left-wingers the sport's ever seen."

"Yup." I grip my glass so tightly I'm surprised it doesn't shatter.

I'm glad that my brother's memory lives on, truly. And yes, the sport lost a legend, but I lost my brother and best friend. The two aren't comparable. They never will be.

Jake, likely sensing the subtle shift in my body language, jumps in, steering the conversation toward the Chicago Patriots' new defenseman.

When the sponsor's attention drifts his way, I mutter an excuse and step away. If I don't, there's a chance I'll say something I'll regret.

As much as I love the start of the season, it feels wrong not shit-texting my brother about whose team is going to beat whose ass. Before Nate passed away three years ago, the Berrett brothers dominated the sport with a combined three Stanley Cup wins. Nate repped the Miami Trailblazers, and I wore the Boston Bobcats' blue, but he was my biggest fan and I was his. Our dream was to one day suit up together for our hometown team, the San Diego Devils. We made the pact when we were six, lacing up our skates side by side. Now that it's just me, I have to work twice as hard to leave a legacy for us.

Needing a breather and a chance to shake off that conversation, I head to the bar. As the bartender pours me another drink, I turn, scanning the room, the toe of my velvet dress shoe tapping against the black marble floor. The DJ is set up on one side of the room, and a good chunk of guests dance on a black-and-white checkered floor. Others are huddled at high tops, mingling and sipping on craft cocktails. I continue my perusal until I catch sight of a hidden alcove off to the side. *Bingo.* Hiding out with my drink isn't the most mature move, but I need a moment of peace to collect myself.

As I step into the hidden nook, I find it already occupied. Curled up on the navy velvet couch nestled in the corner is a brunette with a cocktail in one hand and... an e-reader in the other.

She's literally reading. At a party.

I'm not sure whether I should be offended. Sure, this isn't the Grammys, but it's an invite-only party, not a quiet Sunday afternoon at home.

I cough subtly to announce my presence. Rather than flinch, she holds up a finger in a "one second" gesture, her eyes never leaving the device.

As I bring my glass to my lips, I fight back a grin. I can't remember the last time someone dismissed me so casually. Maybe high school.

A minute or two later, she glances up, and when I get a good look at her, I nearly stumble back. Damn, she's gorgeous. Her beauty isn't flashy. It's not the kind that'll stop men in their tracks. No, it's the understated kind that sneaks up on a person. Her heart-shaped face is smooth and creamy and complemented by deep brown hair that cascades down her shoulders in loose curls. Add in the black dress hugging her curvy figure, and she's my walking wet dream.

"Hi. Sorry, did you say something?" she asks, head tilted.

I shake my head and gesture to the empty space beside her. "Mind if I sit?"

There's no trace of recognition or excitement in her midnight-blue eyes as she gives me a once-over; just pure, genuine confusion, like she can't comprehend why I want to join her. Eventually, though, she gives me a small shrug and a polite smile. "Go ahead."

I take my time getting settled, racking my brain for a conversation starter. Asking why she's holed up in a corner reading at a party feels too accusatory, so I go with the safest, most boring question known to man: "What're you drinking?"

Because the three coffee beans floating in the glass don't scream espresso martini or anything. Good one, Cole.

"Espresso martini." She takes a small sip, watching me over the rim. Nodding toward my rocks glass, she asks, "Whiskey?"

"The one and only," I confirm.

She nibbles on her bottom lip, her eyes searching for a moment, before asking, "Did you know that during Prohibition, physicians could write prescriptions for medicinal whiskey?"

A bolt of surprise mixed with satisfaction hits me. It's rare I speak to a perfect stranger who doesn't lead with a hockey question or some version of *are you ready for the season?* "No, I didn't know that."

Lips pressed together, she nods. "I read a book a few weeks ago that took place during Prohibition. One of the main characters worked for a pharmacy that prescribed whiskey as a treatment for everything from indigestion to cancer. He got caught up with some mafia-type people who ran speakeasies across the city. I'm sure you can guess how that went."

I flash her an amused smile. "My whiskey and mafia knowledge come mostly from *Peaky Blinders* and the *Godfather*."

She lets loose a raspy laugh. "*The Godfather* was actually a book before it was a movie. So was *Goodfellas*."

Ah. The e-reader is starting to make more sense. "Yeah?"

"Yep. Most good movies were books first. *Forrest Gump, Jurassic Park, Fight Club, Call Me By Your Name*. And those aren't even the obvious ones like *Lord of the Rings* and *Little Women*."

I take a sip of my drink, letting the liquid fire soothe me, and nod toward the device in her hands. "I take it you're a big reader?"

She glances down, grimacing a little, as if I caught her doing something naughty. "Mm-hmm. I wasn't planning to bring this bad boy tonight, but one of my favorite authors surprise-dropped a new release. Figured if I'm not the Bobcats' target audience, missing some of the party isn't that big of a deal."

I arch my brows. "Why'd you come, then?"

"Blackmail sounds dramatic," she says with a guilty shrug, "but my best friend threatened to dog-ear my books if I didn't attend. She's the one who made the massive puck-shaped cake everyone's talking about, so I'm here to support her."

I nearly choke on my drink. "Dog-earing pages, huh? That's serious stuff. You must really not like hockey."

"It's not that I don't like hockey," she says, wrinkling her nose. "I just don't understand it. I don't know how anyone can follow the puck. It's microscopic. Everyone is moving so fast; it's impossible to figure out what the hell is going on half the time. And the fighting is brutal. I witnessed more than my fair share of coked-out frat boys wrestling during my college days. I don't really need to rewatch it on TV, you know?"

Before I can stop it, a deep laugh bursts from my chest.

She cringes. "Shit. You probably work for the team or something like that, don't you?"

The use of the word *work* instead of *play* confirms my suspicion. She genuinely has no idea who I am. If she did, there's no way she would've just referred to me as a coked-out frat boy. "Something like that," I confirm simply.

I don't tell her my name. I don't tell her that I'm the team's center. The anonymity is refreshing. When people discover who I am, they treat me differently. They behave differently, whether it's out of jealousy, respect, or lust. I'm no longer Cole. I'm Nicholas Berrett, the NHL superstar. Because hockey is such a key part of my personal identity, it's rare that I get to be myself with someone I've just met.

"I do like sports romances, though." Her smile is sweet, as if she has no clue that her comment about hockey just shredded a tiny bit of my soul. "If that helps at all."

A scoff escapes me. "Before my brain implodes from your *very* incorrect opinion of hockey, please explain how reading about a sport is better than *watching* the sport."

She throws her head back and sighs, as if answering my question will cost her precious moments that she'll never get back. "Because the authors don't dedicate entire chapters to sixty-minute halves where no one scores." She smirks, her eyes sparkling. "Well, someone may score, but in the biblical sense, not athletic."

Head hanging, I give it a shake. There isn't a sport in existence with hour-long halves. *Dear God.*

We sip our drinks while arguing the finer points of athletics. She's not ignorant about sports in general, she just really doesn't care. She's lived in Boston her whole life but has never attended a single professional sports game. And damn if that isn't refreshing.

"What's your favorite sports romance?" I ask. "Maybe I'll check it out."

I won't, but her eyes light up, which was the reaction I was going for. I listen intently as she chatters on about a soccer romance where the star player dates the coach's daughter. I didn't expect a whole SparkNotes version of the book when I asked, but the way she discusses tropes and character arcs and something called the third-act breakup has me rapt.

I truly can't remember the last time I was interested in spending time with a woman. I've spent my whole life focused on hockey, which doesn't leave room for much more. If I had to do it over again, I wouldn't change the choices I've made, but I don't particularly enjoy that I've become the cliché sports player who's married to the game. Especially as my childhood friends are getting married and starting that "next chapter" of their lives. My next chapter has always just been hockey, my happily ever after a spot with the San Diego Devils.

"What do you do for work?" I ask. "Please tell me it has something to do with books."

She flashes me a mischievous smile that has my balls tightening in my slacks. "I'm actually Punxsutawney Phil's travel agent, believe it or not."

Her expression and tone are so deadpan that I genuinely can't tell whether she's kidding.

Before I can confirm, a figure storms into the alcove and growls, "For the love of the original cast of *Hamilton*, if you're in here with your—"

The interloper catches sight of me and snaps her mouth shut. The way her eyes widen is a dead giveaway that at least one of the women in this alcove recognizes me. Her dark blond hair swishes against her back as she looks from me to my companion and back again, brow furrowed.

"Sorry, hi," she says, snapping out of her confused trance. "I did *not* mean to interrupt... this. When I couldn't find you, I figured you'd snuck off somewhere to read, but..." She waves a hand at me. "I can see I was mistaken."

The woman beside me brushes my arm as she covertly slides the e-reader behind my back. "I would *never* do something so antisocial. This is a party, for God's sake, not a book club, Kennedy."

"No reading here," I confirm with a nod. "Just quality conversation."

Clearly, this is a common occurrence, and I kind of like that I'm partnering up with her to cover up her crime.

"Ah, well, I'll just be on my way then," the newcomer—Kennedy—replies with a mega-watt smile and eyebrow waggle. "Continue on with your... quality conversation."

Her tone drips with innuendo, making the phrase sound absurdly sexual, which makes my mystery reader's cheeks turn redder than a tomato.

For a moment, she doesn't move, like she's stunned. But when she snaps out of it, she hurriedly shoves her e-reader into her purse and stands.

"I should go find her." Her eyes move to mine, and she gives me a shy smile. "It was nice talking to you…"

"Cole," I supply.

"Maya," she responds on her way out. "Enjoy your whiskey, Cole."

It hasn't been *that* long since I got laid, so why the hell does my name on her tongue send very explicit images through my mind?

I'm so caught off guard by my body's reaction that it doesn't even occur to me that I should've asked for her number, or Instagram handle, or quite literally anything. *Fuck.*

I knock back the rest of my whiskey and stand. As I leave the alcove, I survey the room, but she's nowhere to be seen. It's ironic, this situation. This woman who loves a good story has gone ahead and turned our meeting into a real-life *Cinderella* scenario. I may not have her shoe, but I've got her name, and that's all the information I need to find out who she is.

CHAPTER TWO

THERE'S nothing better than the smell of books. The almond and vanilla tang is better than any perfume, freshly baked cake, or bouquet of flowers. The instant I step into the Book Nook, I'm surrounded by it. Shoulder-high bookshelves divide the store into sections and line the walls. New releases occupy the endcaps, and top sellers and timeless classics adorn square tables scattered throughout the space. Tucked away in the back are comfy reading chairs, where customers can curl up with a book in one hand and a coffee in the other.

The owner of the store went prematurely gray last year when we added a counter for coffee and pastries. For months, each clank of the hammer and whir of the power drill were a personal affront to her existence. But the new setup draws in fresh faces. While our prime location gives us constant foot traffic, we can always use a little extra boost in an industry that's increasingly digital. And having a best friend who knows the best bakers in town is a bonus, since her pastry connections have the bookstore smelling like a dream every morning. Not even Blythe can deny that freshly baked cinnamon rolls and Danishes add to the store's welcoming atmosphere.

I take a sip of my large Boston Bean coffee and survey the store, relishing how quickly the warm liquid fights off the haze of exhaustion. Sunday shifts always suck, especially after being out late the night before. The three espresso martinis I put away had me up until three a.m., and that's enough to turn anyone into a grouch. So here I am, bleary-eyed and far from bushy tailed.

The morning passes by in a blur. A small group of college-age girls wander in with hot chocolates, and we chat about cowboy romances before they leave with a couple of steamy novels and a new historical fiction pick. I recommend a few sci-fi books to a pair of twin boys who—according to their mother—are addicted to video games and need to put their brains to good use. After I had to gently explain to them that while aspects of science fiction could be based in fact, they were not replacements for their science textbooks, I agree.

I'm pricing new merchandise in the back office when Katrina, my assistant manager, pops her head in to tell me I have a visitor.

Before I can ask who it is, she's hurried off again. *Okay, then.*

I make my way to the front of the store, dusting off my hands. But I stop dead in my tracks when I catch sight of my visitor. Hovering over the round table that houses our staff picks and recommendations is Nicholas Berrett. Yep. The two-time Stanley Cup winner and star center of the Boston Bobcats. I thought he looked familiar last night, but I chalked it up to alcohol and his insanely good looks. Because this man is seriously gorgeous enough to be on the cover of one of my spicy romance books. It wasn't until Kennedy nearly had a panic attack after finding us talking that I learned "Cole" is actually Nicholas.

There's no way he just happened to wander into the Book Nook. Especially when he more or less admitted that he hasn't read anything other than the directions on a bottle of laundry detergent in the past year.

So why the hell is he here?

I will myself to focus on that question instead of how good he looks. Because damn, does he look incredible. His espresso-colored locks fall over his forehead in a way that's too sexy to be accidental and his jeans and jacket hug his toned body, making it obvious that he sees the value in both arm day and leg day.

How I carried on a normal conversation with him rather than stare at him like a love-struck teenager is beyond me. Because men as beautiful as he is—especially famous athletes —don't come around often. And if they do, they're not coming around for me.

Swallowing the knot of nerves building in my throat, I take a steadying breath and make myself walk over to him.

"Anything catching your eye?" I greet him, praying I come across as cool and casual. Internally, my stomach flips like it's training for the Olympics. I'm about five seconds away from becoming a gold medalist.

At the sound of my voice, he looks up, and a slow, easy smile spreads across his face. It sends a shot of adrenaline straight to my lady bits. He's just as muscular and manly as I remember, with a jawline that's likely sharper than his skates.

"Most definitely," he replies, wearing a smirk.

I ignore the pointed comment and gesture to the book in his hand. "So you're into alien smut?"

Cole flings *Mated to the Alien Mercenary* onto the table like it's a hot potato. "What?" His eyes go wide and he stumbles back a step. "No. I don't read... alien, uh, whatever."

"Don't knock it till you try it." I bite back a smile at his awkwardness. "Openly reading smut is part of the newest wave of feminism."

Cole has already composed himself. So much so that he

shoots me a wink that should be cheesy but somehow lands dangerously close to charming. The way his amber eyes sear into mine like they're cataloging my every reaction has me blushing like I forgot to put on SPF before a day at Franklin Park. "Please enlighten me about this smut you speak of, Maya."

"Maybe another time, Cole." Eyes narrowed, I cock my head. "Or should I say... Nicholas?"

The dimple in his right cheek softens his sharp features marginally as he holds up his hands in apology. "I'm sorry; but it's rare that someone doesn't recognize me. All my close friends do call me Cole, though. I only go by Nicholas professionally."

Scrunching up my toes in my boots, I shrug it off. I've learned from my mother that the omission of the truth can be as harmful as a lie, but his explanation makes sense. I didn't sense any underlying motive then, and I don't now. "Apology accepted."

"And in my defense, you told me you were a travel agent," he says, his grin firmly in place, "to a weather-forecasting groundhog."

A compulsion to flee hits me hard. When the memory surfaces, I want nothing more than to hide under one of the reading tables in the back. I've never hated that weird habit of mine until now. My throat closes up, so though I don't dart away, all I can do is stare at him dumbly, which only adds to my mortification. At least I didn't tell him I was a paranormal bounty hunter who sells rare *Twilight* paraphernalia on the side.

"Hmm." He picks up *Mated to the Alien Mercenary* again and lazily thumbs through the pages. "I shouldn't have been surprised when I found out you worked at a bookstore, considering you brought your e-reader to a party."

Nerves skitter through me. "It's no different from people bringing an emotional support dog with them to a party," I blurt, like that's a completely normal and valid comparison. "So you shouldn't take it personally."

Did I just imply I have an emotional support e-reader?

"Fair," he concedes, his lips twitching, "but I *do* take it personally that you think so poorly of hockey." He slips a hand into his pocket and pulls out two tickets like he's a magician revealing that he's had my card all along. The right side is emblazoned with the Bobcats' blue and gray logo. There's a barcode on the left, and in bold black font, the words *Reserved Club-Level* are spelled out. "These are for you."

I frown down at the tickets. *Why is he giving these to me?* Gingerly taking them from his hand, I force my expression to morph into something resembling a smile. "Thank you." *I think?*

He grins at my lackluster response. "Don't get too excited, My."

I don't comment on the over-familiar nickname, even as my heart thuds against my breastbone. "Of course I'm excited. Do you know how much money I'll get when I resell these online? I'm about to pay off my credit card and treat myself to dinner."

His smile falls, turning into what can only be described as a pout. An annoyingly adorable, offensively cute pout. No man over six feet with stubble should be capable of pouting like that.

"I'm kidding," I reassure him with a laugh.

The edge of his lips quirks up. "Come to the game. We'll grab a drink after, and I can answer any questions you have about what the hell happened on the ice."

I haven't been asked out in person since the invention of dating apps, which I haven't bothered to redownload since I ended things with my ex, but that doesn't mean I don't recognize that flicker of interest in his eyes.

I am, however, mildly confused as to why it's there. He's so far out of my league, it's borderline pathetic. Just looking at him ruins all other men for me, and we've done nothing but talk.

"Oh. That's… well, that's an interesting proposal."

"It's tickets to a game, not an engagement ring." He shoots me a lazy grin.

Warmth creeps up my neck and into my cheeks. Though I take a step back to create some space between us, I keep my chin lifted and my tone nonchalant. "Are drinks included with these tickets?"

"Are you negotiating your attendance?"

"If I was, my lawyer would be here." I cross my arms over my chest in mock defiance. "Although if you are open to negotiations, I wouldn't mind if nachos were on the table as well."

He licks his lips, those amber eyes glinting. "If I provide you not only with seats but with nachos and unlimited alcohol, you'll come to the game? It's a private box, by the way."

I bite my lower lip as I pretend to think about it. All the while, my heart is leaping all over the place. Eventually, I nod once.

"I've never had to convince someone to attend a hockey game." He runs a hand through his hair, his expression full of humor.

"You've also never read alien smut," I point out.

This earns me a laugh that makes me melt like a stick of butter. It's official. I'm a puddle on the floor.

While Cole doesn't purchase the book he originally picked up, he does buy a collector's edition of *Grimm's Complete Fairy Tales*. It's a beautifully designed tome, with bonded-leather binding and distinctive gilt edging, so I make sure to wrap it carefully.

The moment he exits the shop, I power-walk—because I refuse to run unless I'm being chased—to the back of the store and video call Kennedy.

Her pearly white teeth fill half the screen almost instantaneously. There's a smudge of flour or baking powder on her left cheek and her honey-blond hair is tied up in a messy bun. My best friend only succumbs to the messy bun look when she's in the throes of a new recipe. As her favorite test subject, I'd usually ask what she's working on, but my mind is too preoccupied.

"Guess who just showed up at the store?" Before she can answer, I hold up my hand. "It's rhetorical, Kennedy. You know Cole showed up here because you told him where I worked."

Eyes dancing, she licks some type of batter off a spoon. "It wasn't rhetorical because I didn't know he'd do that. And technically I didn't tell him. I merely passed along some basic info on where, when, and how to find 'someone named Maya' when asked."

"You cannot just—"

"Don't get mad at me for hyping you up as any good bestie would." She flashes me a smile that's anything but innocent.

After twenty years of friendship, I know this look all too well. She gave it to me when we met on the first day of second grade, when she tried to charm me into trading erasers—her green one for my sparkly purple one. It was obviously a shit deal. Even eight-year-old me knew that. I told her to shove it up her ass in a way that was much more age appropriate. Her response? She giggled and announced we were best friends. We have been ever since. Although I'm debating the merit of such friendship right about now.

"He gave me tickets to his game," I tell her, not bothering to hide the utter skepticism in my voice. "They're box seats."

I can't figure out his angle. Is it because I said I didn't like hockey? Or that I didn't fall all over myself when I realized what he does for a living? I've been told by almost every ex that I'm ball-breakingly stubborn, so maybe he sees me as a challenge and is trying to break through my indifference just to prove he can.

"Anything else? Did he ask you for a kidney? Threaten to throw you out of a window? Trick you into giving him your social security number?"

Frowning, I zero in on her. "Well, uh, no."

"Then stop being so suspicious."

"Yeah, but—"

"No buts." She levels me with a look that means she's not fucking around. "He wants to get to know you better. Let him. It's a damn hockey game. Nothing more, nothing less. Bring your brother and enjoy the VIP experience."

After a pregnant pause, I sigh, exhaling the questions still floating around in my head. "Fine. But I'm bringing a book in case I get bored."

The tension drops away from the corners of her eyes. Chuckling under her breath, she says, "I'd be worried if you didn't."

CHAPTER THREE

STANDING outside Airwave Arena three nights later, I shift my weight from side to side, shivering. I thought I'd be fine in a light jacket, but as the fall winds wrap themselves around me in a frigid hug, I'm seriously regretting my decision. I could wait for my brother inside, but I'm not in the mood to be bounced around in the crowds of people.

My fingers have turned to icicles by the time I spy Elliott's tall frame. He's only twenty-two, but his height and the stubble dusting his jaw make him look older than me.

As he steps up to me, I sink into his hug, happy to steal a little of his body heat. "Hi, E."

Elliott chuckles and tightens his hold, tucking my head under his chin. "Sorry I'm late, Yaya. My meeting ran long."

The childhood nickname sits warmly in my chest, and I forgive him for his tardiness and for my frozen toes. As a toddler, Elliott couldn't pronounce Maya, but he attached to the last syllable of my name. Ya blossomed into Yaya, and he's called me that ever since.

"How are things at work?" I ask as we push through the thick wooden doors of the arena.

"Very busy." He gives me a small smile, but it can't hide the bags under his eyes that weren't there the last time I saw him. "But I like my manager, and the people on my team are nice so far."

Since he started working at one of the big Boston finance firms, I don't see him nearly enough. I'm proud of him for landing such a great job straight out of school, but he works an insane number of hours, which, of course, makes me worry. I've taken care of my siblings since we were kids. When our mom went on her extended vacations with whomever she was dating that month and left us with nannies, babysitters, or random friends, I was their constant. The one who gave them at least a semblance of family and home.

I went to all of Elliott's baseball games and sat through Ava's countless dance competitions. I taught my brother how to parallel park and bought my sister her first box of tampons. And even though they're both legal adults, I can't help but worry about them. I can't help but stress about whether my brother's happy at his job, and there's no stopping the fretting I do over Ava, who's a college freshman still working to balance coffee-fueled study sessions and booze-fueled parties.

"Are you getting enough sleep?" I ask as we walk by the museum-like displays that house memorabilia.

Cole better not have been kidding about the nachos; the aroma of fried foods coming from the concession stands as we pass tempts me to join one of the long lines.

"Yes, so stop stressing out." Elliott nudges me with his elbow and lifts a brow. "And don't deny it. You're giving me devil horns."

With a huff, I smooth out my brow. According to my siblings, my brows crease when I'm overwhelmed or anxious, creating two lines that resemble little devil horns. *Whatever*.

"Seriously, Yaya. I'm good." He flashes a boyish grin. "If

anyone should be stressed about a sibling, it's me. You haven't said two words about Josh. Are *you* okay?"

His tone is gentle, like I'm a deer he's trying not to spook.

"There's nothing to say. I'm fine." I lift a shoulder in a casual shrug. "Thanks for asking, though."

My relationship with Josh never got too serious—I didn't let it—but his cheating still stung. It wasn't his loss that hurt. It was how it made me feel. As if I wasn't worth staying for in the first place. Proof once again that book boyfriends are better than the real thing.

Elliott opens his mouth to argue, his expression fierce. Instead, he deflates, sighing loudly. "So where are our seats? I can't believe you, of all people, wanted to go to a hockey game. I didn't even think you knew Boston had a team."

"Okay, rude." I give him a very abbreviated rundown of how I met Cole, conveniently leaving out the part where he showed up at the bookstore with tickets. No need to give him anything to overanalyze.

By the time the elevator doors open on the club level, Elliott's beside himself with excitement. Apparently, two tickets to a hockey game are all it takes to go from overbearing sister to cool friend. Go figure.

"Do we just go in?" Nerves skittering through me, I wipe my sweaty palms on my jeans and peer down the wide hallway. With the patterned oriental carpet under our feet and the sleek walls filled with eclectic art, it feels more like a boutique hotel than an arena.

Elliott rolls his eyes. "No, we have to perform an Irish jig and solve three riddles first."

My brother and I may look nothing alike, but when his sarcasm comes out to play, there's no doubt we're 100 percent related. Well, 50 percent, I guess. Different dads and all that.

Before I can hit him with a smart-ass reply, the door to our private suite swings open. An Airwave Arena employee who looks like Batman's butler scans our tickets, then silently escorts us into the room.

Two walls are dominated by sleek flat-screen TVs, despite the incredible view of the ice from our club-level seats, which are plush and far more comfortable than I would have expected. We sink into them as modern-day Alfred Pennyworth launches into a rundown of the room's amenities. In-seat dining from a chef-curated menu. Access to some ultra-exclusive club. A mixologist serving craft cocktails. It's all so over-the-top. Cole may regret his choice to seat us up here when his plan backfires because I'm too distracted to actually watch the game.

Pennyworth takes his leave—after letting us know which button to press to summon him, of course—but the door opens again moments later. A woman wearing an oversized Bobcats jersey steps in, a small smile on her lips. With her big ocean-blue eyes, pale blond hair, and high, delicate cheekbones, she looks like a Polly Pocket doll come to life.

Her steps falter a bit as her gaze lands on Elliott and me, but she quickly recovers, donning a small smile and striding our way. Stopping beside my seat, she says, "Hi. I'm Sophie."

Her introduction is pleasant enough, though there's a subtle uncertainty just below the surface, like she's unsure of how she'll be received.

"I'm Maya." I give her a small wave. "And this is my brother Elliott."

Taking his eyes off the ice where the teams are warming up, Elliott smiles. "Nice to meet you, Sophie."

"You, too." Her response is aimed at him, but she's still focused on me, her expression full of curiosity. "I, um, heard Cole invited someone. He usually only brings family, so I wanted to introduce myself. Do you mind if I ask how you two met?"

I uncross then recross my legs, trying to ignore the hint of unease that swirls in my belly at the scrutiny. "At the Bobcats opening party thingy. We're... friends."

Friends is probably a generous term. He's more of an acquaintance. *Man I want to ride like a cowboy* is definitely the most honest, though it's the least appropriate answer.

"How do you know him?" I brace myself for her response. Is this Cole's thing? Lure multiple women into a private box and then make them duke it out like they're in an episode of *The Bachelor*? Because if so, she can have him.

She nods at one of the TVs in the suite. A camera is zoomed in on a player with the number 35 emblazoned on his jersey. The ticker at the bottom of the screen reads *Cameron Davies*. "That's my brother."

I blink, hit with a mix of surprise and relief. And maybe embarrassment over my brief burst of jealousy.

The screen shifts to another player—Logan Clark, according to the caption. He's got the sun-kissed California surfer thing going on with his shaggy blond hair and bright blue eyes.

"He's hot," Elliott murmurs, barely loud enough for me to hear.

My brother and I don't usually have the same type, but even I can agree that blondie is objectively hot. Especially with his "fuck around and find out" smile.

With the whole reality-show scenario officially off the table, I relax a little. Sophie sits beside me, and the two of us fall into easy conversation as the players stretch and warm up. When she mentions she's going to the bar after the game, I sigh a breath of relief. I'm not exactly nervous about seeing Cole again, but I'm guarded. I can't tell what he wants, and as someone with enough trust issues to send their therapist to therapy, that puts me on edge.

By the time the puck drops, Sophie and I have followed each

other on Instagram. I've picked up details about hockey from reading romance books, but without Sophie explaining the finer points of line changes and penalties, I'd be lost.

It's a challenge to focus on the game when Cole's on the ice. He moves with a fierce grace that makes me warm, despite the chill of the arena. Every time he jumps the boards and backs onto the ice, I find myself ignoring my nachos in favor of standing and cheering alongside the cacophony in the stands.

The game is full of nonstop action, and I don't have to be a hockey fan to recognize Cole's talent. He hurtles toward the other team's goalie like it's his life mission, and every time the puck races into the net, I'm on my feet screaming like I'm at a sold-out concert. I thought Cole was attractive before, but seeing him in his element adds a whole new level to his appeal.

It's only once he scores the winning goal for the Bobcats that I realize I haven't even touched the book buried in my bag.

CHAPTER FOUR

IF MY TEAMMATES are surprised that I'm out after a game, they do their best to hide it. It's not that I don't like celebrating our wins or commiserating over our losses. It's just that I'm in bed by ten unless we have a late game. During what little free time I have, I'm typically too tired to do anything but sleep or lounge around. I tend to turn down plans if there's a chance they could interfere with my sleep or training schedule.

Tonight? I didn't just say yes to these plans, I initiated them.

The moment I step onto the semi-sticky bar floor of O'Leary's, the team's go-to bar, I'm met by a crush of regulars. The TVs are all playing games, each a different sport. Guinness flows like water, and the whole place hums like a quintessential Irish pub.

As I weave my way to the back of the bar, I spy Maya sitting with Cameron, his younger sister Sophie, and a guy I don't recognize. A guy I instantly dislike, purely because of his clear familiarity with Maya. Her dark brown hair is tied back with a hot pink scrunchie that clashes horribly with the Bobcats' gray and blue color scheme. Not that it matters, since Maya isn't wearing team colors. Just a black sweater and jeans.

Ignoring the teammates jostling to get my attention, I head over to the high top where she's parked.

As I approach, the mystery man greets me with a welcoming smile. "Hey, man. Great game."

I level him with a blank stare. He's objectively good-looking: dimples, stubble, the works. Logan thinks so too, based on the way he's not so slyly checking him out from across the bar.

Cameron elbows me in the ribs, and I snap out of my one-sided glaring contest.

"Thanks," I grind out, turning to Maya. "Hey. I'm glad you made it."

"We shook on it." The smile she gives me is infectious, her dark blue eyes glinting. "And I'd never miss out on nachos."

The guy nods a little too enthusiastically. "The nachos were unreal. The jalapeño they put on top was amazing."

The thought of the two of them sharing nachos has my hackles rising. "I'm sorry... who are you?" The question comes out more aggressive than intended. I'm not the kind of guy who flexes for dominance, but seriously—who is he?

Cameron coughs loudly in a bad attempt to cover up a laugh, which isn't appreciated by me *or* Sophie, who shoves him so hard he wobbles in his seat.

"Elliott," he answers. Like he's Cher. Or Madonna. No last name necessary.

"Her *brother*." Sophie gives me a chastising look.

I wince. I've never seen Cameron's sister with anything but a sweet smile on her face, so her rebuke makes me feel like an even bigger asshole. For someone who looks like Tinkerbell, she can be surprisingly intimidating when needed.

With a long breath out, I force my shoulders to relax and give Maya's brother a brief nod that's half acknowledgment, half apology. "Nice to meet you, Elliott."

He raises a brow. "I'm sure it is."

I snag an empty stool from a nearby table and maneuver myself next to Maya. There's more room on the other side of the table, but that doesn't deter me. "You don't think it's a bit too early for me to be meeting the family?"

A pink flush creeps up her neck and into her cheeks. *Damn.* It looks cute on her. "Don't be a smart-ass."

I raise a hand to my chest. "You've been checking out my ass? I'm honored, baby."

She gives a brief shake of her head and lowers it, rubbing her forehead with her fingertips.

As a server passes by, I order a drink, then turn back to Maya and ask the question I've been dying to have answered. "What'd you think of the game? Way more exciting than one of your hockey romances, I'm sure."

She rewards me with a smile. "I didn't even consider reading, if that tells you anything."

I preen like a fucking peacock, feathers and all, my chest filling with air and my head lifted high. A few more games and I guarantee she'll be sporting Bobcats colors with pride.

Within minutes, Jake and Logan have made their way to our table. My single-minded focus on hockey has only intensified since Nate passed, and it hasn't gone unnoticed by my closest friends, so they don't bother covering their surprise over my presence as well as Maya's.

Logan zones in on Elliott, the one-named wonder, and wastes *zero* time on pleasantries. "I'm Logan, and you are gorgeous."

Elliott simply accepts the compliment with a lopsided smile.

"So, Maya," Jake asks post-introductions. "What do you do for work?"

She nods absently, her knee knocking against mine under the table. "I write bereavement cards for Hallmark."

Jake's unruly chestnut hair bounces as he eyes me, then Cameron, as if he's unsure that he's heard her correctly. Finally, with a slow blink, he says, "Uh, um, that's interesting."

With a roll of his eyes, Elliott snorts. Tilting his head toward me, he says, "She once told my teacher that she tutored underprivileged zoo animals. Whatever the hell that means."

Maya tips her head forward. "And it made your parent-teacher conference a lot more fun, so you're welcome."

"Why were you at his parent-teacher conference?" Logan asks, the question blunt though not unkind.

Elliott and Maya exchange a look before she shrugs. "Our mom wasn't around a lot, so I went instead."

Elliott looks to be a year or two out of college, and according to Maya's LinkedIn—which I most definitely stalked—she's twenty-eight. Yet she played parent?

Maya shifts her weight on the stool, her eyes darting away, and takes a long sip of her wine (which I didn't realize this bar served until she ordered it). As she pulls it away from her mouth, a drop slides down her bottom lip. Her perfectly pink and plump lip that I am absolutely thinking about nibbling on.

Arousal spikes deep in my belly, but I swallow it down. Now is not the time, considering her brother is nearby. Although I won't be surprised if he and Logan leave together sooner rather than later.

"I think it's adorable that you manage a bookstore, by the way," I say, leaning back in my seat.

She waves off my comment and dabs at her mouth with a napkin. "That's because men hear the word *books* and automatically think of a sexy librarian."

"False." Straightening, I shake my head. "Sort of. For the record, I do think you'd make a sexy as hell librarian, but more than that, I admire your passion for books."

"I used to want to be an author," she blurts out, the distinct beginnings of a flush traveling across her cheeks. "I just never found the time to pursue it."

She glances at her brother, who's drifted over to the bar area with Logan, the move almost enough to hide the flash of guilt that crosses her face.

My chest tightens at the idea that she might feel bad for even wishing she could do something for herself.

"Is it just you and Elliott? Or do you have other siblings?" I ask, sensing the need for a change in subject.

"Younger sister. Ava." Maya's already sweet face softens tenfold. "She's a freshman at Vanderbilt."

"My sister Emily went there," I tell her. "Although that was about fifteen years ago."

Growing up, it was always Nate and me against Darby and Emily. Now that Nate's gone, I feel like a third wheel when I'm with my sisters. It's in my head, I know that, since they simultaneously mother-hen and annoy me, but I can't seem to shake the idea.

Maya regales me with stories of her college days, and somehow, we end up on the topic of drinking games. It's dangerous, considering my overly competitive nature. A nature that even got me banned from coming to O'Leary's on trivia night.

"I have a game we can play," I suggest, dancing my fingers against Maya's spine.

For a moment I'm sure she's going to shrug off my touch. Instead, to my surprise, she leans into it.

"More like a wager, I suppose."

She glances up at me, her dusk blue eyes filled with suspicion. "Why do I get the feeling this is a trap?"

There's no fighting the grin spreading across my face. "Under or over an hour—how long before Logan and your brother leave together?"

She arches a brow, fiddling with her wineglass. "That's assuming they do. My brother's not really the one-night-stand type."

I survey Logan and Elliott, who are standing close, murmuring into one another's ears. I can practically feel the heat of their sexual tension from here. They're definitely going home together.

"Fine, I'll change it," I concede, tapping my fingers against my drink. "If they don't leave together, I'll read a book of your choice. But if they do... you owe me a kiss."

Maya tenses a fraction, her pouty lips forming an O at the boldness of my wager. "This feels rigged."

A deep laugh escapes from my chest. "I never claimed to play fair, but I do play to win."

At that comment, she throws me a haughty look. "I cannot *wait* for you to read *Alien Lovers of Planet Dexxar*."

With a title like that, I'm even more grateful when, forty-three minutes later, Elliott and Logan slip into their jackets and murmur their goodbyes. I barely hold in a laugh at the way Maya gapes, dumbfounded. When her brother claims he's heading home early because he's had a long day, she stammers a goodbye.

"Looks like you need another drink." I chuckle. It's late, and we have a game tomorrow night in Atlanta, but I don't want the night to end. Cheesy, yes, but true all the same. I can't remember the last time I had this much fun off the ice.

Our next drink turns into two, then three, and somewhere between debating which nineteenth century president was the hottest and plotting our hypothetical zombie apocalypse strategy, my cheeks begin to hurt. I haven't smiled this much in years.

At closing time, I reluctantly settle the tab and schedule a rideshare. I have Maya add her address as a stop so I know she gets home safely. It's a crisp night, so I use that as an excuse to wrap my arm around her as we step outside.

"I'm going to regret that last drink in the morning." She chuckles a little darkly. "I have to be up early to open the store."

"What time do you have to be there?"

She taps her chin. "Eight-thirty."

A scoff escapes me before I can stop it. "That's *early*?" I'll be up at six-thirty to train and to get Goose and his collection of toys dropped off at his sitter's house before my flight.

She jabs a finger at my stomach, and I instinctively flex my well-earned abs. "Anything before ten-thirty a.m. is early for a night owl, Cole. Stop looking so offended."

Chuckling, I rest my forehead against hers. But before I can collect my winning kiss, my phone buzzes, notifying me that our ride is here. *Shit.* Zero stars for him for cock-blocking me.

We clamber in, and when we're settled side by side in the back seat, I rest a hand on Maya's thigh, my thumb tracing idle circles. The driver chatters nonstop during the fifteen-minute ride to her Back Bay apartment, blissfully unaware of the silent tension thrumming between us.

I climb out on the passenger side and offer Maya my hand. "I'll walk you up."

"You really don't have—"

"I want to."

Ignoring her insistence that she can get into her own apartment without issue, I tell the driver I'll be back in a minute. Maya lives on the fifth floor of an older building with no elevator, which she grumbles about the entire way up. I have no complaints, considering the view of her ass is top tier.

"Thanks for tonight," she says once we make it to her floor. Outside her apartment door, she shifts from foot to foot and nibbles on her lower lip. "I had a lot of fun."

I take a step forward, and another one, until we're chest to chest and I've got her back pressed against her door. The electricity between us could power a Tesla indefinitely. Tucking a piece of hair behind her ear, I lower my head. I move slowly, giving her ample time to push me away. She doesn't.

With one last inhale, I capture her lips with urgency. Our tongues twirl against one another in a heated dance, tasting and teasing. I grasp her waist and pull her closer, and when she responds by rubbing against my aching cock, a rumbling moan comes from deep in my chest. A burning hunger builds inside me, an adrenaline rush that can only be compared to the one I experience during a face-off.

When we finally break apart, we both suck in quick and shallow breaths. *Fuck.* I've kissed a lot of women, but I've never ended a kiss and immediately been desperate for another like I am now.

Maya toys with the hair at my nape. "Your rating is going to plummet if you make the driver wait any longer."

I nuzzle into her neck and gently nip the sensitive skin with my teeth. "I'll text you tomorrow, yeah?"

"Okay."

Her breathy whisper is almost my undoing. I consider diving in again, fuck the rideshare rating. But I'm stopped when she slips inside her apartment and gives me a small, shy smile as she closes the door.

I rest my head against the solid wood for a moment, reining myself back in, then jog back down five flights of stairs.

I pass out almost immediately upon arriving home and have the best night's sleep I've had in a long time. It's not until Goose whines that I begrudgingly open my eyes the next morning. My alarm hasn't gone off, yet my room is lighter than I expect.

Rolling over, I rub a hand over my face and snatch my

phone from the nightstand to check the time. When the display lights up, I'm greeted with a whole slew of messages.

<Bobcat Boys Group Text>

JAKE REID

Yo, Berrett. Are we riding to the airport together?

Hellooooo?

LOGAN CLARK

Can we focus on the fact that I'm in love?

CAMERON DAVIES

I'm sure Berrett got laid and that's why he's sleeping in.

LOGAN CLARK

He could've been kidnapped for ransom or some shit.

JAKE REID

Adults can't be KIDnapped. Idiot.

LOGAN CLARK

Semantics.

So... do you guys want to be groomsmen at my wedding?

CAMERON DAVIES

All right, now I'm a little worried too.

LOGAN CLARK

Why? Elliott's a great guy. 10/10.

CAMERON DAVIES

Oh, fuck yourself, Clark. You know what I mean.

JAKE REID

Don't tempt him. He definitely would if it were anatomically possible.

Cole. Our flight's in less than an hour. Wake the fuck up.

Turns out I had the best night's sleep because I slept three hours past my alarm. *Shit.*

CHAPTER FIVE

"IS THAT…" Kennedy's voice trails off as she takes a step closer to the sculpture in front of us.

"A woman's reproductive system that doubles as a gumball machine?" I supply, biting back a smile. "Yeah. I think so."

"Okay, cool. Just making sure."

She circles the piece of artwork, as if that will help it make sense.

Good luck. The exhibit we're at is called *The Politics of Rubbish: Figuring the Avant-Garde.* I have zero idea what the hell that means. When Sophie invited me to the opening of her friend's art gallery, I accepted easily, brushing off her warning about the *disruptive* and *paradoxical* nature of the art. But now that I've seen a gumball-producing uterus sculpture, it's starting to make sense.

Kennedy and I move on from the female anatomy and meander around the space. The gallery is set up like a living room, with couches scattered throughout. The side tables adorned with lamps and books help make it feel as though we're at home with all the art. And it works. This place is surprisingly homey for a gallery displaying pieces in the six-figure range.

Side by side, we inspect an oil painting of some European king with *Fuck the Patriarchy* spray-painted over it.

"Now this one I can get behind." My best friend nods resolutely, then snags some type of fried appetizer from a passing waiter. When she pops it into her mouth, she groans like a porn star. "This mac and cheese ball just gave me a better orgasm than any man ever has."

As I sample one of the orgasmic treats for myself, I realize I can't even call her dramatic. They're that delicious. We continue our self-led tour around the studio, switching off between making keen artistic observations and gushing over the food.

The woman in that painting looks like she just found out her husband of ten years is cheating on her with her Pilates instructor.

This zucchini fritter is better than being accepted as an ARC reader for a new fantasy series.

Holy shit, is that a mouse trap made of condoms and flowers?

I think I'm going to hire this chef for my wedding. And my funeral.

We're considering whether the artist who created the piece in front of us is extremely passionate or off their rocker when I finally spot Sophie. She's in a sage green satin slip dress paired with strappy heels, making her look every bit the ethereal fairy I described her as when I talked Kennedy into accompanying me tonight.

Her eyes light up when she spots me. "You came."

There's real surprise in her voice, even though I texted her to confirm the address a few hours ago. I introduce her to Kennedy, and within minutes, they're chattering like old friends. If I'm the moon, content to disappear into stories and imagined worlds, Kennedy's the sun, radiating warmth with a charm so effortless it pulls people into her orbit instantly.

"Maya says you're an artist, too." Kennedy waves a hand, gesturing to a nearby piece. The little tag below it says *Inquire about price*, which means it's way out of my range. Though that's not a surprise. The only thing here I can afford is the free catering.

Pink patches bloom across Sophie's cheeks. "Oh. Sort of. Nowhere near this caliber."

Kennedy scrunches her nose up. "You and Maya with your technicalities. If you create, you're an artist. If you write, you're a writer. Doesn't matter if you're in a gallery or not, or if you're published or not."

Sophie's eyes widen in surprise. "You write?"

"Hardly." Now I'm the one who turns shades of strawberry.

"Liar," Kennedy snaps.

Discomfort creeps down my spine. "Am not."

"Are, too. I read the Valentine's Day poem you wrote to Johnny L. in second grade and—"

My stomach sinks. "It wasn't a love poem! Oh my God."

I cringe at the memory of the cheesy card I wrote him: *Roses are red, violets are blue. Puppies are cute, and so are you.*

Kennedy smirks. "Seemed romantic to me."

With a huff, I snap, "You haven't read anything I've written."

"*A-ha.*" She pumps her fist in the air. "So you admit you write."

Eyes narrowed, I give her a look that I hope will shut her up. I should know better. So I abandon the effort and turn back to Sophie. "It's more of a hobby than anything. And not one I've participated in in a *long* time."

Kennedy may roll her eyes at my self-deprecation, but it's true. No one's ever read my writing, so who is she to say it's more interesting as an Ikea instruction manual? And I haven't written much of anything since I graduated from college over six years ago.

"I'm sure your writing's great," Sophie reassures me with a warm smile. "Want me to give you guys a tour?"

"Yes," I nearly shout, desperate to change the subject. "I need to know the inspiration behind that cyclops statue."

Sophie leads us around the space, pointing at some of her favorite pieces and sharing tidbits of juicy gossip about the artists. Van Gogh's removal of his own ear has nothing on the guy who made the marble statue of Cupid on one side of the gallery. The cherubic angel is wearing a bandit's mask and holding a bomb instead of a bow and arrow. It's all very representative of the artist's "love me or die" motto, considering that, according to rumors, he was stamped with a few stalking charges and still wears his ex's hair around his wrist like a bracelet.

"I need to say hi to a few more people, but then I can leave. Do you guys want to stick around for a few? If so, we can grab a drink after." Sophie smiles, her blue eyes full of hope.

"Absolutely," Kennedy answers before I can object. Coming out on a Tuesday was wild enough for me. Adding drinks on top of that is really going to push my social battery to its limits.

Sophie claps, bouncing on her toes, her contagious smile making it difficult to wish I could head home now and curl up with a book.

Once she's out of sight, Kennedy turns to me with a twinkle in her eye. "You made a friend."

I meet her expression with a glare. "I'm not incompetent. I know how to make friends."

"You just choose not to," she points out, chin lifted.

"There's nothing wrong with choosing quality over quantity."

I can count on one hand the number of people I trust enough to have ingratiated into my everyday life.

"No, there's not, but it'll be good for us to branch out," she replies with a look that dares me to disagree. "It can hardly be considered a girls' night out with just two of us, you know."

When I don't respond, she sighs and flings her arm around me.

"All I'm saying is that putting yourself out there is a good thing."

We both know she's right. With the way my mom has always disappeared and then suddenly reappeared just to stir things up, I've grown uneasy with change. I can admit that my hyper-independence means being alone is my default. I tend to assume that the people I meet will all become footnotes or short chapters in the story of my life rather than reoccurring characters.

"Yeah, yeah." I grab a fried mac and cheese ball from a passing waiter and shove it into my mouth to discourage further conversation.

Thirty minutes later, the three of us are huddled at a high top at a nearby wine bar with a carafe of their house wine, chatting as if we do this every week. Our conversation flows easily, moving from funny stories about bad hookups to tales about a Facebook Marketplace meetup gone wrong. We spend far too much time guessing who Pete Davidson will date next, which somehow leads to a conversation about how Kennedy's parents named her and all of her siblings after presidents.

"Have you talked to Cole lately?" Sophie asks with a tipsy giggle. Her question lacks even a hint of subtleness, which I blame on the wine. "You guys seemed to hit it off."

I take a sip of my drink, having known this would come up at some point tonight. "We haven't talked since the game."

She waves her hand as if it's no big deal. "I wouldn't worry too much. My brother goes MIA when the team travels. Their schedule's insane."

It's been over two weeks since the Bobcats game and the Kiss. Kiss with a capital *K* because it was so damn good that it deserves the recognition and respect a capital letter brings. But Cole hasn't reached out since, and I haven't yet decided how I feel about that. So, as usual, I've tucked thoughts of him away and focused on other things. It's not like I'm looking for anything from him anyway. He seems like a genuinely great guy, the kind of guy I tend to stay far away from. Why? Because they want things I can't offer. But I also wouldn't say no to the chance to trace his abs with my tongue.

And when my phone buzzes in my pocket, a small, radicalized group of butterflies in my stomach annoyingly hope it's Cole. *Assholes.*

DEIRDRE SILVER

Keith and I are going on a cruise and won't be back until after Thanksgiving. Will you tell Elliott and Ava for me? Xx

I truly wish I could say I was surprised by, or even sad about, my mom's text. But it's so typical of her that the only feeling I can muster up in response is relief. I haven't seen her in months—she didn't fly back for Elliott's graduation or to spend time with Ava before she left for school—so what's a few more weeks? And God forbid she bite the bullet and tell my siblings themselves.

Swallowing past the lump in my throat, I pick up the wine carafe and fill my glass nearly to the rim. "Guess who's bailing on Thanksgiving? Again."

Kennedy grabs my phone from the table and reads the text aloud. "God, your mom is the fucking worst."

"I'm sorry," Sophie says. A tight frown furrows her features. "That's really shitty."

I shrug and pick up my drink. I'm used to the constant disappointment otherwise known as my mother. "One would think a woman so uninterested in kids would've invested in better contraception."

A surprised laugh escapes Sophie, making wine spray out of her nose. "Is she really that bad?"

"Yep," Kennedy confirms, straightening in her seat. "Maya missed prom because her sister had the flu, and Deirdre was out of town and wasn't picking up the phone."

I snort. "When is my mother not out of town?"

"Speaking of out of town," Sophie says in the world's worst segue. "The team will be home tomorrow. I think you should text Cole. Make the first move. Or second move, I guess."

I twirl the stem of my glass between my thumb and pointer finger, willing my nerves to remain settled. Before I can look too hard into why I'm even considering this, I ask, "What would I even say?"

Kennedy refills her glass and Sophie's. "You could try something like 'Hey, Cole. My vibrator ran out of battery. You around to make me come instead?'"

It takes more effort than I'd like to admit to keep a straight face, because that's scarily accurate.

Sophie leans forward, her face alight. "You should go with a hockey pun. Want to Zam-boney?"

"Oh, I've got one," Kennedy shouts, making the people seated around us glance over. "You might not like tie games, but what about tying me up instead?"

"What's the difference between me and a hockey fight?" Sophie continues with a shy smile. "They may not like getting nailed, but I sure as hell do."

I slap my hands over my face, half in laughter, half in mortification. "How about *puck no?*"

CHAPTER SIX

"SHIFT your balance to the left, Davies!" Coach Henderson shouts, his voice carrying across the rink. "Push yourself! Atta boy."

"You heard the man!" Logan whoops, the sound a little maniacal. "Shift left!"

Cameron grumbles an insult at Logan as he skates past me. He doesn't do well with constructive criticism, focusing on the criticism aspect instead of learning from the constructive part. For someone who's six-four, over two hundred pounds, and could give Oscar the Grouch a run for his money, he's very sensitive.

"Brush it off, man," I advise in a stern voice. The ozone smell of the arena—the one I've associated with home for so long—surrounds me as I sweep past him. The air here is always chilly, but our constant movement keeps us warm. "Unless you want to repeat this goddamn drill."

"Then tell Logan to stop being so *him*," he responds with a scowl.

Since the guy's natural disposition can be described as scowly, the way his dark brows are pulled together over his dark green eyes isn't anything out of the ordinary.

Coach makes us run the drill again anyway. And again. And again, until the sweat dripping down my face almost obscures my vision. *Holy hell.* The edge work drills can best be described as a methodical way to slowly kill someone's will to live. Though I give it my all, my legs and lungs burn. And that's saying something, considering I push myself harder than just about any of the guys on the team. Apparently, last night's win wasn't enough to prove to Coach Henderson that we do indeed know how to play nice with one another.

He claps, praising Logan as he takes a sharp turn. "Nice and tight, Logan. Keep it up."

"Oh, I can keep it up." His sky-blue eyes light up with mischief. "Especially when it's nice and tight."

Cam's bigger size gives him an advantage as our goalie, but on top of that, it makes people underestimate just how fast he is. His reflexes and speed are just as honed as the nimbler play-ers. It's why Logan doesn't move out of the way in time before Cameron barrels into him, side-checking him into the board.

Once he's steadied himself, Logan simply grins at Cameron, unflappable. Though his borderline sociopathic tendency to incense people is usually directed at the other team, none of us are safe from his constant chatter. It used to drive me insane, but I've learned to tune him out.

I bring myself to an abrupt stop, ready to intervene, but Coach Henderson blows his whistle to end the practice before it can go any further.

"That's it for today, boys. Be at the arena by five tonight." He dismisses the team with a flick of his arm. "Berrett. I need a quick word."

"Someone's in trouble," Logan sings as I skate past him. I swear he's worse than a mouthy grandma playing bridge.

While the rest of the team shuffles off the rink to guzzle

water and towel off, I skate to where Coach is camped out on a bench a good distance away.

Every inch of the worn seat is covered in printouts of plays and strategies. I've always admired Coach Henderson. Not only is he one of the most successful hockey coaches in history, but he somehow balances his professional life and personal life with an ease I've never seen from anyone. He's got stress lines on his forehead and laugh lines around his eyes and lips to prove it.

"You good?" he asks, his brows dipping.

I take a swig of my Gatorade and swipe at the excess that dribbles down my chin. "Yeah, I'm good."

"You've been ballsy with your defense," he notes with a raised brow. "Something going on?"

I grab a nearby towel and run it over my face. "Honestly?"

He folds his arms over his chest, his gaze steady. "I don't pay you to lie to me."

"You don't pay me for my opinion either," I point out with a teasing grin.

His lips twitch, but that's the only reaction he gives me. "Fair enough, but I'm curious. Humor me."

Glancing over my shoulder, I confirm that none of my team-mates are close enough to overhear our conversation. "Jeffer-son's favoring zones."

Coach nods but doesn't speak, signaling I should continue.

"He needs to know when to swap spots," I say, dragging my towel over my sweat-soaked hair. "Momentary two-on-ones are fine, but he needs to communicate better with the other defenseman on when to move, especially toward the support zone."

"Hmm." He leans back, arms crossed. "Any idea who to pair him with?"

"Erickson," I reply without hesitation.

Freddy Erickson is a beast of a defenseman. He's intense, but he'll correct Jefferson in a way that'll make the rookie scared to fuck up.

When I've explained my logic, Coach nods thoughtfully. "Smart thinking. Your mind for strategy is one of the reasons you've been chosen as our team's new captain."

I squint, as if that'll help me make sense of his out-of-pocket comment. "What?"

"Not exactly the response I was hoping for," he says with a gravelly chuckle.

Our longtime captain retired from the sport at the end of last season, leaving a vacancy. The team turned in their nominations anonymously, but Coach has been clear that there's no rush to fill the big shoes he left behind, leading us to believe that a decision wouldn't be confirmed by management until much later in the season.

My throat constricts with emotion, making my words gruff. "Wow, um, no. Thank you. I'm shocked, is all. I thought—well, I thought you were holding off on the decision."

With a shrug, he runs a hand through his thick gray hair. "We just wanted to make sure the player with the most nominations from the team lined up with our opinion of who would emerge as the team's unofficial leader."

Nerves zip up my spine. "You think I'm that leader?"

"I know you're that leader," he says without hesitation

"Thank you," I mutter, my cheeks heating in a way that has nothing to do with my work on the ice. "I won't let the team down."

Coach Henderson explains when and how they'll make the announcement, but it all goes in one ear and out the other. Captains are chosen for a variety of reasons, mainly for their leadership abilities, communication skills, and knowledge of the game and team. It means the rest of the team respects and trusts me to lead them in the right direction. It's a huge responsibility and honor.

I'm still on cloud nine as I head out to my car after I'm dismissed.

"About damn time," Jake calls from where he's leaning against my slate-gray Porsche Cayenne. We live in the same neighborhood and carpool to practice, saving the environment one shared drive at a time. "What the hell took so long, Berrett?"

"That's *Captain* to you," I share, unable to tamp down on a wide smile.

Jake's eyes widen, and he barrels into me. I grunt as he half tackles, half hugs me, his full weight pushing me back a few steps.

"Fuck, man," he shouts, pounding me on the back. "You're serious?"

I sketch a dramatic bow and slip my keys from my pocket. "Yup. They're announcing it tomorrow after the game."

As I slide into the driver's seat, I relish the sensation of the cool leather on my still heated back. Jake hops in a little less gracefully and messes with the heat as I navigate out of the parking lot, then settles in for the thirty-minute drive back from the practice arena.

"Have you talked to your girl recently?" Jake asks.

My chest pinches, but I ignore the sensation. "My girl?"

He snorts. "Seriously? Don't play dumb with me, Berrett."

I keep my focus trained on the road. Considering I haven't shown interest in anyone but Maya in months—years, really—I don't have to ask for clarification. Honestly, I can't get her out of my head. I feel like a goddamn teenager when I get myself off imagining her hips pressed against mine as I kiss her breathless. But... "This isn't a good time for me to get involved with someone."

"Why?" he demands. "Please don't tell me you're going to act all high and mighty now that you're captain."

I press my lips together, still avoiding his gaze. "It has nothing to do with that."

Although it does make things more complicated. Now I'll be the one who's studying practice and game film with a magnifying glass. I'll be the first one at practice and the last to leave, and I'll be the guy making sure our strategy is executed on the ice. Being captain means the margin for distraction shrinks down to zero.

I don't need to look at Jake to know he's studying me. He majored in psychology in college, and despite never having experience in the field under his belt, he likes to think he can accurately analyze us all. It's funny when I'm drunk but annoying as hell when I'm trapped in a car with him.

Eventually, he sighs. "Then what is it?"

"I missed my flight." I shift in my seat. The answer is lame as fuck, but there's no point in lying.

For several seconds, he stares at me. Then, abruptly, he throws his head back and laughs far too loud for such a confined space. "Cole, dude. You've got to be shitting me. You slept through your alarms and missed the flight, and you're blaming Maya for it?"

I shake my head, frustration trickling into my veins. "No, no, I don't blame her at all. But I've been playing professional hockey for almost ten years, and the one time I miss a flight just happens to coincide with the one time I show interest in someone. There's a correlation there. I need to stay focused."

"Man, you can't—" Jake sighs and runs a hand through his unmanageable hair. "Listen, Cole. Enough is enough. It's time to stop this. You can't spend the rest of your life basing every decision you make on whether it'll affect your training or sleep. That's not healthy."

"I don't—"

"Yes, you do." He hits me with a stern lecture-ready scowl. "The only people you hang out with outside of the arena are those of us you already see there. Your whole life is the game. Balance isn't the enemy, bro. Since Nate died, you've thrown yourself into hockey even more. I get it, I do, but at some point, you have to step off the ice long enough to actually live."

The words hit harder than I expect. I suck in an unsteady breath, caught somewhere between shock and uncertainty. Silence settles between us, broken only by an Ed Sheeran song humming through the speakers.

"I'm not trying to be a dick by bringing up Nate," Jake adds, his tone gentler, "but you need something in your life that isn't hockey. When was the last time you did anything for yourself? Not for your career?"

I grip the steering wheel harder, making the leather creek beneath my hands, and open my mouth to argue. But nothing comes out. I snap it shut again, pissed at my lack of defense. Since Nate died, I've dedicated myself even more wholly to the game. The rink is where the two of us grew up, and when I'm out on the ice, surrounded by the sound of a puck thumping into the goalie's glove, blades scraping across the surface, and the roar of the crowd, I can drown out the missing part of me and pretend that he's not gone, even if for a short while.

"He wasn't my brother by blood," Jake continues, "but he was my family, too."

I pull the car to a smooth stop at a red light and glance over, heart thumping painfully against my sternum.

He's frowning, his usually easy-going demeanor darkened. Nathan and Jake played college hockey together and got drafted to the same team as rookies. Back then, people joked that Jake was our triplet. That's probably the only reason I haven't thrown a punch. It's for the best. He'd be more likely to come out on top in a fight between the two of us; the guy's got a mean left hook.

"I know, man," I finally say, shoulders deflating.

He surveys me, his expression thoughtful. "He'd want what's best for you, just like I do. I'm not saying that's Maya, but I don't think it'd be the end of the world for you to fucking text her. Ask her on a date or slide into her DMs. Whatever the kids are doing these days."

Running my hand through my hair, I shoot him a small smile. "Can't believe I'm considering taking dating advice from someone who's sworn off relationships."

Jake narrows his eyes at me, his mood darkening. "If you'd had four stepmoms before you hit thirty, you'd understand why."

"Fair enough," I admit.

"And despite my lack of dating knowledge, I'm almost positive asking the woman out is a solid step one."

I chuckle at the annoyance in his tone. "I'm sure I can figure it out."

"I'd sure as shit hope so." He breaks into a satisfied grin. "You are captain now, after all."

CHAPTER SEVEN

I FLICK my wrist in a sad attempt to flip the pancakes in the pan and immediately regret it. Instead of turning over, one pancake shimmies into a lopsided oval shape, causing the unset batter to shift awkwardly into a blob. *Lovely.* I'm not a bad cook by any means, but dinner is more my specialty. I tend to lean toward granola bars for breakfast, since I'm usually running late. I've practically earned a PhD in hitting snooze. Honestly, why *is* Apple's default alarm nine minutes? What kind of sadistic math is that?

A shuffle of footsteps behind me has me peering over my shoulder.

"Morning," Ava grumbles as she appears at the threshold of my tiny kitchen. Her Bambi-brown eyes are at half-mast as she surveys the stove. "Are those pancakes?"

With the spatula I snag from the utensil holder beside the stove, I manually turn the pancakes. They're a little too brown to be light and fluffy, but they'll do. *I hope.* "They may not look like 'em, but I promise they'll taste like 'em."

Mumbling unintelligibly, she drops into a barstool and drapes herself over the counter. She flew in yesterday and has been catching up on sleep since. Between midterms and a delayed connection, she was running on fumes when she landed.

"What time is dinner tonight?" she asks with a yawn.

"We haven't even had breakfast, and you're already thinking about dinner?" I chuckle at her predictability. "Slow down, Aves."

She sticks out her tongue. Glad to see college hasn't completely matured her.

"Not until seven," I say. "Elliott's finishing up a project."

"He's always working." Her lips twist into a frown. "It's Thanksgiving, for fuck's sake."

"Language," I chide with a raised brow. Even though I swear regularly, and even if she's an adult herself now, the caretaker in me feels obligated to police her language. "He's bringing babka from Goldblatt's for dessert."

Her mood immediately lifts at the mention of her favorite treat. No one loves chocolate chip babka more than Ava, and I've never been above bribing her with it. Once, when she was six, I convinced her not to scream bloody murder at the dentist by promising she could have as much as she wanted that evening. She ate half a loaf. It probably counteracted the cavity-preventing work completed during the appointment, but oh well. I was sixteen and working with limited resources.

With a dreamy look in her eye, she asks, "He's bringing his not-boyfriend, too, right?"

"Yep," I confirm.

Though the thought of Cole is a tender spot for me, meeting him led to not only my friendship with Sophie, but Elliott's introduction to Logan. They've only been seeing each other a few weeks—and Elliott refuses to define the relationship yet, hence Logan's not-boyfriend status—but it's obvious already that the blond hockey player is good for my brother. When he worked late last week, Logan had dinner from his favorite restaurant delivered to his office to make sure he ate.

When Elliott told me, I melted a little. Okay, a lot.

"Need any help?" Ava asks as I slide the pancakes onto a plate.

I roll my eyes. "Thanks for asking *after* I've finished cooking."

"I can make coffee." She grins, knowing I won't turn down another cup. "Almond or skim milk?"

A few minutes later, we're curled up on the couch with mugs of hot coffee in hand and weirdly shaped but surprisingly tasty pancakes on our plates. Since it's Thanksgiving and we have no plans to leave the apartment, we stay in our pajamas and spend the day watching *Gilmore Girls* for the billionth time and catching up on life. We text and talk on the phone a few times a week, but none of that comes close to replacing sitting beside her, where I can feel her body vibrate with excitement as she talks about the friends she's made. And it doesn't allow me to really study the way her lower lip twitches in distaste as she complains about her atrocious English 101 professor.

Since she left for school, I've been filling the quiet with work and slowly making my way through my TBR list. Yes, I've missed her desperately, but I didn't realize just how much until she came home. It's only been two months since she left, but it feels like a lifetime.

She doesn't need me like she once did, and while I'm thrilled she's thriving, my demotion from a main character in her story to someone standing just offstage is bittersweet.

———

I've just finished sprinkling the final layer of breadcrumbs onto my famous mac and cheese when a thunderous *bang* rattles my front door.

If I didn't know any better, I'd assume I was seconds away from being the victim of a break-in. But by now, I can easily pick out the specific sound of my brother's knock. He's the only person on earth who knocks like he's trying to escape a killer clown. Granted, my neighbors are questionable—I'm convinced the guy in 4D performs satanic rituals during full moons—but Elliott's earthquake-inducing knocks are overkill. As if on cue, my upstairs neighbor (who plays the violin at all hours, yet never improves) bangs a broom against the floor in protest. Definitely *not* thankful for her this Thanksgiving.

I yank on the knob and zero in on him. "I'm not going to get my security deposit back if you dent my front door."

With a lopsided smile, he shoves a to-go bag from Goldblatt's into my arms as if that'll make up for his obnoxious entrance. "Hey, Yaya. Where's Aves?"

Before I can respond, his eyes drift over my shoulder and he pushes into the apartment, his face lighting up. And just like that, I'm forgotten. Not that I mind. Elliott won't admit it, but he hates that Ava goes to school so far away. He stayed local for college, like I did, so we kept up with Sunday dinners even during his frat-star phase.

The six-four hockey player lingering in the hallway gives me a sheepish smile.

Confused by the expression, I frown, giving him a once-over. That's when I notice what's at his feet.

A dog.

A ridiculously cute dog with big brown eyes, a pink tongue lolling out the side of its mouth, and a green and blue striped bowtie around his neck. Did I say cute? I meant the cutest freaking thing I've ever seen.

What the hell?

"Who's this handsome fellow?" I crouch down to pet the chocolate lab, who thanks me by licking a layer of moisturizer off my face with his kisses.

"This is Goose," Logan says, his chest puffed out a little. "Elliott said he texted to tell you we were coming. Is it okay?"

Elliott most definitely did not text me, but Logan looks nervous, like I'm about to turn them away. And the dog is practically smiling, already charming his way into my heart. "Yes, of course. I totally forgot. Come on in."

As if he's thanking me, Goose barks, which is quickly followed by another bang of the broom upstairs. With a sigh, I lead Logan inside, taking his coat and the bottle of wine he holds out with a dramatic flourish.

Drinks are poured and a bowl of water is set out for Goose, and soon we're squeezing around my tiny kitchen table (a table meant for two, maybe three, but definitely not four plus a nosy dog), piling our plates high with honey BBQ wings, creamy three-cheese mac and cheese, creamed spinach, and cornbread biscuits. It's not a traditional Thanksgiving feast, but I don't know how to baste a turkey, and I don't plan to learn anytime soon.

"My trainer's going to murder me," Logan moans, scooping a third helping of creamed spinach onto his plate. "What is in this stuff, Maya? It's crack."

"I helped, you know," Ava pipes up, pointing her fork at our guest.

"Taking the dish out of the oven doesn't count," Elliott teases.

"Says who?" She flashes him a mischievous grin before turning back to Logan. "What do you usually do for Thanksgiving?"

"Not much," he says with a shrug. "I'm Canadian; born and

raised in Ottawa. Our Thanksgiving was a month and a half ago."

Lips pressed together, I survey him. I envisioned him being from Los Angeles or Dallas. I blame the lack of an obvious Canadian accent.

"I've lived in the US since I was nineteen, but we usually have games on American Thanksgiving, so it hasn't been on my radar," he adds. "The team's pretty pumped to be with their families this year. It's why I'm on Goose duty."

"He's not yours?" Ava pats her lap in a failed attempt to lure Goose over to her.

He's doubled as my shadow throughout dinner. I haven't given him any under-the-table scraps, but he's been curled up at my feet, nonetheless.

"Oh, hell no." Logan barks out a laugh. "I'm not nearly responsible enough to have a dog. Goose is Cole's. He went home to San Diego, but his usual sitter's out of town, too, so I volunteered to babysit."

"That was nice of you," I say coolly. Focus fixed on my wineglass, I bring it to my lips, pretending the sound of Cole's name didn't make my heart skip a beat.

"Mm-hmm." He shoves an enormous forkful of stuffing—his second serving—into his mouth. "Not sure if he'll like this, though," he mumbles around the food. "Having to compete with his dog for your attention."

"Who's Cole?" Ava asks, suddenly sitting a little straighter, her dark eyes full of curiosity.

"Logan's teammate," I answer.

At the same time, Logan says, "Maya's love interest."

Elliott chimes in, too. "The new captain of the Bobcats."

I narrow my eyes at Logan. *Asshole.* I'm 100 percent not offering him a slice of babka for dessert.

Ava's like a dog with a bone when it comes to my love life.

One mention of a man, even if it's someone I chatted with in line at Boston Bean, and she's mapping out our wedding and picking out our kids' names.

"Oh, c'mon, Maya," Logan says with a chuckle. "You can't deny that you and Berrett have chemistry. It even got me all hot and bothered."

"Okay, ew," Elliott grumbles.

The boyish grin on Logan's face makes it hard to be annoyed with him. He's so damn charming. Add in the dimple, and it's no wonder my brother's infatuated.

Even so, unease prickles at me. "Cole isn't interested. Trust me."

Logan's blond brows bend together in confusion. "Of course he's interested. Do you know the last time he invited someone who doesn't share his DNA to a game? Never. Because he hasn't shown any interest in a single topic that isn't hockey since his br—" He dips his chin and straightens his napkin in his lap. "Let's just say it's been a while. So trust *me* when I say he is interested."

Unwilling to argue with him over something so pointless, I take a sip of my wine. Cole never reached out after the Kiss. And yeah, that sucked a little, but it's fine. Not a huge deal on its own, right? Right. But the other morning, I saw an article about the growing popularity of alien romances and sent it to him, figuring he'd find it funny. Thought it was an appropriate way to reach out. He gave me tickets to a hockey game; I sent him a text about books. Harmless.

Except he ignored the message.

I didn't even get a stupid thumbs-up or a simple *ha ha*.

No, I was met with absolute radio silence.

It shouldn't bother me. It *really* shouldn't. I promised myself I'd never give anyone—especially a man—the power to affect my emotions. Hence the reason I tend to stick to casual relationships and very rarely allow myself to be deeply invested in the people I date. With one foot constantly following a new man out the door, my mom instilled in me—incidentally, of course, because she rarely took the time to teach me anything —a sense of self-reliance. I've depended on no one but myself for as long as I can remember. In fact, I'm probably a little *too* independent, as illustrated by my ability to move on from a relationship without dwelling on it too much. Case in point: Josh.

I suppose being more hurt by Cole's lack of response than I am about my ex—who, annoyingly, won't stop texting me— hooking up with another girl while we were still dating is somewhat alarming. One stupid Kiss, and my brain is ripping off its yellow caution tape like it's performing a striptease. It's probably for the best that things didn't go further.

"You don't believe me." Logan gives me an exaggerated pout, though the expression quickly morphs into a wicked grin. "That'll just make it all the sweeter when I prove you wrong. I've known Cole for years. Once he figures out what he wants, there's no stopping him. And he wants you, Maya."

I don't bother correcting him. And honestly, if Cole's looking for a real relationship, he's barking up the wrong tree. Am I interested in riding him like a cowboy? Absolutely. But sex and relationships don't go hand in hand for me. Thanks to my mother's many failed relationships and the unrealistic expecta- tions that romance books have given me, I don't plan on falling in love anytime soon. If ever.

Ava leans in with a protective look in her eye and steals a sip of my wine. "If a guy doesn't realize how amazing Maya is right off the bat, then he isn't worth her time."

Before Logan can argue with her, the oven timer rings.

I've never loved the *saved by the bell* cliché more than I do right now. I hurry to the kitchen, and Ava trails behind me, leaning against the counter as I take the warming babka out of the oven.

"You've been holding out on me," she remarks. "I want to hear about this man."

I give her a noncommittal noise in reply. "There's nothing to tell, Aves. Promise."

"Then why are you giving me devil horns?" Rather than lunge for the babka, she crosses her arms over her chest. That doesn't bode well for me. "Are you okay?"

I smooth out my features and twist my lips up into a reassuring smile, despite the slight pit in my stomach. "I've got both of my siblings home with me for the first time in months. I'm better than okay, Aves."

cole

THE SCENT of onions sizzling in butter hits me as I step into the kitchen. For weeks, I've stuck to the rigorous diet of protein and veggies my trainer created for me, and I haven't snuck in so much as a chocolate bar in months. The smell of real, indulgent holiday food? It's enough to make me lightheaded.

My mom is in her element, moving around the room like a conductor leading an orchestra, mixing this and whisking that. She stirs, sprinkles, and taste-tests with a precision only earned through decades of creating holiday meals. It's an achingly familiar sight; one that hits me in the chest with enough force to steal my breath.

"Hi, Ma," I call out. My voice is barely audible over the whirr of the MixAid, so when she doesn't so much as twitch in my direction, I try again. "Mom!"

Startling, she presses a hand over her heart. "Jeez, honey. Warn a woman, why don't you?"

I could've walked in waving a red flag and blowing a foghorn and she still wouldn't have noticed me. Not when she's in the zone. My dad likes to joke that he's nearly lost fingers interrupting her mid-baste.

I kiss her cheek in apology anyway. "Need any help?"

Her eyes widen as if I suggested she add mayonnaise and grape jelly to her stuffing recipe. "Thanks, honey, but absolutely not."

The last time she let me help in the kitchen was back in elementary school, when Nathan and I volunteered to make cookies for a bake sale. I accidentally dumped a little flour on him, which led to a food fight that somehow ended in us sacrificing our allowance money to cover the cost of new cabinet faces. They had to be replaced because the two of us managed to stain them with egg yolk and food coloring.

"Noted." I fight a smirk. "I think—"

Twin squeals echo through the house, cutting me off, followed by the unmistakable sound of tiny feet thundering down the hallway. Before I can call out a hello, my nieces barrel into me, shouting, "Uncle Coley! Uncle Coley!"

"Hey, peanuts." I scoop up Violet, holding her in my left arm so she doesn't latch on to my right shoulder, which is still sore from a brutal hit into the boards a few days ago. Lily's going through a stage where she's too big to be picked up "like a baby," so she quickly hugs my waist and grins up at me. She's missing her front tooth, which earned her five dollars and earned me a five-hour story about how magical the Tooth Fairy is.

I only hold their attention for another minute before they race off in search of Darby. Emily and her husband, Zach, appear moments later, arms full of steaming platters. I'm surprised my mom let Emily bring anything, but I hold my tongue. If I question her, I'm liable to get a smaller piece of pecan pie for dessert.

As we gather for dinner a short while later, a pang of

sadness runs through me. It's times like this—when my family's circled around the table—that Nathan's absence hurts the most.

Often, the comfort of home makes me feel closer to my brother. There's the familiarity of the perfume we bought for Mom for Mother's Day back in middle school—the scent she still wears to this day. The smell of stale cigars in my dad's office and the memory of when we stole a few to smoke during high school, only for Nathan to have an asthma attack. The dent in the front door from when he threw a skate at it after we'd lost a game, and the rundown treehouse in the backyard where the two of us spent hours planning our futures as the next Wayne Gretzky and Bobby Orr.

Everywhere I look, there are reminders of him. As comforting as they can be, they can also bring a pain I never experienced before we lost him. And sometimes they're accompanied by a guilt that blankets me completely. Because while I get to keep making memories in this home, with our family, all he'll ever be *is* a memory.

"Uncle Coley," Lily chirps, pulling me back. "Can I sit next to you?"

"Me, too." Violet scrambles to occupy the seat on my other side. "I'm sitting next to you, too."

Clearing my throat, I smile at them and help them settle into their seats.

My mom refills everyone's drink, even topping off Violet's and Lily's cups with more grape juice.

"Mom," Emily sighs, rubbing her forehead. "No juice during dinner."

"Bah, let me spoil my grandkids." My mom dismisses her with a flick of her hand, then homes in on me. "It's not like anyone else is giving me more to spoil."

Here we go again.

"Darby doesn't seem to be catching heat for her lack of offspring," I argue, sinking into my chair.

"At least I'm actively dating." My sister shoots me a smirk.

One brow arched, I snort at her. "Oh? Is that what we're calling it these days?"

My dad groans and buries his head in his hands. "No fighting. Be thankful that you have one another."

That shuts us up instantly and sends my heart sinking into my stomach. For all the jabs and bickering, he's right. I may want to strangle Darby half the time, and Emily might try to micromanage my life like she's got a clipboard and whistle, but I'd be lost without them.

Darby and I mumble out apologies, and my dad's frown softens.

While we fill our plates with turkey, glazed carrots, cranberry sauce, and green bean casserole, my mom steers the conversation in a different direction. Violet chats about her ballet class, Darby shows me pictures of the DIY renovations she's done at her condo, and Lily repeatedly tells me that she can do a "super cool" cartwheel, thanks to gymnastics.

By the time dessert appears, everyone's in a cornbread coma, including me. The second helpings may have been a mistake, since I have a game tomorrow, but it's impossible to turn down my mom's candied yams.

Violet rests her face in her tiny palms, fighting to stay awake. Neither of the girls napped today, too energized about dinner, and the combination of excitement and carbs is clearly taking its toll.

Tugging on one of Violet's pigtails, I ask, "Want to open the present I got you before bed?"

Her tired eyes pop open, and on my other side, Lily perks up, her hands clasped in front of her. "Presents!"

"You can open it once you're in pajamas and your teeth are brushed," Emily says. The warning look she gives her daughter is so similar to our mom's that it makes me chuckle. "Deal?"

"Deal!" they shout in unison as they clamber out of their chairs.

Once they've bolted upstairs, I head into the bedroom I once shared with my brother and dig into my suitcase. The gift—*Grimm's Fairy Tales*, wrapped with care by Maya—is still tucked safely inside.

At the thought of her, a mixture of discomfort and longing flows through me. I should've texted her back, but I considered how to respond for so long that when I finally decided what to say, too much time had passed for it to not be awkward. I'm not the best texter, anyway, so I figure I'll swing by the Book Nook, apologize for more or less ghosting her, and ask for another chance.

I've probably put far too much thought into the plan. It's not like I'm asking for her hand in marriage. I can practically hear Nathan telling me to stop being a "bitch ass" and ask her out. My brother never let his career get in the way of his social life, that's for sure.

Lily bursts into my room wearing pajamas covered in smiling butterflies. "Is that my present?"

With a nod, I tuck it under my arm. "Let's go get your sister, and we can open it together."

She latches on to my hand and leads me to the bedroom they're staying in. Violet's already tucked under the frilly floral comforter, so Lily climbs in beside her and pats the empty spot between them.

It takes effort, especially after the massive quantity of food I consumed at dinner, but I manage to wedge my tall frame between their tiny bodies.

I hold out the wrapped book while they tear the paper with unfiltered joy, each working on her own side. "It's a book of fairy tales."

"Ooh," they murmur. Lily traces the gold-foiled flowers and vines etched onto the cover while Violet runs a reverent hand along the pages.

"Will you read one to us, Uncle Coley?" Lily asks, flipping the book open to a random page.

The Juniper Tree is written in a fancy cursive font at the top. Although I've never heard of the story, I agree. Lily snuggles into me as I begin. Quickly, though, it becomes clear to me that this is not the innocent fairy tale I thought it was.

"Why'd you stop?" Violet asks halfway through.

Maybe because the stepmom beheads the son and sticks his head in a box and then turns him into black pudding?

"Uh, sorry," I cough out an excuse. "I lost my place."

Instead of continuing to read, I bullshit my way through the rest of the story. Instead of using an apple to trick and kill him, I tell the girls that the stepmother feeds him so many apples that he becomes as strong as a tree. I truly don't know what the fuck comes out of my mouth, but my nieces love it and soon demand another story.

I discover quickly that the original stories from *Grimm's Fairy Tales* are indeed grim. Very grim. And so the pattern continues, and I create off-the-cuff stories in a way I didn't know was possible.

I learn that Cinderella's stepsisters get their eyes pecked out by birds and that the prince in *Snow White* is a necrophiliac corpse thief. Thankfully Lily and Violet are too interested in the hand-drawn images on the pages to question my versions.

"Uncle Coley?" Lily taps on my arm, motioning me to bend down.

"Yeah, sweetheart?"

Her lips tip up in a small smile. "I'm happy you're home."

Without Nathan, home will never truly feel like it once did, but I kiss my niece's blond head anyway and say, "Me, too."

"SLOW DOWN, BOY."

Tugging on Goose's leash does me no good. He zigs and zags across the sidewalk, chasing each new smell like he's a detective on a case. The late November winds bite the skin not covered by my jacket as we pass one locally owned shop after another. We pass a bakery, dispensary, deli, and two coffee shops before I spot the book-shaped wooden sign reading *Book Nook*.

"Heel," I demand, my tone firm. "Goose. Heel."

When he *finally* listens, I bend down and scratch behind his ears. "That's a good boy. You ready to wingman me?"

He sniffs the front door, which is as good a response as any. According to the website, the Book Nook is dog-friendly—a bonus since I'm banking on Goose to help soften Maya. Logan spent Thanksgiving with the Silver family and reported back that Goose has a crush on Maya. *Like father, like son.* He didn't even whine for food; he was just happy to snuggle up against her.

Inside, the dry scent of paper and pine shelving washes over me. Maya's easy to spot, tucked behind the front desk, with her head bent over a thick book, her hair cascading in curls around her shoulders.

My heart thuds at the sight.

Okay, yeah, she was right. Something about seeing her surrounded by books sends my brain straight into sexy librarian territory.

Goose spots her an instant after I do and barks at her like she's a squirrel who just darted up a tree. He rears up on his hind legs as if he's about to waltz on over.

"Goose," I chastise under my breath as he tugs on his leash.

Maya's head snaps up at the sound of my overexcited dog and a smile illuminates her face. As beautiful as it is, it doesn't disguise the glint of apprehension in her eyes. But at least she seems pleased to see us. And by *us*, I mean Goose.

He lunges again, desperate to get to her. I don't fight it this time, following his lead since he's got the right idea anyway.

Maya steps out from behind the counter to meet us, and holy hell, her sweater clings to her like it was custom-made. Her painted-on jeans aren't doing much to help my self-control either. When she bends to pet Goose, I barely manage to keep my eyes on her face and not her perfect ass. I'm only human, after all.

"Hi, handsome man," she croons with a soft laugh. Her voice alone is like a siren call. Gentle yet sultry. It's clear she's referring to my dog and not me, but I soak in the compliment anyway.

"Hey," I greet with a welcoming smile.

She peers up at me. The smile is still in place, but confusion clouds her eyes. "Hey yourself. How are you?"

Without waiting for a response, she focuses on Goose again, showering him with attention, peppering his face with kisses.

I've never been jealous of my dog until now. For reasons unbeknownst to me—maybe it's my newfound possessive streak flaring to life—I start rambling. "I'm okay. No complaints. We're twenty-four games in and we've got more wins than losses, which is always good for morale. Especially since none of them have been consecutive losses and only one was an OT loss." My lungs burn from lack of oxygen, but I don't stop. "Clifton's injury means he'll be out the rest of the season, which sucks, but it'll give Peruzzi a chance to help fortify our defensive depth..."

Tilting her head to the side, eerily similar to the way Goose is looking at me, she laughs. "So... you're good?"

Heat creeps up my neck. Because for a minute there, I became the most painfully stereotypical athlete in history. "I'm good," I confirm. "How have you been?"

"Busy with books, so the usual."

"Reading anything good?"

Straightening to her full height, which isn't very tall, Maya hits me with an adorably grumpy pout that shouldn't make my dick twitch but does. "What a ridiculous question. Life's too short to read bad books, Cole."

"You should get that printed on a t-shirt." The corners of my mouth curl up into a smirk. "I'm actually looking for something to read on the road."

Or at least that's my excuse for being here. In all honesty, there's a chance motion sickness will kick in if I try to read on a plane or a bus, but the way Maya lights up and bounces on her toes makes me keep that detail to myself.

"Then you've definitely come to the right place," she says, all her hesitation melting away. "What sort of book are you looking for? Memoir, thriller, historical fiction?"

"Uh... All of the above?"

Maya throws her head back and lets out an indulgent laugh.

Goose gives a happy yip at the noise, butting into Maya's

legs in a bid for her attention. No amount of training has rid him of that needy habit, but she doesn't seem to mind.

Tapping her chin, her lips twitching, she asks, "Okay, what's your favorite TV show? Or movie? That'll give us a place to start."

I list the last few shows I binged, and without another word, she turns on her heel and waves, motioning for me to follow. It's sexy as hell watching her take charge.

Goose and I trail behind her as she expertly weaves through the shelves filled with colorful spines. A few other customers browse the aisles, and an older gentleman reads a newspaper in a nearby chair, but my focus stays on Maya.

She finally stops near the back of the store and pulls a book off a shelf. As she examines the cover, she lets out a sigh, as if finding this book has given her a deep sense of satisfaction. "This one's supposed to be really good. I've sold three copies this week alone."

I take it from her outstretched hand and inspect the cover like it will share the book's secret with me. "Have you read it?"

Brows lifting in surprise, she shakes her head. "Oh. No, I haven't, but a lot of customers say it's like a mix of *Succession* and *Yellowstone*. Full of family drama and angst."

With a shake of my head, I hold the book out to her. "I want something you've read."

I need an *in*, and yes, I absolutely will use her love of literature to endear me to her. In my defense, I did tell her I play to win.

A light pink hue blooms across her cheeks. "I'll put this one away, then."

When she reaches up to return the book, her sweater rides up, showing off the curved flare of her waist. Images of my calloused hands gripping her hips as she rides my cock play through my mind. *Fuck, get it together.*

When she wobbles on her toes, I close the distance between us and slide the hardcover back into place, brushing my body against hers in the process. It does the exact opposite of helping me get my shit together.

"Um. Okay. So, like, *any* book I've read?" Maya sidesteps away, her eyes darting around the shelves, focusing on anything but me.

"Your favorite book of all time," I amend.

"That's... that's like asking me to pick my favorite child." Lips parted and eyes wide, she looks borderline scandalized. "The answer is also dependent on so many things. I could tell you my favorite comfort read, my favorite motorcycle club series, my favorite contemporary romance, my favorite classic. The list goes on. I can't give you just one."

Then she really dives in, listing titles, her favorite characters, and plot twists that wrecked her. I simply listen in rapture. Goose, too, who's stopped sniffing everything in sight and sits silently to my left, head cocked and eyes locked on Maya like she's reciting poetry just for him.

After a solid five minutes, she goes quiet, nibbling on her lower lip. "Sorry, I didn't mean to ramble. I get a bit carried away sometimes. Don't even get me started on book boyfriends."

I throw her a curious look. "What's a book boyfriend?"

"What's a *book boyfriend?*" The heated intensity of her stare cuts through the shield of confidence I wear like a well-earned badge.

"Book boyfriends fill the gap where men fail to deliver," she explains. "They're everything a person *wishes* existed in real life —romantic, emotionally available, committed. They know exactly what to say. And if they annoy me or disagree with my very correct opinion? I can shut the book and shove them back on the shelf."

"Sounds healthy," I note, holding in a laugh. "Although I doubt a book boyfriend can offer you certain kinds of *relief* a real man can."

Her loud, carefree laugh tightens my balls like a warm fucking hand. "You'd be surprised."

Fuck.

"Want to make a bet?" I waggle my brows, because *fuck*, that is one bet I'm sure to win. No doubt in my mind.

Maya's cheeks burn instantly. Yeah, she clearly remembers our last bet.

I let a self-satisfied smirk take over.

"Nope." She shakes her head resolutely. "No more bets."

"Mm-hmm." I take a step closer. "Now you've got me curious. I want to read something with a book boyfriend who can apparently compete with the real thing."

Maya's eyes brighten deviously. "Oh, I know just the book."

We work our way to the front of the store, passing sturdy bookshelves that line the walls and curve around hidden reading nooks and tables.

When she points to a book featuring a shirtless purple alien with a furry tail, I can't help but chuckle. "I walked right into that one, didn't I?"

"Aliens make good book boyfriends," she says with a teasing grin.

"It looks promising," I lie through my teeth. I'm going to get my ass handed to me if I read this in front of my teammates.

She snorts at my forced tone. "Don't judge a book by its cover. I thoroughly enjoyed this one. But if you'd rather read something else—"

"Maya," I cut her off, gently taking the book from her hands and holding it the way she did, like it's something to be revered. "I asked for a book you've read so we can talk about it. And so I have another excuse to see you."

Her pouty lips part, and a slow, telltale flush crawls up her neck. "Why?"

"Because I like you."

This may only be our third encounter, and maybe none of them could be considered romantic, but Jake's words hit home. Not that I'll ever admit that to him. If anyone can make a relationship work, it's me. Perseverance is my middle name. I just have to approach dating like I would a game: show up, commit, work hard, and fight for what I want.

Maya folds her arms over her ample chest, careful not to spill the coffee she's been carrying around. "I haven't heard from you in over a month."

There's no anger or annoyance in her tone; she says it like she's stating the weather.

And that may hurt more than if she were upset.

Rubbing my fingertips against my forehead, I sigh. "I'm sorry I didn't reach out or answer your text. I've never had to make time for someone else, and I got in my head about it. It's a lame excuse, but it's the truth."

"While I appreciate the apology, it's unnecessary," she says, keeping her chin lifted. "You don't owe me anything, considering we barely know each other."

"I'd *like* to know you," I tease, flashing my most disarming grin. "That's what dates are for, right?"

Her eyes narrow into a skeptical squint. "I'm not going on a date with you."

My shoulders deflate. Dammit. I knew I'd messed up, but I didn't think I'd get an outright *no*. It throws me off just enough that instead of going with a smooth or persuasive line, I blurt, "Can we be friends?"

She shrugs as if she doesn't care one way or the other. "Sure. If that's what you want."

"I want to take you on a date," I correct, my brain functioning again. "But until you agree to go out with me, we can be friends."

"All I'm offering is friendship," she reiterates with a put-out sigh. "I can't—I'm not looking for more."

I nod, even though I'm full of it. "Friends it is."

She juts out her hip. "Then why are you looking at me like that?"

My lips twitch. "Like what?"

"Like it's *cute* that I want to be friends," she huffs.

She looks like an adorable puppy trying to act like a wolverine, but I keep that observation to myself.

"It *is* cute." I smirk. "Because I assure you there's nothing *friendly* about the things I want to do to you."

An honest-to-God gasp flies from her lips. "You can't say shit like that."

I nod at a display covered in books featuring half-naked men with glistening abs, fangs, and wings. If they can show off all of *that*, then I'm in the clear. And considering Maya's nipples are taut beneath her sweater, I'm pretty sure her complaint is all bluster.

"Friends," she repeats, as if trying to hammer the word into my skull. "That's what I'm offering. So none of that *babe* nonsense."

"Friends have nicknames," I point out. I've never called a friend babe before, but I've also never wanted to kiss a friend this badly.

She shifts, one hip popped out, her attitude on full display. "But babe isn't a nickname. It's a pet name."

I flash an innocent smile. "What can I call you, then?"

She takes a small sip of her coffee. "This is a weird concept, but you *could* call me by my name."

I wave off that simple suggestion. "How about bookie?"

"Bookie?" she asks, her lip curled up on one side. "What am I? A back-alley gambler collecting debts?"

Biting back a laugh, I rub my chin. "Hmm. Paperback princess?"

"Pass. That sounds like a literary porn star, which I don't think is a thing."

"Worm?"

"Worm?" She reels back a step, nearly spilling her coffee. With a gasp, she yanks her cup away from any books in the potential splash zone. "What did I ever do to you? Why would you want to call me *worm*? That's so—"

"It's short for bookworm," I explain before she can hurl a hardcover at my head.

That doesn't diminish the horror in her expression.

Damn. It's not like I said she *looks* like a worm.

"I'm not exactly good with nicknames," I defend. "I call my friends by their last names. And before you ask, no, I am not lumping you into that group."

I've already been friend-zoned, and the whole point of giving her a nickname is in the hope that it'll transition into a pet name. Calling her by her last name just further cements me as a friend. A person can't call someone they have sexual interest in by their last name. It defies the laws of physics.

"It seems we're at an impasse." Maya's eyes meet mine over the rim of her coffee cup as she takes a long sip.

The name comes to me like a flash of lightning. "Bean!"

Her lips twist in concentration as she lowers her cup. "As in *flick the bean*? Because of the smutty books?"

If I had my own coffee, it 100 percent would be decorating everything within spitting distance. "What?" I cough out. "Christ. No, Maya. Bean as in *coffee bean*."

Her face flushes fire-engine red. "Oh. Well... I don't hate that, then."

"Great. Bean it is." I nod once, then twist the knife in a little deeper. "So, bean. If I had asked you out on a date before I disappeared, would you have said yes?"

Focus downcast, she pets Goose's thick fur. "Honestly? Probably not. I just got out of a relationship. And I like you."

"Isn't liking me a *good* thing?"

"Depends on how you look at it." She cocks her head, her lips tipped up in a wistful smile. "Now, are you actually going to read the alien book? Or should we find something less anatomically creative?"

"I'll take the book," I confirm. "And your friendship."

If I need to tread lightly, take this slowly, in order to prove myself, then that's what I'll do. Maya doesn't know it yet, but in the short time she's known me, she's accomplished something no one else has. She's made Cole show up. Not the player, not the teammate, not the captain. Just me.

And if reading about purple aliens falling in love proves that I'm interested in her? So be it. I've never walked away from a challenge and I won't start now.

CHAPTER TEN

"OUT OF ALL THE books in the store, you sold him *that*?"

A slow, moody song hums through the store's speakers. I let it wash over me, tuning Katrina out. She saw Cole's name on a receipt and, being a die-hard Bobcats fan, nearly fainted in the stockroom. And for the last few days, the staff has been gossiping about how I sold him an alien romance.

"Does he read other paranormal romances?" Katrina props a large stack of books against her hip like a baby. "Shapeshifters? Vampires? Witches? Oh my God, do you think he knows about knotting?"

"Kat," I groan, rubbing my eyes. "I've already recounted our conversation. More than once."

Well, the highlights at least.

Cole's insistence that he read a book I already have so we can talk about it still makes my pulse race. And we've texted every day for the past week. Well, he's texted me and I've answered. He asks about my day, what managing the shop is like, how I pick what book to read next.

It's... confusing, to say the least.

Maybe Logan was right, and Cole was freaked out by the

Kiss, but that doesn't change anything for me. My whole childhood, I was caught in this vicious cycle of hoping my mom would stick around, only to watch her disappear time and time again. Now, as an adult, I distrust situations where there's potential to get what I want.

And I want Cole. Badly. Hence why I've relegated him to the friend zone and padlocked the gate that keeps him there.

"Do you think he'll come back for the next one?" Katrina asks. "There are, like, eleven books in the series."

If she'd asked me a month ago, I would've said absolutely not. But with the attention Cole's been doling out?

"There's a chance."

Kat claps, her silver bangles jangling against one another. "I need to be working when he comes back. If I'm not, you owe me an autograph."

"Yeah, yeah." I wave her off. There's no way I'm asking Cole for an autograph. That would only give him the wrong idea about what I want. "You sure you're good to close tonight? You don't need me to stay?"

She rolls her eyes and gives me a playful smile. "I've worked here for three years, Maya. I think I can handle a book club."

I nod and give her a reassuring smile, despite the worry that pricks at the back of my mind. "Okay, okay."

We host all kinds of book clubs. It's good business—they buy their books through us, rent the space for a small fee, and bring in their own snacks. We've got the Due Date Book Club, full of exhausted but enthusiastic new moms. There's the Paranoia & Probes Book Club, made of readers who enjoy books with high stakes, high tech, and mind-bending twists. My favorite is the Pinot and Prose Book Club. The members are just as serious about their merlot as they are about their plot twists.

Tonight's club can be a handful, and that's putting it mildly. They call themselves the On the Same Page Book Club, which is ironic, because they're never on the same page. By the way they behave, one would think they aren't even reading the same genre. Last month, one woman punched another in the boob when they disagreed over the pronunciation of a character's name. I grew up playing ref when my siblings argued, and they argued *a lot*, so handling them doesn't faze me. Katrina, on the other hand, abhors confrontation, despite her badass persona.

"I'll call you if anything catches fire," Kat says with a grin. "Or if someone smashes a wine bottle. Now get out of here and go have fun. One of us deserves to enjoy our Friday night."

"Fine, fine." I shrug on my parka as Katrina practically shoves me out into the cold.

As I walk home, shoulders shrugged and chin tucked into the collar of my coat, I wonder for the hundredth time why I didn't move somewhere warmer. Florida. Texas. Literally anywhere that won't turn my nipples into glass shards the instant I step outside. I don't fully thaw until I'm curled on my couch, eating carry-out Pad Thai and cradling a book in my hands. This probably isn't what Katrina had in mind when she told me to have fun, but what she doesn't know won't kill her.

Before long, I'm thoroughly lost in my book. My living room fades away and is replaced by a setting in the distant future, where a farmer's daughter finds out she's actually a princess.

When my phone rings, I'm not sure whether it's been five minutes or five hours. Though the off-key screech of my neighbor's violin tells me it's at least ten p.m. I know it's a good book when not even her abysmal attempt to play Vivaldi distracts me.

I dig my phone out from between the couch cushions, but when I see the name flashing on the screen, I briefly debate dropping it back into the crevice and ignoring it.

My heart thuds as I gape at the device a little longer. Why is Cole video calling me?

Our exchanges have been limited to text messages. *That* I can handle. That's safe. He can't see the way my cheeks turn a dark shade of pink every time he casually refers to me as "bean." The nickname shouldn't be so cute; there's nothing adorable about lima beans or black beans. But it is, thanks to my coffee addiction and love for Boston Bean. And yes, maybe the smirk I know Cole is wearing when he types it out is, too.

I should probably ignore the call. But I'm too curious, so I swipe Accept.

Big mistake on my part.

"Uh, hi," I croak.

He's so gorgeous it's a miracle I can even get that much out. Water droplets slide from his hair onto his nape and run in rivulets over his bare shoulders—

Like a record scratch, the world screeches to a halt around me. *Bare shoulders?*

Why isn't he wearing a shirt?

Cole chuckles and a triumphant grin bursts across his lips.

The air evacuates my lungs when I realize I said that last part out loud. Damn his sexiness for making it impossible to keep my thoughts to myself.

"I think we should focus on your shirt. Does it say *Bookstore Whore?*"

Oh God. Kill me. Kill me now.

"It was a gift from Kennedy," I explain, my face burning. "I forgot I had it on."

I don't mention the other shirts she gave me: *Smut Slut* and *Always Tired (from reading all night)*. It's bad enough that I got caught wearing this one.

I mentally shake off the mortification. Why do I care? Cole's just a friend. Honestly, he's just a tiny step above acquaintance. Maybe it's a cop-out to relegate him to that role, because it's clear already that he wouldn't be like other guys I've dated. He wouldn't let me keep him at arm's length. He'd steamroll his way into my life, make himself integral, then vanish just as fast, leaving me to watch him through my TV screen.

"I like it, bean." His smile widens. "And I'm not wearing a shirt because I just got out of the shower."

Don't think of his naked body. Keep your thoughts PG. Focus on his face.

"And you're calling me right after the shower because..."

"Since I'm out of town and can't take you on a proper date this week, I figured a video call was the next best thing." He lifts one sculpted *bare* shoulder in an easy shrug.

"That doesn't answer my question," I say. "And need I remind you that friends don't go out on dates?"

He rolls his eyes and lets out a huff. "Okay, fine. Since we can't 'hang out'"—he uses the fingers of his free hand to do air quotes—"I figured I'd call you instead. And..." He leans in closer to the phone, his lips kicking up on one side. "Friends also don't drool at one another, but you're practically salivating at my naked torso."

"I am *not*," I sputter, my heart lurching into my throat.

Was I? There's a very high likelihood. But come on. His muscular chest is wide, though his torso tapers down into a taut six-pack. I don't mean to objectify him, but the hours he spends on the ice are clearly doing wonders for his physique.

He leans back against a headboard, giving me a peek of crisp white sheets as he gets settled. "Mm-hmm."

"That's a nasty bruise on your side," I comment.

"What was that about you not checking me out, baby?" He smirks, though as he ducks, eyeing the injury I pointed out, his caramel-colored eyes widen as if he's just now noticing it. "Eh, I've had worse."

Hockey player. Duh.

"Oh, you had a game tonight."

Sophie invited me to meet her at a bar to watch the Bobcats play, but I graciously declined, and we agreed to do drinks next week instead.

"I did indeed." He chuckles. "Ended about an hour ago."

"Did you get into a fistfight?"

"This isn't the MMA, bean, but yeah, I got checked a few times." The corners of his lips tug up. "We won, too, by the way. If you were curious."

I roll my eyes at his teasing tone. "That was my next question, but congrats. That's exciting. The team doesn't do anything to celebrate?"

He shakes his head. "Nah. We have an early flight tomorrow. Figured I'd chat with you, then read some of my book."

I arch a brow. "And what book would that be?"

Cole's cheeks instantly flush. "*Alien Lovers of Planet Dexxar.*" His voice tilts up at the end, making the answer sound more like a question.

"This is my Super Bowl." I laugh, bouncing a little on the couch cushion. "Or should I say my Stanley Cup."

He grins at my hockey reference. "Interstellar relationships? Or making me flustered?"

I shake my head, batting at the strands of hair that have escaped my ponytail and fallen into my face. "No, introducing someone to a new book. It's a form of therapy for me, I guess."

"Even if the book is about purple aliens falling in love?"

"You've only just started it," I chastise him with a mock scowl. "You can't already be judging."

"I'm not judging," he promises. He holds up a hand, his middle and pointer finger crossed. "I'm just genuinely curious about how this book has such a big cult following when the plot is so outlandish."

"That's the point. No one's picking it up expecting a Pulitzer Prize winner. They're reading it to escape. If I'm having a rough day, I don't want to lose myself in a heavy story. I want something like *Alien Lovers of Planet Dexxar*. A book that pulls me out of my own head and makes me forget about the real world, if only for a few hours," I say. "When people are down, they want comfort. When they're happy, they want something that amplifies that joy. Books meet you where you are."

I snap my mouth shut, only for Cole to stare at me.

Now it's me who flushes. Big time. I break eye contact and nibble on my lower lip as if that'll turn back time so I can go back and stop myself from word vomiting.

"It's really damn cute when you go into book mode," he comments, his eyes soft. "Have you always been such a big reader?"

"Pretty much. I got my first library card at, like, six years old, so I honestly can't remember a time when books weren't my constant companion."

"Are other people in your family big readers, too?"

The question sobers me up quickly. "Uh, not really, no." I straighten a little, my spine stiff. "My dad's not in the picture and my mom"—*how do I nicely say my mom's only into herself?*—"has other interests."

Cole doesn't ask me to expand or give me the sympathetic look I've become so used to when the topic of my dad comes up, but his brow does furrow. "My dad played basketball growing up. He tried to get my brother and me into it, but we were obsessed with hockey."

My brows raise at the mention of a brother. "I didn't know you had a brother. Does he play hockey?"

"You didn't google me?"

Umm.

"Nope," I half lie. I definitely did, but I quit after reading about two sentences of his Wikipedia page. It was full of too many numbers and stats and phrases like "second-longest point-scoring streak."

"Hmm," he says, as if he doesn't quite believe me. "Yeah, I have two sisters and a twin brother, but he passed away a few years ago in a car accident."

"Oh my God," I blurt out, my hand flying up to cover my mouth. "I'm so sorry, Cole. I had no idea."

"Probably because you didn't google me." He chuckles and throws me a small smile. "But yeah, he played for the Miami Trailblazers."

"Who the hell names these teams?" Head dropped back, I mutter the words to the ceiling. This isn't my smoothest segue, but based on the pain in his eyes, he could use a change of subject.

Cole lets out a mock gasp, the sound easing the tension I hadn't even realized was coiled in my shoulders. "What's wrong with the Trailblazers?"

"Nothing," I say slowly. You know what? *Fuck it.* "That's a lie. All hockey team names sound ridiculous. It's like someone scribbled a bunch of random nouns and a few adjectives on scraps of paper, tossed them into a hat, and had team owners or coaches or whatever pick them out, and voilà—whatever they pulled out became their team's name."

Cole clenches his jaw in an attempt not to laugh, though his amber eyes are still a bit dull. "That's a very astute observation. My hometown team is the San Diego Devils, and I never could figure out the meaning behind the name."

Sensing he still needs a change of topic, I blurt out, "Want to hear a funny story about devils?"

"Duh."

"Okay, in elementary school, a few days before Halloween, my class played this game where we could each give our class-mates one clue about what we planned to dress up as for

Halloween. If you guessed correctly, you'd get an extra piece of candy from our teacher. I wanted to dress up as the devil. Want to guess what my clue was?"

"Lucifer?"

"Nope." I cringe. It's been over fifteen years, and my body still goes into fight-or-flight mode at the memory. "I announced to the entire class that I was horny."

Cole throws his head back and laughs from deep in his chest. The throaty sound makes me clench my thighs together. "Oh, God. That's amazing."

I wince. "If you mean amazingly embarrassing, then sure."

"We've all got our embarrassing childhood stories." He waves me off. "I once accidentally said orgasm instead of organism in science class."

"I once inadvertently started a rumor that a girl named Mary Juana was found hiding in a locker because I overheard teachers talking and didn't know marijuana was a drug."

His wide smile is almost blinding. "I think I have you beat. When our childhood fish died, we flushed him down the toilet, but I was convinced he'd jump back out, so I refused to use the toilet for over a week."

My breath catches. "Wait, you didn't go to the bathroom for *a week?*"

"Oh, no, I did," Cole says, rubbing at his nape. "I snuck outside and went in my mom's vegetable garden."

"Cole!" I gasp, though I quickly dissolve into a fit of giggles. "Oh my God."

"My parents were appalled," he admits. "Rightfully so."

"I cannot believe you told me that," I wheeze, my body sinking farther into the couch. "If I were you, I would've taken that shit to the grave. No pun intended."

He pouts, that luscious lower lip stuck out. "C'mon, I was just a kid. I didn't know any better."

For the next hour, we go back and forth, exchanging funny stories and sharing childhood memories. He tells me about the time he and his brother switched places to take one another's tests, and I tell him about the time Kennedy and I got locked in an Old Navy after hours and the fire department had to come get us out. It's not a date, and yet somehow, the conversation is better than any I've ever had when out with a man.

Cole Berrett is a genuinely good guy. One I could easily see myself falling for, which is exactly why I can't.

CHAPTER ELEVEN

I LAY my hand on the horn, and a few moments later, Jake storms through his building's front door. He loads his luggage into the trunk clumsily, then slides into the passenger seat with downturned brows over bleary eyes. We probably didn't have to leave quite so early this morning, but I'm not taking any necessary risks after my missed flight, and if he didn't want to leave at five thirty, then he could have driven himself.

There's nothing wrong with flying commercial, but packaged pretzels, cramped middle seats, and sitting near crying babies can't compete with extra legroom and first-class finishings. And missing a flight while wearing the captain's *C* is, to use Lily and Violet's vocabulary, a *big no-no*.

"Don't be cranky." I chuckle at his pout. "I got you a coffee. Extra cream, one sugar."

I hold out the Boston Bean coffee—Maya swears they make the best espresso in town—and the lightly caramelized and nutty aroma defrosts some of the ice in his glare.

He leans back into the leather seat with a mumbled *thank you* and a yawn. "Sorry. I'm exhausted. Didn't get much sleep last night."

I peer over at him, one brow cocked. "Something, or some-one, you want to share?"

He rolls his eyes over his to-go cup. "I'm sore, jackass."

"Ah," I commiserate.

He took a few rough hits during yesterday's game. It's no wonder he spent the night twisting and turning.

"Rest up on the plane," I suggest. "Plenty of time to sleep before we get to San Diego."

His responding grunt is the last sound he makes on the ride to the airport. Our team's chartered jet departs from a private terminal at Boston Logan International Airport, so I park my car at the nearby enclosed lot, then huddle into my jacket, pushing through the winter winds as I make my way to our plane. A bundled-up flight attendant waits at the bottom of the steps, a familiar branded parka zipped up to his chin.

"Morning, Samuel," I say.

"Nicholas," he replies with a slight nod. "Good to have you with us again."

I've told the crew to call me Cole, but it hasn't stuck. At least he's no longer calling me Mr. Berrett.

With a dip of my chin, I take the warm, scented towel from him, then wipe off my hands as I climb the steps.

The assistant coaches are deep in conversation near the front of the cabin, likely working out plays and strategies for the upcoming game. With a brief greeting, I pass them and shuffle to my usual spot. Our seats aren't assigned, but we follow an unspoken seating chart, nonetheless.

I slide into the Italian leather seat next to Cameron and buckle myself in. My seat buddy is already half asleep by the window, head lolling onto his neck pillow.

"Morning," he mumbles without opening his eyes. Despite years of early practices, flights, and workouts, he's mostly useless before six a.m.

"I wish this flight wasn't so long," Logan complains from a row over. "San Diego's so far."

"If you slept, it wouldn't feel so long," Cameron snarks. He pulls his eye mask on, indicating his participation in the conversation is over.

Logan flips him off with a lazy hand gesture. "Anyone want to play *Grand Theft Auto*?"

"I'm good," Jake says beside him, already reclining his seat. "I need to catch up on sleep, too."

"Lame," Logan says with an exaggerated eye roll. "Berrett?"

"Nope." I shake my head and stretch my legs out. "Got some reading to do."

The flight from Boston to San Diego is about six hours, which means I have plenty of time to dive into the world of *Dexxar*. As much as I hate to admit it, the book's decent. It won't be studied in college lit classes anytime soon, but it's held my attention so far. Sure, it's a bit difficult to completely suspend my grasp of reality, but that's the fun of fiction, I suppose.

Cameron lifts his eye mask up and squints at me. "I'm sorry. What?"

"I know you've taken a few hits to the head recently," I retort, "but surely you know what reading is."

He elbows my side. "Yeah, asshole, I've just never seen you read anything longer than a text message."

Jake leans forward in his seat and grins like he knows a secret. "It's because of Maya, isn't it?"

I ignore them both and unzip my duffel. I'm not particularly excited about how my teammates will react to the washboard abs of the purple alien on the cover, but you know what they say. Never judge an alien book by its cover.

———

Sweat trickles down my back as adrenaline surges through me. Fans decked out in the Devils team colors roar from the stands, stomping their feet and waving at the camera in hopes of being on the Jumbotron. It may not be a home game, but I practically grew up in this arena, and the energy rolling across the rink is electric.

As the Devils take the ice, I skate to the center for face-off. Rolling back my shoulders, I tune out the noise of the stands and the pep talk Logan's trying to give, focusing completely on the puck. The moment it's dropped and the whistle blows, my world shifts. Nothing matters but the win.

After a deadlocked opening period, we spend the second period making up for it. The Devils are great, but we've been working our asses off in practice, and with a combined eleven shots across the period, Jake and I both end up on the score sheet. And despite the Devils refusing to roll over, we establish a towering lead through the remaining forty minutes of play.

The win is ours; I can almost taste it.

During the next line change, I swing my body over the wall and chug my water. I've played most of the game, and my lungs burn with the exertion. As a center, I've got more freedom to move across the ice than my linemates, but that also means I'm covering more ground.

"Solid defense out there," I tell Jefferson as he joins me off the ice.

He mumbles his response through sips of water and gasps of air. Pairing him up with Erickson whipped him into shape better than Coach Henderson expected and, consequently, cemented his belief that he made the right call when he named me captain.

In the third period, we have a comfortable lead, but I won't be confident in our win until the buzzer times out and the announcer declares it.

Cameron is ruthless in his defense of the net, preventing goals with applause-worthy accuracy.

Jake strips the puck from the opposition's center and flies down the ice like a missile. I fall in beside him, running interference and blocking an overly aggressive left-winger. Their goalie is so focused on Jake that he doesn't notice Logan setting up, and by the time he's figured out our play, it's already in motion. Logan smacks the puck with swift surety, and it whizzes into the net, hitting the back with a satisfying snap.

We may be in Devils territory, but our fans showed up, and they make themselves heard. I'm almost positive it's my mom that starts the "Bobcats" chant when I score the winning goal in the last few seconds of the game.

After a quick round of post-game interviews, I head for a long, scalding shower in the visitors' locker room. From there, the majority of us pile into cars and head to my childhood home for a late dinner. Every season, my parents insist on hosting the guys for a home-cooked meal. It's a feat, considering eighteen well-muscled hockey players don't just take up a lot of space but require a lot of food, but my mom has never been one to back down from a challenge, and she's been feeding hockey players for decades, from peewee league to the pros.

I'm bombarded with congratulations and hugs the moment I walk through the front door. Despite my parents both being born and raised in San Diego, the house is decked out in Bobcats colors. It's only accentuated by the gear my friends, family, and teammates wear.

As I make my way across the crowded family room, greeting my parents' friends and someone's cousin's uncle's ex-wife, my phone buzzes in my pocket.

MAYA SILVER

Don't let it get to your head, but I watched the game (it was either that or Jeopardy reruns). Congrats on the win!

Hope your butt's not too bruised after that hit.

I snort. My tailbone's definitely feeling the aftermath of getting steamrolled by a player nearly double my size after Logan mouthed off about his haircut.

COLE BERRETT

Thank you!

Glad to know you're keeping an eye on my ass.

How'd it look in my shorts?

MAYA SILVER

Remember how I told you to not let it get to your head?

COLE BERRETT

You miss me. Admit it.

MAYA SILVER

I miss the days when I could get a good coffee for less than $5.

A small blonde barrels into me, stealing my attention from my phone. My niece grins up at me, a half-smeared Bobcat face painted on her cheek. "Hi, Uncle Coley. I'm hungry."

"Hi, princess." I hoist her up into my arms, relishing the way she snuggles into my neck. "Let's go get you a snack."

Violet nods, making her tight curls bounce. "Yay!"

I find my mom in the kitchen with an exasperated frown hardening her features. It only takes an instant to locate the reason for the look. Across the room, Logan's hovering over the dip bowl, dunking pita chips in like it's an Olympic event. I swear he doesn't even chew before he swallows and goes for another. Jake and Cameron watch with horrified fascination while Lily—who's wrapped around Cam's back like a tiny monkey—giggles uncontrollably.

We cross the room to run interference. "Save some for the rest of the room, man."

Logan pouts, his bottom lip stuck out. "I may be your future brother-in-law. Cut me some slack."

The asshole shoots me a saccharine smile, fully aware that he's opening me up to a level-five interrogation. If my hands weren't occupied with holding Violet, I'd stab him in the eye with the serving fork on the counter in front of me. The last thing I need is for my mother to get involved in my love life. Or lack thereof, considering I'm stuck in the friend zone.

My mom pushes the spinach artichoke dip closer to him. *Traitor.* "What do you mean?"

Logan happily scoops a heaping glob of dip onto a chip and pops it into his mouth. "We're dating siblings. That's like one degree of separation from being brothers."

My mom's jaw nearly hits the tiled floor, and her golden-brown eyes that so closely resemble my own widen. "You—*what*? I—you have a girlfriend?"

"No, I d—"

"Nicholas Henry Berrett, how could you keep this from me?" Before I can answer, she launches into a breathless string of questions.

For a moment, I massage my temples, letting her wear herself out. "Mom," I finally interrupt. "*Mom.*"

With a sharp inhale, she rests a hand on my forearm. "Sorry, honey. I'm excited is all. You haven't been interested in a relationship since... it's just been a while."

Briefly shutting my eyes, I take a deep breath. "I'm not dating anyone, Mom. Logan's just being a... D-bag."

"What's a D-bag?" Violet whispers not so loudly.

My stomach sinks. Dammit. "Um… it's a diaper bag."

"Because Logan's smelly," Cameron adds with a chuckle.

Jake bites his lip. "And you want to throw him in the trash immediately."

"So you *aren't* seeing anyone?" my mom asks, her brow creased.

I shake my head, my lips pressed together, and her face falls, as if I just told her that I hate her raisin crumb cake.

Violet leans over and taps on my mom's shoulder to get her attention. "It's okay, Nana. Don't be sad. Mommy said we have to be patient for Uncle Coley to bring home my new auntie."

Lily nods over Cam's shoulder, as if my dating life is a common dinner topic. "Or uncle," she suggests. "My friend Angela has an uncle who is married to her other uncle."

Violet tilts her head and eyes the ceiling, then nods. "Yeah. As long as Goose likes him, we'll like him, too, I bet."

Logan chokes on the pita chip he's munching on, and Jake pats his back, although he's buried his face in his shoulder to hide his laughter. Cam cackles, not even bothering to hide his amusement. *Assholes.*

"That's right, girls," my mom says, giving them a reassuring smile. "Your uncle can be with whoever makes him happy."

"I have seen him check out my junk a time or two." Logan pops another chip into his mouth and crunches it with his teeth obnoxiously. "So you may not be wrong."

Cameron whoops out a laugh, startling me from my thoughts. My mom fights a smile as she takes Violet from my arms and helps Lily off Cam's back. "Why don't we go get ready for bed, girls? You can show the boys your cool hockey pajamas."

My nieces practically drag my mom out of the kitchen, and

the moment they're out of sight, I smack the back of Logan's head. Hard.

"Ow," he whines, rubbing the spot. "I could have a concussion."

"We're hockey players." Cam snorts. "We have perpetual concussions."

"Did you really have to say that to my mom?" I bite out. "She's going to be on my ass for weeks."

I immediately regret the ass comment when Logan wiggles his brows suggestively. He thankfully keeps his trap shut about it.

"What *is* going on with you and Maya?" Jake asks, his expression one of pure curiosity.

He hasn't brought her up since practice a few weeks ago. Likely because he feels unnecessarily guilty for bringing up Nate.

"There's nothing to tell." With a frown, I run my fingers through my hair. "She wants to be *friends*."

The word tastes sour on my tongue. Like I'm stuck in the penalty box, watching the game continue on without me. Spending time with Maya, even if it's mostly via video calls, only makes me want to spend *more* time with her.

Logan nods, as if this makes complete sense to him. "Take it slow and prove yourself. I have a good feeling about you two."

Cameron's jaw drops. "'Take it slow'? This coming from the guy who fell head over heels after what, six weeks?"

Logan waves him off, unbothered. "Elliott's different. He's open to finding his person, whereas Maya doesn't like change. And she only dates guys who are safe. Ones who have no chance of sticking around longer than she wants them to."

"Why would taking it slow help, then?" Jake asks, taking the question from my mouth. "Wouldn't it be better to rip the Band-Aid off and dive right in?"

Logan pops a chip into his mouth. "You can't build trust overnight. Especially not with someone who's only ever depended on herself. You rush her, she bolts. I'm not psychological, but—"

"Do you mean you're not a psychologist?" Jake gives him an incredulous look.

Logan swats his words away with the flick of his hand. "Yeah, that's what I said. Anyway, I'm not saying she won't date you, but if you rush her or push for more than she's ready for, I think she'll run."

"Minus the way you mixed up *psychological* and *psychologist*, that has to be the most emotionally mature thing you've ever said." Cam lets out a low whistle. "Elliott's good for you."

"He's good at a lot. Especially blowj—"

"Nope. Absolutely not." Jake rears back. "I haven't had nearly enough whiskey for that conversation."

"How come you guys can talk about your sexual escapades and I can't? Just because—"

"Don't pull that crap." Cam snatches the dip bowl off the counter and points the chip in his hand at Logan. "Us ignoring your extremely inappropriate questions about our sex lives hardly qualifies as talking about our sexual escapades."

I tune Logan out as he grumbles about how we're no fun at locker room talk and take out my phone again.

COLE BERRETT

It's okay to admit you miss me, bean. I'm sure the Book Nook sells self-help books that cover how to handle your overwhelming feelings.

MAYA SILVER

We only sell books that help egomaniacs tone down their narcissism. Happy to put a copy on hold for you!

COLE BERRETT

I'll pick it up tomorrow when I'm back in town. We can discuss it over tapas once you've finished working.

MAYA SILVER

I'm more of a chips and guac girl.

COLE BERRETT

I know a great Mexican spot.

MAYA SILVER

Will there be margaritas? My yes is contingent on that.

COLE BERRETT

Are you negotiating with me? Again?

MAYA SILVER

Duh. If you need help with a counteroffer, the Book Nook also sells Negotiating for Dummies. I'll even give you my friends and family discount.

Yep. It's going to be hard to take it slow when she makes my heart race so fast.

CHAPTER TWELVE

COLE BERRETT

Okay. Hear me out. This alien simply believes that destiny has chosen this random chick as his person, and that's it? Done deal. He's ready for marriage and babies and the whole she-bang?

MAYA SILVER

It's the fated mates trope, so yes, lol.

COLE BERRETT

Sounds suspect.

Are you working today or do you have the day off?

MAYA SILVER

Day off! Meeting Sophie for coffee this afternoon.

COLE BERRETT

Nice. Tell her I say hi.

I'm about to start practice.

Talk later?

MAYA SILVER

Sure. Good luck, Captain!

UNABLE TO FIGHT A SMILE, I set my phone on the table and take out my book. I sit back, sighing, and sink into the overstuffed chair I've hunkered down in. As I take in the coffee shop, I let the scent of espresso wrap around me like a blanket.

I've only read a chapter when the door chimes. On instinct, I swivel at the sound. Sophie bustles in, brushing a light layer of snow from her jacket, scanning over the customers seated at bistro tables in wrought-iron chairs and standing in front of a glass case filled with a selection of baked goods. When she spots me cozied up in the back corner by the fireplace, a smile brightens her face.

She scurries over and wraps me up in a quick hug before making herself comfortable in the seat I've saved for her. "I am *so* sorry I'm late."

I wave off her concern with the flick of a hand. "Don't worry about it. I'm usually the one running behind, so it's nice to be first to arrive for once. Plus, I have a book." I hold the paperback up and wiggle it.

With a giggle, she peers over at the chalkboard menu hung on a nearby wall. "What's good here?"

I bolt upright. "Hold on. You've never been here?"

"I don't think so?"

"How are we even friends?"

She arches a pale blond brow. "I didn't realize it was a requirement."

A laugh bubbles out of me. It took a few happy hours and late-night hangouts for her sassy side to shine through, but once it did, it never left the party. For that, I'm grateful.

"It is now," I tell her. "This place is sacred."

Sophie may be new to the menu, but this place has been a

constant in my life for years. I've cried into cappuccinos, celebrated Book Nook promotions with pastries, and spent countless hours drinking refill after refill of drip coffee while telling myself "just one more chapter."

"Okay, okay." She tugs off her knit beanie. "So what's good here, O wise one?"

"Everything," I deadpan. "But their espresso is amazing and they have the only coffee cake in the city that Kennedy says is better than hers."

We place our orders—a lavender latte for her and a caramel macchiato for me—and catch up as we wait for our drinks. The place is busy but not chaotic, filled with the usual hum of milk steamers, indie music, and quiet conversations.

Once we have drinks in hand, Sophie shifts forward, her eyes on me as she blows on her latte. "How's work? Still drowning in stacks of books, or have you figured out how to bend time and space yet?"

I laugh. "Not yet, but I'd rather be busy than bored. Work's..." I lift a shoulder and let it drop. "Fine."

She arches a skeptical brow. "Just fine?"

I take a sip of my drink, relishing the way it warms me. "It's good, but that's nothing new. It's always good."

And that's the truth. I love my job. But lately, things feel a little flat. Predictable in a way that makes me antsy instead of relieved. I go to work, and when I'm not there, I'm reading or scrolling through Bookstagram to find my next book. The only parts of my days that stand out lately are Cole's calls and texts.

"You need a hobby," Sophie announces.

A light laugh escapes me. "I'm pretty sure reading is considered a hobby."

She narrows her eyes at me. "Okay, smart-ass. What I mean is a *new* hobby. Like tennis or rock climbing."

I cringe good-naturedly. "Aren't hobbies supposed to be enjoyable, though?"

She smacks the table, causing some of her coffee to spill over the lip of the mug. "You should take a writing class!"

A flutter of excitement I thought had long ago faded lights in my belly, but I do my best to tamp down on it. "I haven't written in a long time," I admit, eyes darting around the room as if the ghost of decisions past is going to appear.

Sophie shrugs. "Did you take any creative writing courses in college?"

"One, but the school didn't offer a degree program." I finger the edge of my sweater, dropping my focus to it. "I wanted to go to Northwestern or Columbia because they have some of the best creative writing programs in the country, but I had Elliott and Ava to think about, so staying local made more sense. Boston has great schools, thankfully." I force a smile to my face. "So it's not like I sacrificed my education or anything."

"You're a good sister," she says gently. "And you'll be an even better writer once you take that class. That's the whole point, you know. To improve and all of that jazz. I took a glass-blowing class last year and loved it."

"Really?"

"Mm-hmm. When I moved to Boston, I didn't really know anyone, so I joined a couple of classes to meet people. I'm absolutely shit at manipulating molten glass, *but* I made a few friends, and it was fun to try something new."

"So you won't be opening up an Etsy shop and selling elaborate glass sculptures anytime soon?"

"God, no," she laughs. "I showed Cameron a vase I made, and he thought it was a bong."

I choke on my coffee, wincing as it burns the back of my throat. "Sounds interesting."

"Speaking of my brother," she says with absolutely no shame. "He said that Cole's been reading a lot."

More carefully this time, I take a sip of my coffee. A puff of heat hits my face, making the stray hairs at my temples flutter. I'm honestly surprised it took her this long to mention Cole. The woman has not been shy about telling me she thinks we're perfect together.

I'm worried that I'll accidentally admit that Cole's the sexiest man I've ever seen, and that'll send her straight to the internet, where she'll use some program that takes individual photos of us and morphs them in a way that swears it's what our children will look like.

"Hmm," I say, keeping my tone even. "Good for him."

"Oh come on." She slumps back in her seat. "You've got to give me *something*."

"There's nothing going on with Cole and me. We're just friends."

I've used that phrase at least twenty times in the past week, since neither she nor Kennedy will leave me alone about it. If I had juicy details to divulge, I'd be more than happy to share, but Cole and I are friends. That's it. And the more I remind myself of that truth, the more apt I am to believe it.

"Either admit you like Cole or promise me you'll look into a writing class," she says with a sneaky grin.

Apprehension swirls in my stomach. "You weren't this diabolical when we first met."

Sophie clinks her coffee cup against mine, sealing the deal. "You're welcome."

CHAPTER THIRTEEN

THE SPRAY of the hot water kneads my sore muscles, pulling an unbridled groan from my lips. I soap my body, digging my fingers into my overworked muscles to rid them of any lingering tension.

Once a month, I take inventory and do a major restocking, which means lifting and carrying tons of boxes. I thought hiking up and down the stairs of my building would've prepped me better for the exertion, but my muscles don't appreciate the strain.

As I run my soapy hands over my chest, I can't help but imagine it's Cole's rough fingers plucking at my nipples. *Fuck.* Friends most definitely do not do this, but in the privacy of my own shower, I let myself live out the fantasy. If he wanted a casual situation that involved hot, heavy sex, I'd be more than down, but he wants a *date*. And that's dangerous. Cole Berrett is a genuinely sweet guy who asks me questions and remembers even the smallest details and is reading alien smut just because I teased him into it. That's marriage material, and I'm... not sure what to do with that. Turning people away is an emotional reflex for me. It saves me from having to deal with the fallout when they eventually walk away. But so far, Cole is sticking like that extra-sticky Gorilla glue from Home Depot.

With a huff, I force my hands from my breasts and run them through my hair, washing out the conditioner. I need to stop fantasizing about Cole and have a date with my vibrator instead. Once I've turned the shower off, I tighten the fluffy white towel around my body and assess myself in the mirror. I bite back a sigh, cursing the winter weather for making my skin so pale. Though I suppose it's better than looking like an Oompa-Loompa, which is what happened when I let Kennedy give me an at-home spray tan. *Never, ever again.*

My phone rings on the counter, so I snatch it and accept the call without looking at the display.

It's a mistake.

"You answered," a familiar voice says. "Does that mean you forgive me?"

Shit.

"Do I forgive you for cheating on me, Josh? No. For some weird reason, I do not."

My ex lets out a dramatic sigh. "C'mon, babe. I told you it was an accident."

My hackles raise and my free hand clenches, like I'm the kind of person who'd ever actually punch someone. *Lord, give me strength.* "Right. Please tell me how one's dick accidentally slips into someone? I'm dying to know."

"She meant nothing," he continues, as if this factoid is supposed to make me feel better. "Why can't we just move on? All couples have their issues. Let's just work through this. Please?"

I bite back a scoff. Did I enjoy spending time with Josh? Sure. But he's certainly not irreplaceable. And I'm sure as hell not interested in giving him another chance when he so epically broke my trust the first time around.

"An issue is when a couple can't agree on where to go for dinner. What you did is an entirely different problem." I cannot believe I'm even entertaining this conversation.

Though I can admit that it's doused all the desire that swirled in my belly while I was in the shower.

"But I miss you."

Tucking my towel tightly beneath my armpits, I take a calming breath. "That sounds like a you problem. Listen. We're done. I shouldn't have to keep repeating myself to get my point across. Please just stop texting and calling. You're only making it harder on yourself."

"But—"

Before he can come up with another lame excuse that has nothing to do with me, I end the call.

I haven't even set my phone down before it rings again. *Jesus H. Christ and the horse he rode in on.*

"For the love of all things holy," I bark into the phone. "What in the ever-loving hell do you not understand about leaving me alone? Should I say it in French to get it through that thick skull of yours? *Va te faire foutre.* Understand that?"

There's an elongated pause on the other end of the line, followed by a throaty chuckle that has the annoying habit of making me clench my thighs together. "I didn't realize you spoke French, bean."

My cheeks heat. Hell, my whole body heats, and not in a good way. "I don't, but I do know a few choice phrases."

It was how I covertly swore in front of my siblings when they were young. Fat lot of good that did me, considering Ava's favorite word is "asshole."

"Clearly," he says, amusement lacing his tone. "What's going on? Are you okay?"

God, I swear he has to gargle gravel to make his voice that rumbly.

"My ex doesn't seem to understand the concept of *we're not getting back together because you cheated on me*," I tell him.

Cole growls. He literally *growls* into the phone, and it sends a shiver down my spine. "He cheated on you?"

I hit the speaker button and set the device on the counter. I'm not embarrassed by it. His cheating has everything to do with him and nothing to do with me, but that doesn't mean I want to get into the nitty-gritty details. "According to Josh, it wasn't cheating. It was a momentary lapse in judgment."

"What a fucking idiot," Cole huffs. "He doesn't deserve your forgiveness or you. And he needs to understand that you're no longer his. Tell him he needs to back off."

Whoa, there. I roll my eyes as I get a second towel for my hair. "Roger that, sir."

"I'm serious, Maya. If he doesn't get the memo, I'll happily deliver it."

My insides light up. *Is Cole... jealous?*

Nope. Not going there. "So, uh... what's up?"

He makes an unintelligible noise, then cuts himself off and takes a deep breath. "It's last minute, so if you have plans, I understand, but my meeting got rescheduled and I was wondering if you wanted to have dinner with me. I leave tomorrow and won't be back until the New Year. I'm fine ordering in; I know restocking takes a lot out of you. But I'd like to see you. If you're free. And want to."

Cole's rambling is more endearing than it should be. And it lowers my defenses just enough for a "sure!" to pop out. I can handle dinner at my apartment with the guy I fantasized about playing with my nipples no less than fifteen minutes ago. I think.

"Okay, great. I'm craving Chinese," Cole continues, "and this new spot just opened around the corner from me. Thoughts?"

"Sounds good. What time do you want to come over? Seven-ish?"

That'll give me enough time to clean my hot mess of an apartment *and* blow dry my hair so I don't look like a troll doll.

"That works. I've got to shower"—*welcome back, inappropriate thoughts*—"but traffic from here to the Back Bay shouldn't be too bad."

My breath catches and my senses tingle. "Uh, how do you know where I live?"

He chuckles, the sound raspy through the phone. "Don't tell me you forgot that we kissed outside your door."

"Oh." My cheeks flush furiously, and it has nothing to do with the post-shower steam fogging up my bathroom mirror. "Right. Well, um, see you then!"

Once I've ended the call, I do a quick tidy of my apartment —a.k.a. shoving every miscellaneous item into my laundry basket and hiding it in my bedroom—then cycle through three different legging-and-sweater combos before landing on one that doesn't look like I'm trying too hard. Or so I hope.

By the time Cole arrives, my apartment is in semi-decent shape and I am, too. Cole, on the other hand? I don't think he's ever been less than extraordinarily handsome in his life. Even in sweatpants and a fitted tee, he looks like he stepped out of an ad campaign.

He leans against the doorframe in all his holy glory. His jaw is dusted in a layer of scruff and his plump lips are fixed into a reckless grin. The kind that urges me to knock the wonton soup out of his hands and climb him like a damn monkey.

It takes more effort than I'd like to admit to remain where I am.

"Hey," he greets me. "I come bearing gifts."

I force myself to look away from his chiseled features and

focus on the *three* packed bags of Chinese food. *Damn*. I didn't think he'd order the entire menu.

Taking one of the bags from his arms, I lead him into the apartment. "How much do I owe you?"

He scowls, his dark brows pulled low. "You don't owe me anything. Don't be ridiculous."

"That's a lot of food," I point out, peering over my shoulder. "Probably enough to cater a Bat Mitzvah."

Or at least a baby shower.

"I'm a big guy." He shrugs, as if that statement wasn't extremely subliminal. "Do you want to eat at the kitchen table or the island?"

Coming back down to earth, I cough out, "Uh, the table is fine."

While I pull out plates and silverware, Cole opens container after container of delicious-smelling dishes. Beef and broccoli, orange chicken, kung pao pork, and General Tsao with tofu. I grab one of my nicer wines—and by that, I mean it cost more than $11.99 but less than $24.99—and pour two glasses.

I set the glasses on the table, and when I look up, I find Cole studying me with keen interest.

"You're taking a writing class?"

Breath stuttering, I dart a look at my laptop, which is open on the seat next to him. There's nothing salacious on there. Just about a thousand open tabs, all holding information about writing courses and classes. Who knew that searching "creative writing class near me" would send me down a rabbit hole of such epic proportions?

I wiggle my fingers, silently demanding he return my private property to me, and sit in the empty chair across from him. "It's considered rude to look through people's computers."

With a completely unrepentant smirk, he closes the lid. But

rather than hand it over, he keeps it on the seat like it's claiming squatter's rights. "Good thing you're not just people."

"Hmph." I pile a bit of everything onto my plate at a turtle-like pace, but when I can no longer pretend to be engrossed by the food, I risk glancing up.

Cole's amber eyes narrow in assessment, the steadiness of his stare an almost physical force. "So are you?"

Playing dumb, I ask, "Am I what?"

"Taking a writing class? You've mentioned wanting to be an author."

I sputter at his question. The word *author* sounds so outlandish and out of reach that I feel ridiculous for ever having admitted that to him. "No, I'm not. Sophie suggested I find a hobby. That's not reading, I mean."

"But you're not sold on taking a writing class." It's more of a statement than a question.

When I don't answer, he puts down his fork and rests his forearms on the table, his focus homed in on me.

"I told you I took a shit in my mom's vegetable garden because I was scared a goldfish was going to resurrect itself from the toilet. I highly doubt anything you could say would be more embarrassing than that, so spit it out. What's bothering you?"

I can't help but laugh at the memory of that story. He has a point, though. My insecurities aren't nearly as embarrassing as *that*.

"I don't know." Fork in hand, I pick at my food, moving it around on my plate. "I guess the idea of turning what's forever been such a pipe dream into a reality makes me nervous. What if I spend months or years working on a manuscript, and then it's not even good? There are *so* many books and authors out there. The Book Nook is big, and we only sell a fraction of a fraction of a fraction of published works. Who am I to compete with the Sarah J. Maases and Emily Henrys of the world?"

His nose scrunches up. "This is how you feel when I name sports players, isn't it?"

A smile blossoms across my face as warmth blooms in my chest. "Yup, pretty much."

"Okay, well, who are they? Besides authors, obviously."

"Obviously." I laugh. "A fantasy author and a romance author, respectively."

"But you read fantasies and romances written by other authors, right?"

I flick my hand, gesturing toward the other side of my apartment, where books live in every nook and cranny. "Of course."

"Just because a reader likes those authors doesn't mean they can't also like *you*." He grins, pleased with himself. "Plus, you already have the perfect plot. You can write a memoir about a bookstore manager falling head over heels for a hockey player."

Cheeks heating, I avert my gaze. What was I thinking, letting him into my apartment? Alone? During my child-bearing years?

"What a great idea for a work of *fiction*," I stammer, shoveling a load of lo-mein noodles onto my fork. I shove them into my mouth, uncaring that I'm at serious risk of choking, because the alternative is to stare at him like an absolute idiot.

"I'm full of great ideas." He licks a drop of sauce from his lips, and suddenly the room feels about twenty degrees too hot. "And I think you should take the writing course. Make it your New Year's resolution or something."

I lift a brow. "And what's your New Year's resolution?"

"To read more," he says simply.

It's impossible to keep the smile off my face. "You're liking *Alien Lovers of Planet Dexxar* that much?"

"I like *you* that much," he corrects, "but the alien lovers aren't too bad."

I'm too dumbstruck by his boldness to do more than gape.

"I know you like me, too," he says, his smile a little arrogant. "If you didn't, you wouldn't be hanging out with me when you could be reading. But I'm more than happy to take things at your pace."

I've never been flustered by a man before. Don't get me wrong, I'm nowhere near cool, calm, or collected, but I rarely care enough to let a guy's reaction or opinion affect me. Cole? He's a different story. At a loss for how to respond, I awkwardly blurt out, "I got you a Christmas gift."

A little too abruptly, I stand, banging my knee on the table in the process. Then I scurry to my coat closet, where I stuffed the box wrapped in snowflake paper.

I'm a decent gift giver, but I usually know how my audience will react. Cole's a wildcard, so I can't help but squirm a little as I hand it to him. "I went shopping with my brother and Logan and saw these. Thought you'd like them."

Cole chuckles. "Shopping with Logan's an experience."

"One I'd be happy to never suffer through again," I agree.

Logan's the most indecisive person when it comes to clothing. He tried on the same pair of pants no less than thirty times before he decided he hated them and left the store with nothing.

Cole unwraps the gift and pulls out the two rocks glasses. They each have a hockey puck embedded into the side, making the glass look warped and broken.

A grin of genuine appreciation causes tiny lines to crinkle next to his eyes. "These are amazing, bean. Thank you."

Hit with a wave of relief, I sink back into the chair and take a large gulp of wine. "Merry Christmas."

"And happy Hanukkah to you," he says. "I got you something as well."

My insides light up with delight. "Really?"

"Really." He shuffles to the front door and picks up a nondescript bag from next to his jacket. One I hadn't noticed among all the to-go bags, I guess.

Wiggling in my chair, I tamp down on the temptation to squeal with excitement. I usually only exchange gifts with my siblings and Kennedy, so this is a surprise. Although maybe it shouldn't be.

I gracefully take out the tissue paper so I don't seem like a complete animal and pull out a forest green fabric-bound journal with *one day these thoughts will be worth millions* embossed on the cover.

"It's a creative writing journal," Cole explains as he sits back down. "There are a bunch of prompts and stuff."

Emotion bubbles up inside me, warming me from the inside out. "This is the most thoughtful gift I've ever gotten." Granted, my mom once got me a gift card for the bookstore where *I work*, so the bar's pretty low, but still. I hold it against my chest like it's a signed first-edition copy of *The Great Gatsby*. "Thank you. It's amazing."

"There's no need to thank me." He grins. "The smile on your face is more than thanks enough."

And the smile he gives me in return makes me wonder if my New Year's resolutions should include more than just giving writing a chance.

CHAPTER FOURTEEN

THE TEAM ENDS the year in the best way: by beating one of our biggest rivals. It's why Logan's throwing back tequila shots like he's at an all-inclusive bar in Mexico. It's why Cam's shirt is completely unbuttoned, showing off his tattooed torso. And it's why Erickson ripped the back of his pants while dropping it low.

With the mix of EDM, hip-hop, and pop, along with killer cocktails and a dive bar vibe with high-end decor, it's no surprise this club is a magnet for celebrities and influencers. One would think my teammates would dial it back with all the phones filming us, but they're not concerned. I don't necessarily blame them.

We're set up at a table next to the DJ booth and dance floor, but instead of celebrating the win or soaking up the scene, I'm checking my phone to see if Maya's texted me back.

COLE BERRETT

How's karaoke? Winning a Grammy anytime soon?

MAYA SILVER

No one can sing Taylor Swift better than Taylor Swift, Cole. Don't be ridiculous.

But I will admit I do a pretty good All Too Well.

COLE BERRETT

10-minute version?

MAYA SILVER

The fact that you know about Taylor's 10-minute version just turned that very innocent text into a sext.

COLE BERRETT

I aim to please. ;)

MAYA SILVER

Time for me to sing backup on Bohemian Rhapsody. Enjoy your strippers!

COLE BERRETT

I'm at a club, not a strip club.

And even if it was one, I'd rather be at karaoke with you.

MAYA SILVER

Well, duh. I'm kind of amazing.

A slender body bumps into mine and I come face-to-face with the redhead who's been eye-fucking my crotch from across the dance floor for the past thirty minutes. She looks vaguely familiar, but I can't place how or why. It's probably because she resembles almost every girl in this club, short skirt and crop top and all. I'm not one to judge, but this place feeds every LA stereotype about influencers.

"Hi there. Want some company?" Her husky voice is like nails on a chalkboard.

The high I was feeling after Maya's last text vanishes, and I fix my expression into something resembling a polite smile. I'm not interested, but I can't flat-out ignore her. I'm not that much of a dick. "You're more than welcome to sit."

"Thank you." She taps her sparkly nails against her overly plump lips. "What are you drinking?"

Humor rolls through me at the question. Not because of this woman, but because I can't help but reminisce about the time I asked Maya that same question in a lame attempt to start a conversation.

The redhead, no doubt assuming the smile is for her, rests her hand on my arm like she has the right to do so. Four or five months ago, I'd be flattered by the attention. Now, I'm slightly annoyed by it.

"I'm drinking a Grey Goose martini with a twist," she says. She leans super close as she adds, "*Extra dirty.*"

The club may be loud, but the innuendo in her voice is clear, nonetheless. She waits for me to respond, probably with a comment about how I like my sex how she likes her drinks, but my lips stay zipped.

"I'm Roni," she says.

If she expects that to mean anything to me, she'll be sorely disappointed. "Nice to meet you. I'm Nicholas."

"I know who you are." She giggles and playfully squeezes my arm. "That workout video you did with Adidas was *amazing.*"

"Thanks."

She pulls an olive off a toothpick with her teeth, lashes fluttering. "What sort of pre-workout do you use?"

I frown at her, confused. Is she really trying to pick me up by asking about my pre-workout routine? It takes more energy than it should not to scoff. "A mix of stuff."

"If you're looking for another one, I just launched my own

whey protein powder line," she announces. "It's called *Ripped by Roni*."

For the next ten minutes and thirty-four seconds, Roni tells me *all* about her life journey from Vegas stripper to fitness influencer who now has her own brand of workout supplements. All the while, I envision ways to fake my own death. I don't have to even look at the ingredient list to know I wouldn't touch her stuff with a ten-foot pole. Not after she tells me her most popular flavor is banana bread.

When one of my teammates interrupts our conversation to ask for a photo with her, I use the distraction to my advantage and make my escape. There's an open seat next to Cameron, so I slide into it quickly, not bothering to worry about why the faux leather is so sticky.

"She's hot as fuck," he says, nodding to Roni. "You're not interested?"

"Definitely not."

He lets out a low whistle. "Damn. Maya's got you whipped already."

"Yup," I admit without an ounce of shame. Maya's a beautiful enigma I'd be happy to spend all my time unraveling. She's open yet guarded. Playful yet serious. Tough yet sensitive. Independent yet deeply connected to those she cares about. Outgoing yet a homebody. She's brought out the laid-back side of me that I thought I'd lost. And based on our chemistry, I have no doubt the sex will be mind-blowing.

"You've got to lock that down before you get a serious case of blue balls, Berrett."

With a grunt, I shrug off his amusement at the deeply intimate relationship I've developed with my hand. I want more than just the pretty parts with Maya. I want the bad days, the ugly crying, and the bitchy moods, too. And if that means taking it at her pace and jerking off instead of fucking her senseless, then that's what I'll do.

"Anyway," Cam says, bringing his drink to his lips, "I heard a rumor."

"About?"

"The Devils."

My ears perk up like Goose's do when I say *outside* or *play ball*. "What about them?"

"Rumor is Rogers is retiring after the playoffs." He turns my way, one brow arched. "His wife just gave birth to twins, and his rotator cuff may need another surgery."

"Madoff can't fill his shoes." I shake of my head. "They'd need to trade…" I trail off as his words connect in my head.

My contract with the Bobcats includes a full no-movement clause. No trades without my agreement. That kind of protection isn't handed out lightly. I earned it. In the four years I've been with the Bobcats, a few opportunities have come up. I listened to each pitch, sure, but moving to a new team mid-season when I've put so much blood, sweat, and tears in with the Bobcats never felt quite right. Besides, moving someone like me isn't easy. The salary cap alone can be a challenge. And I know my worth. It'd take more than one player and a draft pick to balance that scale.

The only team I'd happily be traded to is my hometown team.

And if their star player retires and they're in the market for a new center, especially one with my skill? Then I'd be stupid not to consider it.

Cameron nods at my shell-shocked expression. "As I said, it's just a rumor, but it's something to keep your eye on. Tell Mark."

If my agent wasn't in the Bahamas ringing in the New Year with his new fiancée, I'd already be on my way back to my hotel room to call him. "Thanks for looking out, man. Appreciate it."

"Any time, Cap."

I take a long sip of my drink, sorting through the multitude of thoughts suddenly bombarding me. It may be a very happy New Year, indeed.

———

The hotel breakfast area is filled with familiar faces, most of whom look severely hungover. A ten-a.m. flight on New Year's Day is brutal, and likely Coach Henderson's attempt to keep the guys from letting the night get too wild. Based on the condition most of my teammates are in, his plan failed. Epically.

The breakfast selection features all the staples—oatmeal, mini boxes of cereal, questionable-looking eggs, and a bread and pastry basket. I toast a sesame bagel, smother it in whipped creamed cheese, and pour myself a coffee before sliding into the open seat between Jake and Logan.

"Happy New Year," I greet them.

With a nod, Jake picks up his glass of extra-pulpy orange juice. "You, too. Where's Davies?"

Shrugging, I bring my coffee to my lips. The moment the flavor registers, I grimace. I don't consider myself a snob, but with the money management paid to put us up here, one would think they'd have the funds for an upgrade from this watered-down crap they call coffee. Maybe the Boston Bean has spoiled me, but this stuff is terrible. "I don't know. Still sleeping, I would assume."

We started the night together, but we sure as hell didn't end it that way. When I dipped out at exactly 12:04 a.m., Cameron's night was only just beginning. The last I saw him, he was being pulled to the dance floor by a five-foot pixie. His size may help him on the ice, but it most definitely does not lend well to the dance floor. I briefly debated staying longer just to watch him make an ass of himself, but in the end, I decided a decent night's sleep was more important.

Logan slices into the soggy pancake on his plate but doesn't say a word. He's being uncharacteristically quiet, which puts me on edge.

"Hungover?" I nudge him with an elbow, baiting him into a conversation.

Rather than answer, he slowly stuffs a piece of pancake into his mouth and chews. *Okay, then.*

"He's mad at you," Jake explains. Now that I'm really looking at him, he's glaring at me as well. *Great.* It's been eight hours since I last saw them, and considering I was asleep for about seven of them, that leaves a one-hour window where I apparently fucked up. If Logan were the only one pouting, I'd brush it off. After all, he once got upset with me for not noticing his haircut. But if Jake's pissed off, too, that legitimizes the claim.

Pushing an annoyed breath through my lips, I place my coffee cup back on the table. "What did I do?"

"More like *who* did you do?" Logan drops his fork to the table with a clang. "I leave the club thirty minutes before midnight so I can have an orgasm as the clock strikes mid—"

Jake lurches forward, peering around me. "I'm sorry. So you can *what*?"

"Have an orgasm at midnight." Logan rolls his eyes. "It's a great way to end one year and enter the next."

Jake opens and closes his mouth like a fish, wide eyes darting to me. Any annoyance he has with me is completely sidetracked by Logan's admission.

I take a bite of my bagel. "You left the club early to jerk off?"

Logan scoffs. "Obviously not. Elliott and I were having phone sex, but had to coordinate—"

"Dude," I cough out and lean back, wishing I could rewind time and stop myself from asking. "No. Keep that shit to yourself."

Logan picks up his fork again, squeezing hard enough that his knuckles go white. "Why? It's not like there's any way he'll be your brother-in-law now. Not after who you spent the night with."

I throw my hands up. "Can someone fill me in? Because I seriously have no idea what you're talking about. I went to bed alone and woke up that way, too."

With a grunt and far too much drama, he slaps his phone onto the table. When I stare at him blankly, he nudges it toward me.

Head shaking, I give in and lean forward. He's got a post from *Page Six*'s Instagram pulled up, and in it is a photo some lucky amateur photographer with a cell phone must have captured. The image is of the fraction of a second after midnight when Roni jumped on me like a damn kangaroo and kissed me like I was receiving CPR.

Fuck.

CHAPTER FIFTEEN

"IS IT ALWAYS THIS LOUD?" The clink of cutlery against a nearby table makes Sophie flinch, and when a waitress close by yells out an order to a fry cook, she can't hold back a grimace. "Because it seems *really* loud in here today."

Kennedy lifts her head up from where it's been resting on her arms against the table. "Or you're just really hungover."

"I wouldn't have had that last tequila shot if *someone* hadn't dared me to do karaoke *and* pick a *Hamilton* song."

Sophie's rendition of "The Schuyler Sisters" was equal parts horrific and hilarious.

Kennedy's two loves in life are baking and Broadway, which Sophie discovered last night. And if there's a microphone—or a spatula—to sing into, you bet your ass she'll belt out songs from *Moulin Rouge!*, *Six*, *West Side Story*, *Funny Girl*, or one of the other million musicals she's obsessed with.

Kennedy picks up her half-empty cup of coffee and grins over the rim. "How was I supposed to know you'd never seen it? It's a classic."

Sophie half-heartedly flips her off and then stands, splaying her hands over her stomach. "I'm going to the bathroom. The smell of bacon is making me nauseous."

She and I matched each other drink for drink last night, but waking up to photos of Cole making out with drop-dead gorgeous Roni Carlyle—my favorite contestant on *Love Island* last season—sobered me up really quickly. Considering he's "just a friend," knowing he spent his night with her shouldn't bother me. And I wish it didn't. This is the exact reason I didn't want to date him. But clearly that backfired, because by keeping him in the friend zone, I'm getting all the hurt without any of the relationship perks—i.e. orgasms and flowers.

Buzz. Buzz. Buzz.

Movements synchronized, Kennedy and I glance at my phone, which is lying face down on the table next to Sophie's now-forgotten plate of eggs and bacon. I don't bother checking the display. I already know it's the same person who's been trying to reach me since early this morning.

"Answer it." Kennedy groans and drapes herself over the table, barely avoiding dipping her hair in syrup. "This is, like, the eightieth time he's called."

It's only the fourth, but I don't correct her. Stabbing a piece of turkey bacon with my fork, I narrow my eyes at her. "You're the one who tells me that it's rude to be on my phone at the breakfast table."

"Well, it's also rude to make my hangover worse by letting your phone continuously vibrate," she argues. "So answer the damn thing and put the poor guy out of his misery."

"I wouldn't use *misery* to describe Cole's situation," I grumble.

He certainly didn't look miserable when Roni was sprawled on his lap with her hands on his cheeks as they rang in the New Year with the kiss to end all kisses.

Every time I close my eyes, I see the image, like it's burned into my retinas, and wonder how it compared to our Kiss.

"The guy's reading an alien romance for you." Straightening, Kennedy rolls her eyes and hits me with a look that would make a grown man's balls shrivel up and hide in his stomach. "You're obviously punishing him."

"No, I'm not," I snap as my phone stops vibrating. "He can do whatever he wants with whomever he wants."

"Really? You're going to tell me that the smooch he shared with Roni Carlyle *isn't* the reason you've been glaring at your pancakes like they've personally offended you?" She lifts an imperious brow. "Yeah, no, I'm not buying into that brand of bullshit, babe. You like Cole, but you don't want to like Cole, because liking him means you're opening yourself up to getting hurt. And you've been hurt by those you should've been able to trust way too many times."

"Aren't you too hungover to be seeing right through me?"

My phone buzzes again. Make that five phone calls this morning.

Kennedy's face softens. "Aren't you tired of fighting your feelings for him? Answer the phone, Maya."

Buzz. Buzz. Buzz.

"And don't be a bitch," she calls after me as I slide out of the booth to take the call in private.

It has to happen at some point, so why not now? As much as I'd love to be petty and ignore him forever, that's not fair to either of us.

I step out into the vestibule, where the noise is muted considerably, and answer the call. At least here, Kennedy can't eavesdrop.

"Maya." The relief in Cole's tone fills me with guilt over not answering. Then I remember the image of him with another woman draped all over his ripped body and that guilt flies out the window and boards a bus to Guadalajara.

"Hey," I greet simply, choking back the anger that's been brewing in me since I woke up this morning. "What's up?"

"I've been calling."

"I've been at breakfast."

Oof. So much for not being snappy.

Cole chuckles at my sassy response. "Anywhere good?"

"It's a twenty-four-hour-diner around the corner from me. Your trainer would have a hemorrhage the second he stepped into the place, considering the amount of oil in their eggs would put eighteenth-century lamplighters to shame."

"I'm sure it's great." He laughs, the throaty sound making my guilt second-guess its decision. "Listen, there's a photo of me and some girl—"

"Woman," I correct. My tone is laced with bitterness. I hate it, but it's woven through me thoroughly by now, making it impossible to hide. "You can't refer to the woman with the most liked ass on Instagram as a girl, Cole."

"So you've seen the photos." There's far less humor in his tone now.

Heat pricks at the backs of my eyes, but I banish the sensation. "Of you playing tonsil hockey? Mm-hmm."

"Nothing happened," he urges. "I mean she kissed me, but I didn't kiss her back," he amends. "It looks bad, but she launched herself at me like a fucking spider monkey to get a New Year's kiss. I pushed her away immediately and—"

Not wanting to hear the details, I put the kibosh on his explanation. "It's fine, Cole."

"No, it's not. Your ex-boyfriend may've been a piece of shit who didn't value you, but I'm not about to break your trust before I've even fully earned it." His voice gets a little louder now, his tone a little crisper. "I swear on my Stanley Cup wins that nothing happened, Maya. I wouldn't fuck up what we have for a quick lay. I hope you know I'm not that guy."

Puffing out a breath, I let his words penetrate. He's *not* that guy. Ever since Cole waltzed in on me and my book, he's done nothing that would make me question his honesty. He's way more open with his feelings and thoughts than I am, anyway.

"Okay," I reply, my tone soft. "I believe you."

"Thank you." He lets out a sigh that muffles the phone line between us. "I just landed in Boston. When are you free? I want to see you."

If they weren't still as nauseous as I am, thanks to the tequila still slopping around in my stomach, his words would make the butterflies in my stomach cheer. "Thursday?"

"I'll be in Florida for a game," he says. "I'll be back Friday morning, though."

I tilt my head back and mentally flip through what I have going on this week. "I have dinner with my brother. What about Saturday?"

"Perfect. We can do something in the afternoon, since I know how you like your sleep."

I bite back a smile. "Oh, how generous of you. I'll see you then."

"It's a date."

For once, I don't correct him.

———

If the sign above the double-door entrance didn't read Bobcats Community Ice Rink, I'd assume this was some fancy tech company's office. The building is compact but striking, its exterior all clean lines and gleaming silver panels, with a wall of oversized windows. It looks more like it belongs in a design magazine than in a suburban sports complex.

The city may be blanketed in a layer of snow, but the sun is out in full force, so I shield my eyes as I climb out of the car. "We're ice-skating?"

Cole's face splits into a boyish grin. "Yup. At our practice arena."

"I've never ice-skated," I admit.

This stops the pro skater in his tracks. Slowly, he turns, and his lips part. "Never?"

I tuck my arms around myself to fight against the wind tugging at my clothes. "Uh... no?"

In a bid to hand me off to people who weren't her, my mom signed me up for tons of classes when I was a kid. Ballet, gymnastics, swimming, art. Somehow ice-skating never made the cut.

"So it's your first time?"

I pinch the bridge of my nose and squeeze my eyes tight. It's cold and I'd like to get inside. "Yes, and phrasing the question in different ways isn't going to change my answer."

Cole either doesn't hear me or doesn't care. "I get to be your first."

"Oh my God," I groan at his insinuation. "You're taking me skating, not taking my virginity. Please chill out."

Just like that, he's snapped out of what I can only imagine is a skating fantasy land. Grabbing my mitten-covered hand, he practically drags me through the parking lot.

"Can anyone skate at your practice arena?" I ask.

"It's open to the public," Cole explains. "Anyone can watch our practices, too."

"What?" I crow. My voice is far too loud now that we've stepped inside, so I step closer, keeping my tone lowered, and ask, "What if your competition comes to watch? Wouldn't that give them an edge on you if they could study your plays and stuff?"

A scene from *Bring It On*, where another cheer squad films their practice and then steals their dance routine during the competition, pops into my head.

"This isn't one of your books, baby." Cole chuckles. "No one has the time for covert operations like that. Plus, recording isn't allowed at practices."

"Oh."

"Mm-hmm." He gives me a half smile. "Now let's go get you fitted for skates."

It's not a simple process. Not when Cole turns a skate rental into a twenty-minute inquisition. The poor high-school kid working behind the desk remains bewildered as Cole grills him about the brands they carry, throws around phrases like *optimal instep height*, and compares the sharpness of various pairs of skates. His presence garners attention from onlookers, the scrutiny making me squirm so violently I hop awkwardly from foot to foot like a backup dancer. He's either completely oblivious to the looks he's getting or he's so used to it that it doesn't register for him.

Once he's narrowed the skate choices down to three options, I try them all on. I'm like Goldilocks—the first pair is too big, the second pair is too small, and according to Cole, the third pair is *just* right.

"These are the winners," he announces with a satisfactory grin.

"Are you sure?" I ask, trying and failing to wiggle my toes. "Because my toes feel suffocated."

The only indication he's heard me is the harsh breath of air that slips through his nose. *Rude.* Regardless, I sit still as he finishes the laces.

"The skates should be snug," he says as he ties the laces into bunny ears. "They have to be a lot more fitted than regular footwear. You want the least amount of negative space." With that, he taps my calf muscles. "Stand up."

I obey, a little wobbly as I go, and immediately, my toes brush against the end of the skates. With a grimace, I eye Cole, who's still squatting on the ground. "Yeah, they're definitely too small."

Ignoring my complaint once again, he wedges a pointer finger into the gap between my ankle and the back of the skate.

Okay, invasive, much?

"Nope. They're good." Standing, he rests his hands on his hips. "Now bend your knees just a little and make sure your ankles and hips are in line with your head."

I awkwardly finagle my body into said position, but when I look at him for approval, he shakes his head. "Keep your weight forward and your head up."

Softening my knees, I bend forward. As I go, my face heats. I feel ridiculous, considering I'm not even on the ice. The only other people on the rubber floor outside of the rink are a group of what looks to be six-year-olds tying up their skates with practiced precision, which makes me feel marginally worse. With an exhale, I force myself to look away from them and zero in on Cole to gauge his reaction to my form.

Rather than assessing my stance, he's focused on my behind like it's a homing beacon.

"Cole," I choke out through a laugh. "At least pretend you're not checking out my ass."

He snaps to attention, his head whipping around violently enough to cause damage to his neck. At least he has the decency to look embarrassed. "Yup. Got it. Staying focused."

Stepping behind me, he places his hands on my hips and tilts them forward a tad. Then, with a hum, he takes a step back and walks around me so he can observe from every angle.

"Good," he comments eventually. "Now stand up straight and try again."

I salute him. "Yes, sir."

Brows lifting, he smirks. "I like you calling me *sir* a little too much."

Dirty thoughts dance across my mind, every one of them involving Cole without a shirt. I'm not into anything too kinky, but I don't mind ceding control in the bedroom, and based on the way Cole's eyes sparkle, he knows exactly where my thoughts have strayed.

With heated cheeks—again—I bend into the skating position, avoiding eye contact like it's my job.

He uses two fingers to lift my chin. "Head up," he gently reminds me.

We do this a few more times before he's fully satisfied. Rather than admit that my thighs are already burning from the weird little skating squats, I shoot him a thumbs-up.

"Let's talk about falling."

I scoff. "Okay, wow. Rude. You're just assuming that I'm going to be a sucky skater?"

"Everyone falls," he states calmly. "And if you've never been on the ice before, there isn't a doubt in my mind you're going to fall. But I'd like to avoid broken bones and bruises, if that's all right with you."

"Yeah," I mumble, properly admonished. "Okay."

I listen with the patience of a saint as Cole goes over what to do when I fall. Because it's a when, not an *if*. Don't tense up, try to land on my butt if possible, and use my hands to cushion the fall. My eyes aren't the only ones tracking his every movement as he talks. I'm going to believe it's because he's a famous hockey player and not because he looks edible in his Bobcats sweatshirt with day-old stubble covering his jaw. In my experience, women tend to end up with one of two guys: the hot bad boy or the cute nice guy. But Cole? He's a hot nice guy; a peacock among geese. Not that we're together. Simply an observation.

"You ready to skate?" Cole asks, bringing me back to reality.

I flash him what I hope is a confident smile and nod. *Ready as I'll ever be.* Then, awkwardly, I waddle across the rubber floor. There's a chance I walk better in heels than skates, and that's saying something.

Cole steps onto the ice and holds out a hand for me. Without giving myself time to read into the motion, I slide my palm against his. Nothing about it feels forced or awkward, and that thought lights me up inside. More than anything, it feels natural. Like it was inevitable.

The moment my skates touch the ice, it's as if every single tip Cole gave me was spoken in a foreign language. Don't lock my knees? Oh, too bad, because they lock up tighter than *Mona Lisa*'s security at the Louvre. Keep my head up? That's impossible when I'm wobblier than a newborn foal.

"Relax," he chuckles. "I've got you, bean."

Holding my breath, I grip his hands like they're a damn lifeline, which they essentially are.

Cole glides backward with ease and pulls me along with him, his lips twitching in amusement.

"I'm doing it!" I squeal as we glide across the ice at a slow but steady speed. "Look!"

He picks up his pace, and a cool breeze kisses my cheeks. The smoothness of each movement lulls me into a sense of security. We glide to the left, then the right, and before I know it, we've been around the rink a couple of times.

Cole slows gradually, eventually bringing us to a stop. "Ready for me to let go?"

My fingers immediately tighten around his. "Um, no. Absolutely not."

"C'mon, you can do it." He gives me an easy, reassuring smile. "I'll be right next to you. Trust me, okay?"

His words hold a request that extends beyond the reach of the ice rink.

Trust him. Over and over, he's shown me that I can. So I take a deep, steadying breath and pull my hands away from his.

Bad idea.

One moment I'm standing upright, and the next I'm flat on my back, the air knocked from my lungs. I burst out laughing; if I don't, I'll cry. And here I was thinking he was a jerk for assuming I'd fall.

Cole stares down at me with a dumbfounded expression on his face. "Fuck. Did not see that coming. Are you okay?"

"Weather's great down here," I force out between giggles. "Did you know that figure skating rinks are slightly warmer than ice hockey rinks?"

"I did know that." He holds out a hand and pulls me up onto my wobbly feet. "Softer ice makes for easier landings. Have you been doing hockey research?"

"If by hockey research, you mean reading a romance where a figure skater and hockey player fall in love despite the odds against them, then sure."

Cole takes a step back as he chuckles, and I latch on to him like a starfish. I do not want to fall on my ass again so soon. A girl can only take so much embarrassment.

"You've got this," he reminds me. "Take baby steps."

"Obviously," I huff. "I'm not about to attempt crazy *Blades of Glory* type shit after I just bruised my butt."

He rolls his eyes. "I mean literal baby steps." He demonstrates by taking two tiny steps, then gliding forward a bit. "It'll help you transition into skating."

"Oh." I mimic his moves, my feet clunking against the ice in a very ungraceful way. "Like that?"

"Good enough," he says, biting back a grin. "Now alternate lifting one foot and then the other."

Despite the cramping in my calves, I do what he says with a strained smile on my face. Soon enough, I'm gliding forward on my own. The squeal that escapes me should be embarrassing, but I'm too proud of myself to care. My motions aren't nearly as smooth as Cole's, but considering he's a professional hockey player who spends the majority of his time on the ice, I'll take the win.

I don't make it very far before I'm flat on my ass once again. And again. And again. My respect for hockey players goes up tenfold. Not only do they skate with amazing accuracy, but they're playing a sport while doing it.

"I think you're done skating on your own for a bit." Cole takes my hands in his once again and glides forward slowly so we're side by side as we make our way around the ice. "Although you do look good in skates."

I blush under his intense gaze. "You look good... always. It's kind of annoying, actually."

He throws his head back and laughs. "It's been a while since I skated for fun."

"Yeah, I can't imagine getting chased around the ice and aggressively slammed into the boards is a lot of fun."

"Hardy har-har."

We do a couple more laps before I give in and suggest a breather. I'm not sweating—not much, at least—but my toes and calves are cramping from keeping the skates upright and I feel every edge of the insoles.

At the boards, we stop next to a group of kids. Their eyes all widen at their proximity to Cole, no longer giving a rat's ass about what their instructor is teaching them. I get it. It's impossible not to be a fan of this man.

One of the bolder kids breaks away from the group and skates up to us. "Hi. You're Nicholas Berrett."

Cole bends down so he's closer to the kid's height and leans in conspiratorially. "I am. But my friends call me Cole. What's your name?"

"Andrew Garrett Klein, but my friends call me Andy."

"It's nice to meet you, Andy. Are you a Bobcats fan?"

He nods enthusiastically, his blond curls flopping against his forehead. "The *biggest*. I've been to six games. I was there when you beat the Tigers during overtime last year."

"I'm our team's goalie." Andy's attention drifts to me, his head tilting. "Are you his girlfriend? Because his Wikipedia page doesn't say he has a girlfriend."

Heat creeps up my neck, but Cole only grins at the innocent question. Rather than answering, he weaves his fingers through mine and pulls me against his side.

The youth hockey coach skates over and shoots me an apologetic smile while squeezing Andy's shoulders. "He's a great goalie, but not so great at subtlety."

Clearly.

I give Andy a small smile, ducking a little deeper into my jacket. "I'm Maya, Cole's friend. He's teaching me how to skate."

Andy's jaw practically touches the ice. "You do private lessons?" He drops his head back, eyeing his coach. "No offense, Tom, but you're totally fired if Nic—Cole—can teach me."

"I'd stick with your current coach, bud," Cole says with an apologetic chuckle. "Private lessons with Maya take up most of my free time."

I elbow him in the ribs, which likely hurts me more than him. "Do you want a picture with Cole? I'm sure he'd be happy to take one."

"Yeah!" Andy shouts. He waves for his teammates to gather around us. "Let's get—"

A blurred figure approaches in my periphery, stealing my attention. If I were a more experienced skater, I could've braced myself for impact. Instead, when the skater crashes into me, all the air whooshes out of my lungs and I'm tossed backward. My body hits the ice, a chill reverberating through my bones, followed by my head thumping against the slippery surface. Starbursts cloud my vision, and then the world goes black.

CHAPTER SIXTEEN

RAW PANIC SURGES through me as Maya's small frame slams into the ice. And when her head hits, memories of my brother's fatal head injury momentarily paralyze me. My heart beats in my ears, making the cacophony of shouts and laughter surrounding us fade into white noise. I push through the gaggle of kids surrounding me and drop onto my knees next to Maya. *Fuck, fuck, fuck.*

"Can you hear me?" I rest my hand against her cheek, careful not to move her neck. She's warm to the touch, a nice juxtaposition to the chill of the ice seeping through my pants. "My?"

A moment later, her dark blue eyes open and slowly blink into focus. Relief slams into me so fast my limbs go weak. A ball of stress still sits heavy on my chest, but seeing her eyes settles the worst of my nerves.

"Hey, gorgeous," I say softly, trying to keep my panic at bay.

Her face twists in discomfort, her eyes a little unfocused.

I brush a soothing thumb against her cheek. "You got hit pretty hard. That's got to hurt. You want to try to sit up so we can make sure you're okay?"

She grimaces but allows me to tug her into a sitting position. When she's upright, I gently probe the back of her head to ensure it's not bleeding. She winces when I press on the spot that took the brunt of the fall and will no doubt turn into a goose egg.

"Let the record state," she says, giving me a strained smile, "that my lack of coordination wasn't the sole cause of this tumble."

"I'll note that," I reassure her. "Let's get you off the ice, yeah?"

It takes a controlled effort to not drag her out of here like a caveman. If I wasn't concerned about jostling her, I'd say fuck it and give in to the urge. But with her best interest in mind, I take her hands and slowly lead her off the ice and onto a nearby bench. Once I'm sure she can sit up without toppling over, I grab our things from where we stashed them in a locker.

Maya doesn't complain when I undo her skates and slip her sneakers back on, but when I pick her up bridal style, her attitude makes a reappearance.

"Put me down," she hisses, squirming in my arms. "I can walk, Cole."

With a grunt, I pick up my pace and push through the doors of the building. "And I can carry you just as easily."

"Cole—"

"Maya," I snap. The instant the word is out of my mouth, I force myself to take a deep breath. "Just please let me take care of you, okay?"

Her pouty mouth drops open, but no words come out for the remainder of the walk to my car. She does shoot me a questioning look as I buckle her into the passenger seat, though. The moment my own ass is in the driver's seat, I dial our team's orthopedic surgeon. He's at every game, evaluating sprains, fractures, and mild concussions, and he's the one I want to take a look at Maya.

Once the ringing sound of the phone echoes through the speakers, I reverse out of my parking spot and speed in the direction of his office.

"Hey, Nicholas." Dr. Greenbaum greets me on the third ring. "How's your shoulder treating you?"

"Fine, thanks," I rush out, my heart still thudding against my sternum. "But that's not why I'm calling. I took my girl skating, and a kid flew into her, knocked her out and—"

Maya squeaks and clutches my arm. "I promise I'm fine. I—"

"You were out cold for over three seconds," I scold, my voice tight. "You need to see a doctor. It's either him or the hospital. Choose."

Her jaw drops open in response, her focus drifting over my face. Clearly catching on to how dead-ass serious I am, she simply leans back against the seat, making herself comfortable.

I should probably apologize for my brusque behavior, but I don't have it in me. This isn't something I'm willing to compromise on.

Dr. Greenbaum's voice fills the awkward silence. "Any other symptoms besides brief loss of consciousness?"

"I'm a little dizzy and my head's sore," Maya admits with a frown. "But that's it."

Her calm demeanor does nothing to alleviate the panic that's constricting my every breath. In fact, it only makes me press a little harder on the accelerator and grip the steering wheel so tightly that my knuckles turn white.

"Swing by my office," he offers, his voice lacking the concern that's overtaken me. "I'm sure you're fine, but it can't hurt to take a look."

"Thanks," I grit out. "We'll see you in ten." I hang up the phone and book it to his office in record time.

A nurse stationed at the reception desk immediately guides us into one of the brightly lit rooms with walls covered in diagrams of human anatomy, where she takes Maya's vitals and asks her a few basic questions.

While I'm relieved that there's no chance Maya could be pregnant—because, in my mind, that means she's not sleeping with anyone else—I do briefly worry her embarrassment may cause her to faint.

"Nicholas." Greenbaum's deep baritone resonates off the walls of the small room as he steps inside. "I'm happy to see you, although I wish the circumstances were better."

Hoisting myself out of the plastic chair that's about two sizes too small for me, I shake his hand. "Hey, Doc. Thanks for squeezing us in on such short notice."

"Always happy to help." He turns to Maya with the same serene expression he wears when he's assessing a player's injury. "I'm Dr. Greenbaum," he introduces himself. "What's your name, dear?"

"Maya." She swishes her legs back and forth off the end of the examination table, making the protective sheet over it crinkle. "Nice to meet you sounds kind of weird, given the situation."

He chuckles and nods. "Why don't you tell me what happened?"

"A kid—about four-five, ninety pounds—railroaded her while we were stationary," I explain, hands clenching into fists. "He wasn't going full speed, but he lost control and slammed into her. She flew back about two feet and hit her head on the ice."

Maya gapes at me with what I'll take as a newfound understanding of just how observant I can be.

"And you were knocked unconscious?" Greenbaum directs the question at Maya, completely cutting me out of the conversation. It's fair, considering I'm not the patient, but that doesn't mean I have to like it.

"For only a second or two."

"Three seconds." I narrow my eyes at her. "And you were dizzy and wobbly when you stood up."

Doc hits me with a warning glance that stops me from adding further details, then turns back to Maya with a warm smile. "Let me wash my hands and we'll take a look."

While his back is turned and the water runs, Maya motions to him and mouths, "He looks like Santa Claus."

I bite back a chuckle. With his protruding stomach, white beard, and perpetually flushed cheeks, the good ole doc does resemble Saint Nicholas.

"So what do you do for work, Maya?"

"I manage an independent bookstore," she answers.

Greenbaum spins around with a paper towel still in hand. "Oh! I'm going on vacation with my wife next week and need a book to read on the beach. Any suggestions?"

Without hesitation, Maya deep dives into a list of books he should consider. It's awe-inspiring, how knowledgeable and insightful she is while describing books she loves. It's a refreshing change from the people I'm typically surrounded by. People who are always focused on the score, the plays, the next game. With books, there's no winning or losing. There's just pure enjoyment.

The two of them continue to talk books while he shines a light at her pupils to test their reactions.

I, on the other hand, sit in silence, my body strung tighter than a guitar string, as he assesses her memory, attention, and reasoning, as well as other cognitive skills.

"Seems to me you have a minor concussion," he announces post-examination, "and a few bumps and bruises."

"You're sure?" I press. "You don't want to do a CT scan?"

"I'm quite sure, Nicholas." He waves me off and gives Maya a little spiel about taking it easy and avoiding physical exertion for the next few days.

She nods along before thanking him for his time, and when he disappears, she turns to me, her expression brighter than it's been since she took that hit. "It's weird hearing people call you Nicholas."

I shrug at the observation. "I'm used to it after so many years."

"Why'd you decide to go by Cole and not Nick? That's the only nickname I've ever heard people use for Nicholas."

"I lost a coin flip."

Her legs stop swinging and she tilts her head. "You what?"

The memory makes me chuckle. "My brother and I did everything together growing up. Everyone knew us as a pair. Nicholas and Nathan. Nick and Nate. We even joked that when we made it pro, our tagline would be 'Nicholas and Nathan: the Berrett Brothers.'"

"You knew you wanted to play professionally when you were that young?"

"Oh yeah," I reply, my chest pinching. "We wanted to play professionally, and *together*, for the San Diego Devils. But outside of hockey, we were super different. I liked pancakes, he liked waffles. I liked thrillers, he liked action movies. I liked my coffee black, he only drank tea. We were always opposites.

"But you were still best friends?"

I swallow to clear my dry throat. "Yup. But because we were so different in so many ways, we wanted our names to be less..." I press my lips together, searching for a word to explain what I mean.

"Matchy-matchy?"

I chuckle. That's not the term I would have chosen, but... "Exactly," I concede. As if changing my nickname could somehow unravel the ties that connected Nate and me. Not even six feet of dirt can sever the bond. When he died, he took a piece of me with him. It's gotten easier to talk about with time, though.

"So we did a coin flip to see who had to change their nickname. I lost, so I chose to go by Cole."

Maya holds up her hands like we're in school. "Question. If Nathan lost and couldn't go by Nate, what the hell was he going to change his nickname to?" She giggles.

"Ethan."

The giggle turns into a burst of laughter. "Ethan? That's a random choice."

"After Ethan Hunt from *Mission: Impossible*. Nearly sent my mother to an early grave. It's a good thing I lost." I chuckle. The poor woman. Her face turned as white as a sheet when we told her about the coin toss.

With a sigh, I stand and step up to Maya, only stopping when I'm positioned between her legs. "I'm sorry about your concussion."

She frowns, her brow crinkling. "You don't need to apologize, Cole. It wasn't your fault."

Only now, as I stare into eyes the color of the night sky, does my body relax. I've been on edge since the moment her skates left the ice and she flew backward. A shiver racks my body at the memory. "It was."

"You can't possibly blame yourself." Her eyes widen like an owl's. "How was an eight-year-old knocking me over your fault?"

My body tenses. "I should've been paying closer attention. I knew you weren't confident on skates and—"

She angles closer and rests her hands on either side of my face, her fingers pressing into my cheeks. "What's going on? You heard the doctor. I'm fine. A tiny, baby concussion and some bruises, but that's it."

I lay my hands on top of hers, threading our fingers, and gently press my lips against her forehead. And then her right cheek, her left cheek, and her nose. Finally, I brush my lips against hers. She tastes sweet, like ripe cherries on a warm summer day.

"Nathan died in a car accident. He was T-boned while driving through an intersection and died from an epidural hematoma on the way to the hospital." I close my eyes and blow out a shaky breath. "Head injuries set me on edge. Maybe that sounds ridiculous since I play hockey and get and give concussions regularly, but it's true. Head injuries outside of a game are what freak me out."

The words hang in the small pocket of air between us like a noose. Rationally, I know that the hit she took was nothing like what happened to my brother. But tell that to the tiny part of me that's terrified of losing another person I love. Maybe I'm not in love with Maya yet, but the strings of it are there, and the more time I spend with her, the harder I'm going to fall. It's inevitable, and it's probably the only fall I'll ever willingly jump toward.

With the tiniest "oh," she wraps her arms around my waist, resting her cheek on my chest. I lean into her comfort, luxuriating in her soft warmth and letting it thaw the layers of ice still protecting the memories of my brother.

"I'm sorry if I overreacted, and I'm sorry if I was short with you, but you're important to me." I tighten my arms around her and bury my face in her neck, breathing her in. "I don't want to lose you, whether it's because some dumbass kid knocks you down and you hit your head or because you walk away without giving me a chance."

"Cole, I—"

I shake my head. "You don't need to say anything. I'm just glad you're okay."

"I know this is a severely inadequate response, but I'm sorry about Nathan," she breathes. "I can't even imagine what that was like for you. And there's no need to apologize. If our positions were reversed, I'm sure I'd be just as concerned."

My shoulders curl inward at her blanket acceptance. "Hmm. Now what do you say we get out of here, park our asses on your couch, and order an absurd amount of takeout? We can even pick up Goose on the way."

With a dramatic sigh, Maya rolls her eyes. "You're not letting me out of your sight, are you?"

For the first time in an hour, I crack a smile. "Good to know your concussion didn't damage your intellect, bean."

———

The sight of Maya and Goose curled up on her couch loosens the last bit of tension in my shoulders. My dog is very selective, so the instant way he took to Maya gives her an infinite number of brownie points.

Tucked beneath a blanket so only her head is visible, she glances from me to Goose. "I'm surprised you have a dog, given how much you work."

I love how she says *work*, as if I'm a consultant or accountant. As if it wouldn't matter to her one way or the other if I was. "He wasn't exactly planned."

"Cole," she teases, "did you not use protection? Is Goose an oopsie baby?"

"Hardly." I chuckle. "The Bobcats team up with a local

animal shelter for a yearly calendar, and I was paired with Goose for the November photo. We bonded over grilled chicken and naps. He'd already been working on me with those puppy dog eyes, but when they told me he'd been at the shelter for a while, that was it. I knew I had to adopt him. And here we are."

Maya sticks her lower lip out in an exaggerated pout. "That's the cutest thing I've ever heard. And please tell me the players are shirtless in the calendar, because *that* would raise some serious money."

"So you'd buy one?"

She gives a firm nod, her eyes glittering. "To support the animals, of course."

"Mm-hmm. Liar."

"I always wanted a dog growing up." She strokes through Goose's soft brown coat, her focus fixed on him now, her expression a little distant.

"Your mom didn't let you?"

She lets out a sardonic chuckle. "Oh, she would've. But then I would've had to take care of it on my own, and my plate was already a little full."

"You can borrow Goose any time you like. I think he may like you better than me, anyway." Not liking the solemness of her face, I blurt out the first thing that comes to mind "Have you ever seen *Rocky*?"

She scrunches her nose in confusion. "That was random."

I nod to the paperback book on her coffee table. It's called *Fight for Me* and features a very muscular—and shirtless—man wearing boxing gloves on the cover.

Her cheeks flush an adorable shade of pink when she spies the nearly naked–man cover. "Oh. Uh, no. I've never seen it."

"What about *The Fighter*?"

"Nope."

"*Field of Dreams*? *Remember the Titans*? *The Mighty Ducks*?"

"No, nope, and definitely not. Have *you* ever seen *She's the Man*?"

Now it's my turn to frown. "I don't think so."

She wiggles, her face lit in a grin. "Well, then, Cole Berrett, I'm happy to tell you all about it, because it's the greatest sports movie of all time."

I tuck a pillow behind my head and listen as she launches into a play-by-play of her version of the greatest sports movie of all time. And for once, I'm not stressing out about a practice or a teammate's injury. I'm not making a mental to-do list of all the shit that needs to be accomplished before our next game. I'm simply enjoying myself. And it has nothing to do with *She's the Man*, and everything to do with her.

CHAPTER SEVENTEEN

A COLD, wet nudge to my cheek wakes me from a delicious dream where Cole and I—

Oh shit.

Breath held, I take in the warm arm banded around my waist, the hard chest pressed to my back, and the scratchy stubble brushing against my shoulder. *Okaaay.* So apparently my comfy, cozy dream, where the two of us were snuggling on my couch, wasn't exactly a dream.

I force my eyes open, finding Goose's nose an inch from my face. He practically smiles when he notices that he's gained my attention and lets out a little yip, his wagging tail knocking a book off my coffee table. The thump of the hardcover hitting the floor paired with the *whoosh* of my upstairs neighbor's vacuum rouses Cole from sleep. He grumbles into my neck, his hot breath hitting my skin, causing a wave of goose bumps to rise along my spine.

"What time is it?" he mumbles, his voice scratchy from sleep. Because he definitely needs one more thing to add to his insane sex appeal.

Without looking at my phone, I confidently answer. "A minute or two after nine."

Cole grunts. "Can you tell time using the sun's placement in the sky or something? How do you know that without looking at a clock?"

I point toward the ceiling, and as if on cue, a loud thump and bang fill the relative quiet of my apartment. "My upstairs neighbor vacuums every Sunday morning from 9:02 to 9:54 on the dot."

"That's annoying."

"Trust me, I know. Mary Poppins makes it very difficult to sleep in."

"I'm usually up by now to take Goose out and—*fuck*." He sits straight up, and my body immediately misses the heat of his. Noticing Goose beside me, he relaxes. "You okay, buddy? We usually don't sleep this late."

"He woke me up by rubbing his nose against my cheek," I say. "So I think he slept in, too."

Cole releases a deep breath. "Yeah, that's how he wakes me up when he has to go outside."

At the word *outside*, Goose's ears perk up and he wags his tail again, batting another book and the remote off the coffee table.

Cole rubs a hand over his face and clambers off the couch. It's the first time I've seen him be anything but graceful.

Figuring this position can't be flattering, I sit up, only to come eye-to-eye with his crotch. I usually need a minimum of one cup of coffee to wake up in the morning, but I suppose an eyeful of Cole's prominently outlined cock will have to do.

"Um, Cole..." I chuckle, trying not to look directly at the very impressive dick in his pants. "You may want to take care of that before heading outside. Or at least charge my neighbors for the show."

He tucks his chin, frowning, as if noticing his morning wood for the first time.

How could he have missed it? Though we're still struggling to rouse ourselves, his dick is already out and about this morning. So many romances I read glorify the image of men in gray sweatpants, but damn, there's no way even the hottest of book boyfriends has anything on Cole Berrett in black joggers.

"This is technically your fault," he says nonchalantly, "since you ground your ass against me like a pole dancer last night."

I gasp and a throw pillow at him. "Take it back."

He laughs while easily dodging the terrible throw. "I said what I said, baby." He clips Goose's collar onto his leash. "I'll be back in a few."

As the door snicks shut behind him, I flop back onto the couch and sigh. I'm going to need more than a few to get my libido in check. It's very rare that I fall asleep on the couch. I blame the concussion and how surprisingly snuggly Cole's muscular body is. He wouldn't let me turn on a movie because "watching television after a hit to the head is breaking the cardinal rule of having a concussion," so we spent the night giving one another scene-by-scene breakdowns of our top sports movies. I started off strong with *She's the Man*, *Bend it Like Beckham*, and *Stick It*—all phenomenal—before Cole butted in with a very long-winded description of *Miracle*. It must have been during his recap of *The Mighty Ducks* that I fell asleep.

I make two cups of coffee in my very high-end Keurig and am adding a splash of milk to mine when Cole and Goose make their way back inside.

With an appreciative groan, Cole wraps his large hands around the steaming mug. "Thank you."

"Mm-hmm. What's on your agenda for the day? Did sleeping in put you behind schedule?"

"Nah. I'll probably go on a run with Goose and then rest and read about aliens for the rest of the day." He throws me a smirk over the top of his mug, which, embarrassingly, says *Buy Me a Book and Call Me a Good Girl.* "What about you?"

"I, um…" Heat creeps up into my cheeks. "I actually have a creative writing class this afternoon."

I expect him to be pleasantly surprised. Instead, he responds with a look of horror. "You can't go to a writing class today. You're concussed."

Laughter bubbles up and escapes me. "I said *writing* class, Cole, not *gymnastics* class."

"Dr. Greenbaum said to take it easy," he continues, tapping his fingers against his ceramic mug at an increasingly aggressive pace. "That means physically *and* mentally."

Poking my tongue into my cheek, I inhale a long breath. "Well, it's a good thing I'm not taking the SAT, isn't it?"

"I really don't think you should go."

I rear back, clutching my coffee tighter. "And I really think you should mind your own business."

He doesn't back down. In fact, he stands taller. "I've had plenty of concussions and—"

"Great. Good for you. Congrats. I've had plenty of practice taking care of myself. If I didn't feel good or was experiencing any lingering symptoms, I wouldn't go."

He places his mug on the counter with forced gentleness and approaches me slowly, like I'm a wild animal and he's at risk of being attacked if he makes one wrong move. "I know that, Maya. I wasn't insinuating that you can't take care of yourself." He drops his head and roughs a hand through his messy hair. "I'm just worried and want to make sure you're not overdoing it, okay? But if you think you can go, then you should go."

I pull my shoulders back. "I am going."

He sighs and rubs his brow. "I'm trying to apologize here, bean."

"There's technically been no apology."

Lips quirking up, he places his hands on my hips and rests his forehead against mine. "I'm sorry."

"Okay." I nod. "And I'm sorry for getting defensive."

"It's kind of hot when you get all aggressive like that."

I roll my eyes. "Today's class is an introductory more than anything. I won't be mentally exerting myself too much."

He nods, though based on his frown, he's only slightly mollified by this information. It's weird to have someone looking out for me. To be challenged by this man because he's worried. To not be the recipient of an eye roll when I dig my feet in. To be met with a valid argument rather than be labeled as dramatic. It's uncomfortable. Like trying on a new cut of jeans that I swore would never look good on me, only to find that they're not as bad as I expected. In fact, the jeans make me look kick-ass.

"What're you thinking about?" Cole murmurs.

I look up at him through my lashes.

He's beautiful. Breathtakingly, heart-wrenchingly beautiful. And he's here. In my kitchen. Drinking coffee out of an embarrassing mug. Making sure I'm okay. *Nope. Not going to cry.* How pathetic would that be? Someone outside of my siblings and Kennedy does a decent thing by showing care and affection, and I get all emotional?

"That I'm really hungry," I half lie. "And I want toast."

He steps back and smiles warmly. "Then I'll make toast while you tell me about the class."

I hop onto the counter as he moves around my kitchen, looking for a loaf of bread. His large frame takes up most of the space and dwarfs my appliances. The ridiculous scene, blessedly, keeps me from looking at his sweatpants.

"It's called Creative Writing—"

"Very creative name."

I stick my tongue out. "Anyway, the course is taught by a retired English professor."

"How'd you choose this one?" he asks over his shoulder. "Over the million tabs you had open?"

There's no way in hell I'm telling him that I drunkenly signed up for the class at Sophie and Kennedy's urging at three a.m. on New Year's Day. And that I chose it after Sophie said the professor had "kind eyes." Whatever the hell that means.

Regardless, it'd probably have been in my top three if I had decided while sober rather than five tequila shots deep.

"Good reviews. Their website described it as 'a creative space with tutorial-style teaching,' which I'm almost positive means it's interactive. I assume I'll learn about things like plot development and point-of-view, and then put pen to paper in a workshop."

"Will you let me read the stuff you write?"

My heart lurches. "Um, you play hockey, but you don't see me asking to put on your skates and go out there and play a game, do you?" I stammer.

"No, but that's because you'd probably get concussed." He leans against the opposite counter and crosses his arms over his chest. "And that also doesn't answer my question."

Nerves skitter through me at the thought. "Maybe."

"Maybe? Just maybe?"

I take a sip of my coffee. "You're lucky you didn't get a flat-out no."

"Hmm. I'll just have to turn that maybe into a yes." He shifts, the move making his biceps ripple against the sleeves of his shirt. "And I can be very persuasive."

Throwing him a sweet smile—and fighting to keep my focus off his arms or his crotch—I point to the toaster. "Breakfast's ready."

The rest of the morning passes by in a blur of domesticity. Though I'm hesitant to admit it, even to myself, it's the best Sunday morning I've had in a while. Being as independent as I am, I'm often alone with my books. I never realized how lonely that could be until now. Until I'm laughing as Cole lounges at my kitchen table, slyly feeding Goose a piece of turkey bacon under the table.

———

"Honey, we're here!" Kennedy calls as I open the passenger door. "Did you pack your lunch? Do you want me to walk you to the door?"

I level her with a glare. "You're seriously making me regret not paying for an Uber."

"I'm just trying to lighten the mood." She lifts one shoulder and lets it fall, unbothered. "Because whether you admit it or not, you're nervous."

She's right about that. I'm so nervous that I considered emailing the instructor to explain that I had a concussion and couldn't make it. But then I recalled the expression on Cole's face when he told me he was proud of me for taking the leap, and it unlocked some praise kink I didn't know I have, so here I am.

I open the door and step out of the car before I chicken out. "I'll text you after. Thanks for the ride."

"You're going to do great," Kennedy reassures me with a smile. "Knock 'em dead, tiger."

Blowing out a breath, I take in the scene before me. The snow-covered lawn is crisscrossed with sidewalks and surrounded by tall buildings and decorative archways. Overlooking it all is a large clock tower, giving the quad a dark academia vibe.

The cold air encourages me to hasten my pace along the uneven pathway to the building's entrance. Inside, it's eerily quiet, since there're no regular classes on Sunday. Following the directions from the welcome email I received when I signed up, I make a left and then two rights. When I find auditorium 111, I silently open one of the double doors, not wanting to draw attention to myself, and slip in like a ninja. There are already a few people scattered throughout the tiered seating, so there are plenty of available spots to choose from. Not wanting to be too close or too far, I find a seat in the middle row and make myself comfortable.

At four p.m. on the dot, our professor waltzes into the room. Their midnight-colored hair is cropped close to their head, and their glasses have lenses the size of a drink coaster. I honestly can't tell if they're closer to thirty or fifty.

"Good evening, fellow writers! I'm Jaden and welcome to your creative writing safe space." They sit on the edge of the oak desk at the front of the class, gripping the edge on either side of their legs. "Now, you're all here for one reason. Because you've read the first chapter of a book and found it nearly impossible to put down. And *you* want to craft a story like that." They scan the group slowly, expression open. "To evoke emotion so strongly that a reader would rather remain in the world you've created than return to real life. And the good news? Soon, it'll be a reality for you. I'm here to teach you the methods and principles that all the great writers use to create your own masterpiece."

For the next two hours, I listen with rapt attention as Jaden outlines the course guidelines and schedules and then dives into our first topic: storytelling with a theme. As I scribble down notes like I'm Moses receiving the Ten Commandments, a strange feeling of *rightness* floods through me.

This is exactly where I'm supposed to be.

CHAPTER EIGHTEEN

THE SECOND I STEP OUTSIDE, my balls shrivel to the size of grapes. *Fuck.* The frigid temperatures of Boston in late January are enough to make me consider prematurely retiring to Florida. The wind slices through my jacket like it's nothing, and snowflakes slap against my face with zero remorse. Thankfully, I parked near the exit, so in a matter of seconds, I'm sliding into the relative paradise of my heated car.

My shoulder throbs, a reminder of a second-period scrap on the ice, and my jaw's still tender from the elbow I took during a play. All I want to do is go home and take a bath with one of the eucalyptus bath bomb thingies Logan got me for Christmas, but I promised my teammates I'd head to O'Leary's for a bit. It's only nine, making it far too early to pull the "I'm going to bed" card. Even though I'd really like to. We have an away game tomorrow, and I always get less than stellar sleep in any bed that's not mine. Unless it's Maya's couch.

I'm just about to shift into reverse when a call from my agent comes through the speaker system.

"Great game tonight," he says when I answer, his deep voice rumbling through the interior of my call. "Very impressive, and

I'm not the only one who thought so. Just got a call from Jerry Bronson."

I smile at the display on my dashboard. Mark Rodriguez is the best in the business, and every conversation we have is efficient and to the point. It's why our calls never begin with any of the typical niceties like *hello, how are you?* or *how's your shoulder after the blow you took earlier?*

"Thanks," I say as I crank the heat, "but I have no idea who that is."

He clucks his tongue, chastising me. "The Devils' new assistant coach. He wanted to know if your no-trade clause excludes them."

My hands drop from the steering wheel as my heart stutters in my chest. "Oh."

"They want you. Badly," he continues as if he hasn't just knocked me off kilter.

"Rumors about Rogers are true, then, I'm assuming?" I force out. "He's retiring this season?"

"Off the record, yes. If he keeps playing like he has been, he'll end up on long-term injury reserve," he confirms. "It'd be a post-trade deadline deal, since they want Rogers to finish out the full season."

It's a common misconception that trades can't occur after the stupidly named "trade deadline." Teams can make trades whenever they want, but if a player is acquired after the deadline, they're not eligible to play for their new team in the playoffs.

"I'd have a chance at the Cup with the Bobcats." An opportunity to clinch the title as captain.

"You'd also get your shot to play for the Devils," Mark replies evenly, like he hasn't just dangled the culmination of my entire career in front of me. "That's been our goal from the beginning. Unless that's changed?"

"No," I blurt out. "Sorry, I'm just stunned, is all. This is great. Really great."

Then why is the thought of leaving Boston and the Bobcats making me nauseous?

"Good. I'll keep you posted."

Mark ends the call before I get the chance to say goodbye.

In the quiet of my car, I rest my head against the smooth leather of the headrest and take a deep breath to calm my rapidly beating heart. I'm not sure whether it's from excitement or... dismay? I've been working toward this since I was a kid. It's what Nathan and I always wanted. But now that it may be a reality, it feels too soon. Like I haven't done my due diligence as captain of the Bobcats.

But a person doesn't simply give up their dream over a case of cold feet.

I take a few more deep breaths to center myself before making my way to O'Leary's. By the time I push open the creaky wooden door, all thoughts of the Devils are pushed aside. It's time to celebrate this win with my team.

It's not hard to spot the guys. Every one of them is over six feet, with the honed muscle of a lumberjack. With a beer in hand, I make my way over and slide into the open seat next to Elliott. He's another reason I agreed to come out. Getting her brother's approval may not make or break things with Maya, but it sure as hell won't hurt.

"Berrett!" Logan yells, louder than necessary. The excitement in his expression is overkill, seeing as how we've only been apart for forty minutes. "You made it."

"I'm a man of my word." Turning to Maya's brother, I give him a friendly smile. He's calm and collected in a way that balances out Logan's crazy and cockamamie ways. "Hey, Elliott. How's it going?"

He tips his beer toward me and smiles. "Great game out there."

I nod in thanks. "Too bad the person you came to watch spent most of the game in the penalty box."

Logan gasps dramatically. "Rude. I only spent twenty minutes of the game there."

Cameron and I exchange a knowing look. He takes a sip of his beer, then uses it to point at our left-winger. "That's an entire period, bud."

"I'm lucky I got to see you play at all," Elliott chides with a raised brow.

He and Maya look nothing alike. Whereas Maya's all soft angles and fair skin, Elliott's got the build of a quarterback with an olive complexion. But their sarcasm and facial expressions? Scarily similar. I'd know, considering I've been on the end of that sardonic eyebrow raise more than a few times.

"He just can't help but start shit on the ice." Jake laughs, fishing a handful of peanuts from the small dish at the center of the table. "Happens every game."

"I'm definitely dating an attention whore," Elliott agrees.

In classic Logan fashion, he throws a hand against his chest and gasps so loudly it sounds like he's asphyxiating. Rather than rolling his eyes like the rest of us, Elliott smiles like it's the cutest thing he's ever seen.

"Cole," a tantalizingly familiar voice calls out. "You finally made it."

Heart leaping, I spin and blink once, then again, confirming that it is indeed Maya who's just approached, wearing a Bobcats jersey and a wide smile. Now I'm really damn happy I agreed to come out tonight.

Cam bumps my leg under the table, snapping me out of my stupefied surprise. Tonight's really taking me for a ride.

I pull her into my arms and let the familiar smell of her

perfume surround me. Fuck the bath bomb. This right here is what I need. I have no idea *why* she's here, but I'm relieved, nonetheless. "What're you doing here, bean?"

It's hard to miss the not-so-quiet comments of surprise from my friends at the nickname, but I block them out and focus on Maya.

"Enjoying a drink with the team after a win." She bumps her shoulder against mine. "Duh."

"You were at the game?"

She nods. "Yup."

"But you had class," I state dumbly. Every Sunday from three to six, and Tuesday and Thursday from five to seven. Like a lovesick puppy, I have a reminder set in my phone so I can text her good luck before class.

She shrugs and shoots me a shy smile. "Yeah, well, after all the smack talk about kicking the Raptors' asses, I had to see if you lived up to your word."

I can't keep the smile out of my voice. "You even wore my jersey."

She huffs a breath. "It's not your jersey, it's *mine*. I paid seventy whole dollars for this bad boy at the team store."

Turning around, she drags her hair over her shoulder, showing me the back as if I don't already know it'll be Berrett embroidered in all capital letters. It goes halfway down her thighs, making it look like some kind of mini dress.

"Want me to sign it?" I tease. "Since you're such a fan?"

"Hmm, then I could resell it for quadruple its value, right?"

The comment brings me back to when I first gave Maya tickets to the game, when she made a similar comment. I'm just as intrigued by her now as I was then. She's a thirst I can't quench.

"I told her you could get her a jersey for free, but she insisted on being a *real* fan and buying her own." Sophie shakes her head. She slips into the open space next to Logan, making herself right at home.

"I was debating between your jersey or Cameron's," Maya says with a coy grin as she finally sits in the seat next to me. "Lucky for you, I like the number twenty-five better than thirty-five."

A rough grunt explodes from my chest. I haven't been jealous over a girl since Zara Owens chose to go to prom with Nathan instead of me during our sophomore year of high school. It was the first and last time we fought over a girl.

"I did play better than Berrett tonight," Cam adds a little too loudly. "And I've got more abs than him."

Chuckling, Maya brings her drink to her lips. "Good to know."

When she sets her glass down, I grasp the leg of her stool and tug it toward me, putting distance between her and Cameron. He'd never poach, but that doesn't mean I like the fake flirting. "How was class?"

A smile races over her face. "Really good. We dug into determining a character's internal versus external conflict in a novel."

A lightness fills my chest at the joy in her expression. "I don't know what that means, but you sound excited about it, so I take it that's a good thing."

"Very good. I stayed after class to chat with the instructor, so I was a little late to the game." She gives me a sheepish shrug. "But I made it before the halftime show."

Everyone at the table cringes at the term *halftime*. "Intermission, not halftime," I correct.

"That's what I meant." A flush washes over her cheeks. "It was *very* entertaining."

I take a sip of my beer. "What game did they play?"

"Chuck-a-Puck. Two siblings played, and I don't know *what*

happened down there, but one of the boys started throwing his pucks at his brother instead of the target," she informs me. "Do you guys not watch?"

"Berrett was doing his captain duties during intermission," Jake teases. "Whipping us all into shape."

Maya tilts her head. "Oh, really?"

I shrug. "I usually work with the coaches on strategy. Who to put on the ice, which plays to set up, and any adjustments we need to make. That sort of thing."

"Impressive, Captain Berrett," she comments with a smile.

"You know..." I lean in close, my forearm resting on the table. "I can work my magic and get you picked to be on the ice for one of the intermission games. You may even win a Bobcats stuffed animal or something equally amazing."

Maya frantically shakes her head. "Nope. No, thank you."

"You don't want thousands of people cheering you on?"

Her eyes widen in horror. "Absolutely not. Some of us have this thing called stage fright."

"She's not kidding." Elliott breaks into a smart-ass smile. "Remember how you threw up during auditions for your school play, Yaya?"

Her blush darkens to a deep red. "I don't enjoy being the center of attention."

"You *love* being the center of my attention," I tease with a wink. "It's honestly shocking you haven't admitted that you're in love with me yet."

"The day I admit to being in love with you is the day I willingly subject myself to one of those publicly humiliating intermission games." Blinking rapidly, she untucks her hair from behind her ears so it curtains her cheeks. "And I don't think it's a good idea for me to ever get near a skating rink again, anyway."

Elliott tilts his head, frowning at his sister. "Why not?"

When Maya tenses at the question, it hits me. She didn't tell her brother what happened. Of course she didn't. She'd rather suffer in silence than worry him.

Completely oblivious to the tension, Jake rests his forearms on the table and angles forward. "She got a concussion while learning how to skate."

Elliott, who's been spinning his glass in circles on the table, goes lethally still. "You had a concussion?"

With a dismissive wave, Maya takes a slow sip of her drink. "It wasn't a big deal."

"Wasn't a big deal," he repeats incredulously. "You're kidding me, right? Why didn't you call me?"

With a sigh, she leans closer to me, a move that I'm pretty certain is unconscious. "I'm fine now, Elliott."

"Yeah, *now* being the operative word. Clearly, you weren't fine when it happened."

I angle closer to Maya and place my hand on her nape in silent support. I may not agree with her decision to not tell her brother, but what's done is done. And based on the flush creeping up Elliott's neck, he's not letting this go anytime soon.

"I took her to the doctor immediately after it happened," I tell him. "He reassured me it was a mild concussion, and she had no worrisome symptoms after the first few hours."

It's ironic that I'm the one acting cool, calm, and collected about the concussion when I was anything but when it happened.

"See, babe? She's fine now," Logan placates Elliott in a soft tone. In any other situation, I'd revel in his reaction. Because, for once in his life, Logan is soothing instead of starting shit.

"She was concussed." Elliott huffs. "And didn't deem it important enough to tell me."

"Because it wasn't." Maya straightens, crossing her arms

over her chest. "It's not like you could make it go away, Elliott. And if I'd told you, it would have distracted you from studying."

He mirrors her movements to a T. "So my studying for a stupid accounting test is more important than your health? Don't bullshit me, Maya."

"Hey, hey, hey," I cut in, using my captain's voice. "You have every right to be concerned, but why don't we all take a breather?"

"I'm going to get another drink," Maya says, pushing away from the table.

Sophie quickly follows after her while Jake and Cam mumble excuses about needing refills as well. That leaves just Elliott, Logan, and me—as well as a lot of tension—at the table.

So much for getting on Elliott's good side tonight.

"So," Logan says, breaking the silence. "Do you guys want to hug it out?"

Ignoring him, I meet Elliott's icy stare head-on.

"She should've told me," he reiterates, daring me to disagree.

I exhale loudly. "You know why she didn't."

His shoulders slump, his body deflating a little. "I'm not a kid anymore. She doesn't have to pretend everything's perfect all the time."

"You'll always be her kid brother. She's never going to want you to worry."

"I know that all too well." He takes a deep breath, his chest expanding, his shoulders straightening, and levels me with another glare. "I've only seen my sister cry twice, and both instances were because of the book she was reading. Don't be the third reason."

A bolt of surprise flashes through me. I admire him for being protective of his sister, but I could beat the hell out of him with one hand tied behind my back. He may have the build of an athlete, but he doesn't have the muscle to match.

Logan claps and shoots Elliott a rakish wink. "Threatening Berrett is my favorite pastime, so let me know if you need any assistance."

I flash him a brief disapproving look but quickly return my focus to Elliott. My respect for him grows when he doesn't flinch away from my assessing gaze.

If anything, my scrutiny emboldens him. "I like you, Berrett. I think you're good for my sister. But if you do anything to hurt her, intentionally or not, I'll use your skates to slice your balls clean off."

"And use them as Christmas ornaments," Logan adds with a devilish grin. *Asshole.* "Or fuzzy dice for his car."

Despite my inexperience with real relationships, I know full well I'd never purposefully hurt Maya. "She's safe with me."

Elliott nods, holding eye contact. "Will you make sure she's okay?"

"You don't want to go talk to her?"

"I need some time to cool off," he admits with a shrug. "And cornering Maya when she's done talking about something is riskier than skydiving with a faulty parachute."

Logan snorts loudly. "What I think he's saying is good luck, buddy."

Maya's ire tonight is set on Elliott, so I figure my safety isn't at risk. Still, I approach her slowly, taking in her tense shoulders and clenched jaw as I slide onto the barstool next to her. With a long exhale, I rest my elbows on the table and give her an expectant look. "Well?"

She swirls the remaining drops of her drink around the glass. "Well, what?"

"Are you done sulking? Or do you need a few more minutes?"

She snaps her head to the side, her face twisting into a scowl. "I don't sulk."

I pinch her chin between my fingers and move her head around like I'm examining her. "Yep. Just as I thought. The symptoms are all there. I'm sorry to say, ma'am, but you have a major case of sulking."

Jaw clenched, she tries to fight off a smile, but a loud laugh breaks free. "Fine. Maybe I was sulking *a little*. But there was no need for Elliott to freak out like that."

"He's your brother. I get that you don't want him to worry, but I also get why he's upset."

She opens her mouth, ready to argue, but I hold up a hand to stop her.

"No, no, no. Don't get mad at me. Imagine if Elliott got hurt and you found out on accident, in front of a group of people." I lift my brows and lean in closer, giving her a second to consider. "You'd be pissed."

She nibbles on her lower lip, her eyes darting around. "Well, yeah, but it's different."

"No, it's not. You forget that Elliott's an adult. You don't have to hide stuff from him like you did when he was a kid." I turn, my knee bumping her thigh. "As a brother myself, I can guarantee that he worries about you nonstop. Whether or not there's a legitimate reason to. Cut the kid some slack. He loves you, yeah?"

Maya's lips twitch into a frown. "It's really annoying when you make sense and give good advice."

"You also think it's annoying that I look really good all the time," I point out with a teasing smile.

She hits me with an eye roll, but her body relaxes against mine. "Now's when you offer to buy me a drink."

"Shouldn't you be buying me a drink?" I ask, leaning against the bar. "I did score the winning goal tonight."

Her lips twitch. "Yeah, but Cameron *did* block about thirteen—"

I let out a deep grumble, and she erupts in a fit of giggles. The sound is so sweet that any annoyance at Cameron's begrudgingly amazing saves dissipates.

Before Maya, my favorite sound was the buzzer announcing a goal. Now? It's her carefree, unadulterated laugh.

And until Mark called to tell me about his conversation with the Devils' assistant coach, igniting the flame of possibility, I assumed I'd take the opportunity without hesitation.

Now I have questions.

Like: Would Maya take a chance on a guy who might not stick around?

CHAPTER NINETEEN

WHY THE HELL is my sandwich ringing?

Across the spaceship, Kennedy has morphed into an aquatic creature with shimmering, scaled skin and three luminescent purple eyes. But I'm more concerned that my pastrami on rye won't stop going *ring, ring, ring* than I am about my best friend's shapeshifting ability.

Before I can get to the bottom of it, the dream shatters like glass, and reality hits me with all the subtlety of a freight train. I groan, already plotting the slow and painful demise of the person who's decided to interrupt my day off—especially after I stayed up way too late working on a writing assignment for class.

Your characters haven't gotten any sleep. Write about why, and how they respond to being sleepless.

The irony of that prompt isn't lost on me.

Rolling over, I fumble for my phone and swipe to accept with all the enthusiasm of a hungover sloth. "What?"

"Shit. Did I wake you up?"

I rub the sleep out of my eyes. "If it's before noon, then yeah."

The deep chuckle gives away the caller's identity. "Sorry, bean, but I've got a *huge* favor to ask."

The rumbling timbre of Cole's voice is equivalent to three cups of coffee. My body perks right up.

Running a hand through my bedhead, I lean against my pillows. "Sure. What's up?"

"Could you watch Goose? His babysitter is sick and can't take care of him when I'm gone, but I have to leave for the airport in a few hours. I called my backup sitter, but—"

"Cole," I interrupt, eyes squeezed shut. "It's way too early for this much information. I'll watch Goose. Not a problem."

As far as favors go, this one's easy. Kennedy once asked me for a favor that turned into me being forced on a double date to a Haunted House. My "date" had a prosthetic eye, which he proceeded to continuously take out for fun.

"It's not too much of a hassle?" Cole continues. "I'll only be gone for the night."

"That's fine with me."

A deep sigh filters through my speaker. "Have I told you that you're the best? Because you're the best."

"Well, duh," I scoff. "Don't act so surprised."

He chuckles. "Are you okay staying at my place? Goose did well staying at your apartment with me, but I'm worried he'll get anxious if I'm not there."

I stretch my legs out straight, relishing the sensation. "Yeah, you have a guest room, right?"

"You may as well get used to my bed, Maya," he says with practiced seduction. "Because you won't be able to resist me for much longer."

Dammit. Even through the phone, his voice sends shivers up my spine. He'd be an incredible audiobook narrator, though I'll keep that opinion to myself.

"That's very presumptuous of you."

"Hmm." That sound rumbles through me. "If you're that opposed to sharing my sheets, then you're more than welcome to sleep in the second bedroom. Although I'll warn you that Goose doesn't like sleeping in there."

Well, Goose is just going to have to suck it up.

"Okay." I bite back a laugh. "Let me pack up some stuff and then I'll head over. I'm off today."

"I owe you one, My. Seriously."

Thankful he can't see my blush, I say, "As if I could say no to Goose."

Or you.

———

Cole's place is only a ten-minute drive from mine, but our living situations are night and day. Although my apartment is in a nice area, I can only swing the rent because the building itself is... let's say *charmingly flawed*. The garbage disposal works when it feels like it, my showers hover somewhere between lukewarm and disappointing, and the chipped paint on the walls looks like it was slapped on sometime during the Civil War.

Cole's condo, on the other hand, is straight out of a luxury lifestyle spread. It's in one of Boston's more exclusive neighborhoods and is surrounded by restaurants I've only read about in *Eater*. The kind of places with six-month waitlists and prices that would require me to auction off a vital organ just to try the prix fixe.

Turning in a slow circle, I take it all in. Rather than the stereotypical bachelor pad I envisioned, his home is surprisingly inviting. Large arched windows and twelve-foot ceilings let in natural light that emphasizes the color variations in the oak chevron flooring. There are marble countertops in the kitchen and a hand-carved fireplace opposite a couch so over-sized it could probably fit the entire Boston Bobcats team. If I lived somewhere this nice, I don't think I would ever venture outside.

Cole jogs down the stairs with a duffel bag thrown over his shoulder. "What do you think?"

He's freshly showered, and water droplets soak through his shirt, drawing my attention to the way the muscles of his shoulders stretch the material.

"You have built-in bookcases," I comment. That should sum up my opinion. It's like my Pinterest board brought to life. "Did you design it yourself?"

He surveys the room with a pleased grin. "Definitely not. I bought it completely furnished and haven't changed much. Only turned the office space into a gym and added heated floors to the master bathroom."

I lift a brow. "Of course you did."

"You won't be giving me that attitude once you try it out."

The thought of using Cole's shower is unwittingly erotic.

But I don't let myself dwell on dangerous images of him naked and wet. No. With a shake of my head, I turn back to the instructions he left on the counter. They're extremely detailed and include everything from how much time Goose needs outside to how many of each treat he's allowed to have. It's adorably detailed. Who knew dog dads could be so sexy?

"Does everything make sense?" Cole sidles up beside me, the spicy scent of his cologne wrapping around me like a hug.

His whole condo smells like *him*, and it's sent me into a state of arousal. Once again tamping down on the sensation, I clear my throat and take half a step to the side to put a little distance between us.

"I'll have my phone with me if you have questions, but that should include everything."

"We'll be fine." Looking at Goose, who's curled up at my feet, I ask, "Won't we, Goosey Goose?"

Cole nods, though his lips are pressed into a thin line, like he's nervous about leaving Goose with a new sitter.

"Seriously." I try not to let my voice betray how humorous I think his concern is. "We'll be good. If I have questions, I'll call."

He nods once, resolved, and bends down to talk to Goose. "You be good for Maya, okay, buddy?"

The dog lazily blinks at his owner before promptly falling back asleep.

With a deep chuckle, Cole straightens and levels a serious look at me. "He likes to watch me play, so if you could turn the game on for him, that'd be great."

My mouth drops open. "You're kidding me."

"Why would I be kidding?" He frowns, his brows furrowed. "He's a big hockey fan."

"He's a big hockey fan," I repeat dumbly.

Maybe he's had one too many hits to the head, because there's no way Goose knows what the hell is going on when I'm barely beginning to get the hang of it.

Cole tucks a loose strand of hair behind my ear and throws me a lopsided smile. "Mm-hmm. You gonna watch with him, baby?"

The pet name grips my libido like a vise, but I tamp down on the need that threatens to overtake me. Crossing my arms over my chest, I say, "You should probably get going."

"Are you kicking me out of my house?"

"You have a flight soon and you're dawdling."

"Maybe I just like spending time with you." He presses a chaste kiss to my forehead. Then, scooping up his duffel, he strolls to the front door. "Don't forget to text if you need anything."

What I need is a lobotomy, considering all I want to do is bury my face in his chest and soak in his attention.

————

Thirty minutes later, I've given in to the temptation to snoop. Yes, it may be considered a breach of trust, but he never explicitly told me *not* to. Plus, the man suggested I sleep in his bed. What does he expect? Besides, I may as well familiarize myself with my temporary lodgings. If he's a secret axe murderer, I'd like to find out now and not further down the line.

Goose watches me move around with mild interest but doesn't bother moving from his spot in front of the fireplace. He probably thinks I'm an idiot, with the way I'm tiptoeing around when there's no one here to catch me.

Cole's kitchen is annoyingly boring. Based on the sparkly, clean condition of the counters and appliances, I doubt he spends much time in here. The fridge is mostly empty—nothing but a couple of apples, half a bag of carrots, and several bottles of salad dressing—but the freezer is stocked full of frozen meals. And not the Lean Cuisine kind. These are home-cooked and packaged nicely in glass Tupperware containers. Huh. So he's a meal-prepper. That makes sense, given his busy schedule.

His junk drawer is equipped with a few takeout menus—which I didn't know were still a thing, considering Google exists—and a slew of pens, each with a hotel name printed on it.

"Onto the next room," I murmur. My voice echoes off the high ceilings, leaving a creepy chill at the back of my neck. I'm not used to so much quiet. At home, there's always some background noise: the clank of the furnace kicking on, the humming of the fridge, my upstairs neighbor.

I check the coat closet in the hallway next, but I regret my decision the moment I open the door and a mountain of hockey gear tumbles out. The head of a cracked hockey stick smacks the sensitive spot between my neck and shoulder, and I stumble over the shin pads at my feet.

The clattering and crashing sounds interest Goose enough to rouse him from his comfortable position. As he approaches, he looks at me with what I'm certain is judgment. *Yeah, yeah.*

Staring down at the ground, I consider my options. Obviously, I have to put everything back, but based on the cleanliness and order of Cole's kitchen, I have a feeling he doesn't just shove stuff in the closet, slam the door closed, and hope for the best.

Unfortunately for him, in the end, that's exactly how I tackle clean-up.

Okay. Where to next?

The bathroom, laundry room, and dining room reveal nothing exciting. In fact, they contain very few personal details. He wasn't kidding when he said he hasn't changed much about the condo since he purchased it. I resist the urge to snoop in his bedroom and instead head for the bookshelf. It's definitely for aesthetic and decorative purposes, but it's stocked with some of the classics and a few good memoirs.

Eventually, I lie on his couch—which is comfier than my bed—with Goose and my book. As far as days off go, it's a pretty damn good one. The only issue arises when it's time for bed.

"Goose, come here."

He sits in the doorway, his dark brown eyes fixed on me.

I pat the guest room bed in a pathetic attempt to lure him in. Clearly, this isn't his first rodeo. Not with the way he continues to stare me down without breaking eye contact. Maybe he has to go to the bathroom? I force myself out of the comfortable bed and shuffle to the back door, but Goose doesn't follow me. Doubling back, I find him pawing at Cole's bedroom door.

"Dad's not home, buddy," I tell him, using a high-pitched voice I always find myself using when speaking to animals. "Let's go sleep in the guest room. C'mon."

Ignoring me, he continues to attempt his way into the master bedroom. *I'm starting to think that Cole wasn't kidding when he said Goose won't sleep anywhere else.* The moment I open the door for him, he leaps onto the king-size bed and curls up in a little ball at the foot.

Oh, for fuck's sake.

The room is painted dark gray with sleek edges and harsh lines, but as I poke around, I find details that are distinctly Cole. The piece of art above his bed is a black-and-white snapshot of a hockey game. Both bedside tables are cluttered with family photos. And his closet boasts every piece of workout gear ever created by Nike and Adidas. I even find both glasses I gifted him for Christmas residing on his dresser, right next to his cologne.

By the time I've finished my self-guided tour, Goose is fast asleep on the bed. *Shit.* I can either sneak out and hope he doesn't notice *or* spend the night in Cole's bed. A bed that looks extremely comfortable. With Tempur-Pedic pillows. And a cozy comforter. And a dog who refuses to sleep anywhere else.

It takes less time to decide than it should. But in the end, if I'm not sleeping with Cole, I may as well enjoy sleeping in his bed.

CHAPTER TWENTY

OUR TEAM DOESN'T SCORE in the first period. It's hard to when our chemistry is off and we can't get the damn puck past the Rangers' best defenseman. Jason DeVries is a giant dick, known for his out-of-line chirping. And, as a bonus, he despises me. Why? Solely because I look exactly like the man who "stole his girlfriend." It's ridiculous, if unsurprising, that Nathan's love life is stirring up trouble for me years later. Some things never change.

By the end of the second period, we've scored once, but we're still down by two. Jake passes me the puck, but DeVries intercepts and jams me into the board. Collisions are part of the game, and for the most part, they're clean. This wasn't, and yet the referee doesn't call it.

"What the hell is your problem?" I shout, shoving DeVries off me.

He smirks, his eyes lit up with distaste. "Just as shitty of a player as your brother. Can't get a simple puck past me."

I shove his chest hard. I'm not quick to anger during games. Players have to become immune to the constant shit-talking and aggressive testosterone because there are about nine million ways to get a penalty. I can usually stay level-headed enough to avoid the penalty box, but mentioning Nathan? Game fucking over. "Want to say that again?"

"C'mon." He chuckles darkly. "We all know the Berrett brothers never lived up to the hy—"

I slam into him before he can get another word out. Rage, hot and heavy, springs to life and consumes me. The fight escalates with both Bobcats and Rangers players piling on to get a piece of the action, led by none other than Logan. DeVries lands an elbow to my nose, but not before I get in a few solid punches. As a ref pulls me off him, the first person in my line of vision is Coach, and he's angry as hell.

Fuck.

———

I find Maya cuddled under my covers with my dog snoozing at her feet. She may only be there because, for reasons unknown, Goose dislikes the guest bedroom, but I'm not one to look a gift horse—or chocolate lab—in the mouth. I quietly drop my duffel on the floor of the closet and pad across the wood floor to the bed. Since Goose is the worst guard dog known to man, he doesn't so much as flinch at the sound of my steps.

Maya's curled on her left side with her hands resting under her cheek. Her lips are pushed together in an adorable little pout that's at war with her relaxed brows.

I run the tips of my fingers over her cheek, reveling in the smoothness of her skin. *God, she's breathtaking.* I must accidentally say that out loud, because the second the thought crosses my mind, a scream pierces the stillness of the house and a small fist connects with my face.

"Fuck." I reel back, cradling my jaw. If I wasn't already bruised from the on-ice fight, that would have done the trick.

Warm liquid drips down my lips, confirming that her hit reopened a cut I sustained earlier. It hurts like a bitch, but I can't deny she's got a great right hook.

She squeaks, her eyes going wide in the dim room, and sits upright.

I can't help but chuckle. "Definitely not the warm welcome I was hoping for."

Maya turns on my bedside lamp and cups her mouth with both hands. "Oh my God. I'm sorry! I thought you were an intruder." She turns to face Goose. "What the hell, dude? You're supposed to protect me. Not sleep through an attempted kidnapping."

He simply blinks at her before hopping off the bed and sauntering over to me.

Sighing, she studies my face. "Are you okay? I swear I didn't mean to hit you. I'm usually very nonviolent."

"You seem to forget I take hits for a living." No longer cupping my jaw, I prod at the area, testing the tenderness.

"I made you bleed!" she shrieks, jackknifing out of the bed.

Damn. If I thought her sleeping in my bed was sexy? It's nothing compared to her slipping out from under the covers in only a t-shirt. The smirk that pulls up my lips as I give her body an obvious once-over is automatic.

Maya holds up a hand, her cheeks stained bright red. "Don't say a word unless you want matching black eyes."

Biting back every innuendo in the book, I follow her into my bathroom. Based on how familiar she is with where the washcloths and Advil are, she's done some snooping. I don't blame her. I've done the same at her place. I've yet to figure out why she has enough Q-tips to supply our nation's armed forces, but I can't exactly ask without revealing how I know that they're in the bottom drawer to the left of the bathroom sink.

As Maya holds the washcloth under the faucet, Goose

weaves between my legs, desperate for the affection I've yet to give him.

"Hey, buddy," I croon, scratching him behind the ears. "You have fun with Maya? She give you lots of belly rubs?"

He wags his tail in response and curls up between my feet as I lean against the counter. Am I jealous that my dog has spent more nights with the girl I'm falling for than I have? Definitely. Do I love the way Maya mumbles about how a grown man being cute with dogs is obnoxiously attractive? Abso-fucking-lutely.

When she refuses to let me take care of the injury myself, I hop onto the bathroom counter and let her play doctor. This is not how I thought my nurse fantasy would play out, but beggars can't be choosers. She lightly presses the cloth against my cheek, and I suck in a sharp breath. It's been a few hours since my fight with DeVries, but my face may take a little longer to recover than my ego.

"What are you doing back so early?" Maya stands directly between my thighs. If she noticed, she'd back away, surely, but I'm not going to be the one to bring attention to it. "You said your flight was tomorrow morning. It's the middle of the night."

"I decided to come back earlier."

She runs her free hand through her adorable bedhead. "Yeah, no shit, Sherlock. You could have called or texted so I didn't think I was being abducted, you know."

I snort. I never would have guessed she'd give Logan a run for his money in the drama department, yet here we are. "Sorry. I honestly wasn't thinking. I booked a red-eye back home the moment the game ended."

More like the moment Coach Henderson was done handing me my ass in the locker room.

Motioning to Goose, who's lying happily on my bathmat,

Maya says, "Goose begged me to turn the game on, so we watched."

"Told you so."

"Mm-hmm." Maya gently pulls the now-stained washcloth away from my cheek. "Let me take a look at you."

"You don't need to use my injury as an excuse to check me out."

"If your narcissism has returned, then you must be okay," she says with a smirk.

I sit stock-still as she skims her fingers over the bruise on my cheek. She ghosts them against my skin like a whisper, equal parts tantalizing and caring. When she nears my mouth, she stops. "You cut your lip."

"Still works just fine." I cover her hand with my own and brush my mouth against her palm in a sweet kiss. "See?"

She sucks in a startled breath. "Sort of."

"Sort of?" I wrap my legs around her, and as I hoped, she loses her balance just a little, forcing her to place her hands on my chest to catch herself. "I'm happy to more thoroughly demonstrate."

Her lips part, but she doesn't say a word.

Taking the opening, I gently press a kiss to her exposed collarbone. Slowly, I give every inch of her neck attention, relishing the way her chest rises and falls in rapid succession. I swirl my tongue over her pulse point, spurred on by how fast her heart is beating.

"Cole," she murmurs as I nip beneath her chin.

Pulling back, I meet her gaze. "Hmm? Something you want?"

She nibbles on her bottom lip, as if warring with herself. But before I can tease her further, she arches forward and slams her lips to mine. There's no hesitancy in the way she kisses me. Like

I could float away at any moment, and she needs to tether us together.

The room is warm and electric, the air radiating with the demolition of the sexual tension we've spent months ignoring. I slip my tongue between her lips, eager to taste her, and devour her mouth like I've been wanting—no, *needing*—to for so long. Her small hands roam over my back, exploring the planes of muscle, pulling me tighter against her. There's no hiding how hard I am, and by the way she rolls her hips against mine, desperate for friction, she's not the least bit put off by it.

Not one to deny Maya anything she desires, I toy with the waistband of her underwear, dragging my finger back and forth over her soft skin, eliciting a shudder from her. When I slip my hand in to cup her warmth, it's a goddamn miracle I don't come right there and then.

"Already so warm and wet for me, baby," I praise, nipping lightly on her lower lip. "You want me to make you come?"

"Yes," she mewls.

"Hmm. Well, I want to take you on a date. Do we have a deal?"

"Are you negotiating an orgasm for a date?" She rears back, her jaw unhinging. "Seriously?"

"What can I say?" I brush my thumb lightly against her clit and she jerks at the contact. "That *Negotiating for Dummies* book you recommended taught me a lot."

She laughs, but when I brush against her entrance to tease an answer from her, she lets out a long, low moan. God, I could listen to that noise every day. She's unbelievably responsive as I push inside her, twisting my fingers until I hit that spot that makes her throw her head back and gasp. Maya drags her hand through my hair and tugs, the sharp sting making my cock twitch in my pants.

Not wanting to get distracted from my mission, I pull my

hand away, causing her to deflate, her body draped against me. "Go on a date with me, Maya. Give us a chance."

"I can't—"

I slip a finger back inside her, and she subconsciously spreads her legs to grant me better access.

"Can't what?" I slip a second in, reveling in the knowledge that she's like this, desperate and panting, because of me, then create a slow, even rhythm.

She throws her head back, her mouth open in a silent moan. "Cole," she eventually says, her voice desperate with need. "Please."

"Answer the question." I brush my lips against her neck. "Why can't you give in to us?"

"Be-because then I'd have to admit I'm falling for you and that this is real." Her eyes widen in panic, but before she can backpedal or second-guess herself, I distract her by flattening my thumb against her clit. Instantly, she clamps around my fingers and pants through an orgasm. I don't stop until she sags against me, our kiss transitioning from frantic to languid.

I like her like this. As desperate for me as I am for her. With a deep, satisfied moan, I tilt my head back to look at her. "Newsflash, My." I tuck a piece of hair behind her ear and flash a knowing smile. "I've already fallen for you. And I'm scared, too."

She searches my face, her expression open. "Yeah?"

"Yep. I may be an insanely good-looking, Stanley Cup–winning, superbly talented hockey player—"

Maya rolls her eyes.

"But," I continue, a little more seriously, "I'm only human. So yeah, what I feel for you scares me, but I'm willing to give it a shot."

She nibbles on her bottom lip, dragging her fingers over my chest. "I guess I can give it a shot, too."

Ever the faithful wingman, Goose lets out a deep howl that reverberates through the bathroom. Nothing like a man's dog pretending he's a werewolf on a full moon to kill the romantic mood.

With a tinkling laugh, Maya scratches the top of Goose's head. "Is he okay? I've never heard him make that noise before."

"He probably just needs to go out," I guess with a yawn. "I'll take him before I shower."

And jerk off, because I'm harder than I've ever been.

"Since I'm still on babysitting duty, why don't you shower while I take him out?" she suggests with a yawn of her own. "We can head to bed after. I'm sure you're tired."

I accept her offer and take my time in an indulgent shower. The mixture of hot water and an orgasm washes away my anger and frustration over the game and kneads some of the tension from my taut muscles. Afterward, I find Maya once again curled up on her side in my bed, hands tucked under her cheek, while Goose snuggles protectively against her back. *Cockblocker.*

I swap my towel for a pair of boxer briefs, then corral Goose, forcing him to his spot at the end of the bed, and curl up against Maya under the covers. Her body is soft and pliant against mine, the sensation instantly draining all remnants of stress I'm holding. I run my fingers up and down her forearm, watching the goose bumps erupt against her fair skin.

"Mmm, that tickles." She turns her head against the pillow and opens her eyes. "That was a long shower."

"I didn't cool down the way I should have after the game," I explain. "A shower won't make up for it, but it'll help with the muscle soreness."

"Ah. Smart." She lifts a hand and lightly brushes it against my bruised cheekbone. "Does it hurt?"

"Not any worse than my self-esteem," I say with a sigh. "We lost the game during a power play while I was in the penalty box." Puffing out a breath of air, I pull her closer to me. "Some dickhead player brought up Nate to mess with my head, and it worked. I lost my shit."

Maya's body flies up like she's being exorcised. "He brought up your *brother*? What a motherfucking twat-waffle. You should've taken off your skates and used them to saw off his balls!"

I don't know whether to be concerned that the Silver siblings share a penchant for threatening to cut off people's balls with skates or be flattered by Maya's indignation on my behalf.

A scowl that promises wrath flashes across her face as she waits for me to answer her.

"He's an asshole, but it's his MO."

"That doesn't make it okay," she argues, flopping back down onto the bed.

I pull her onto me and she settles with her head on my chest. "No, it doesn't. It was fucked up of him, but I should have seen it coming. The two of them had a long-standing rivalry."

"Really?"

"Mm-hmm. They played for the same team in college and were ultra-competitive. A few years later, Nathan started dating DeVries' ex-girlfriend. I guess he wasn't over her and thought Nathan only did it to fuck with his head. It got messy. And now he hates me by proxy."

Maya's eyes light up. "Do you have his number? We can add it to a telemarketer's list so he's bombarded with spam calls."

I chuckle into her neck. "Let's not talk about him anymore. How was Goose? Did he give you any trouble?"

She hums, snuggling closer. "He tried to get me to join his pyramid scheme, but other than that, things were great."

"I should let him borrow my *Negotiating for Dummies* book. Maybe he'll have better luck next time."

Maya's airy laugh snaps the remaining threads of anger I was holding on to.

"Thank you again for watching him," I say, burying my face in her hair. "I seriously owe you one."

"You also owe me a date," she reminds me with a teasing grin.

"I'm going to sleep very well tonight dreaming up ideas for that date." I tighten my hold on her waist and press a soft kiss beneath the hollow of her ear. "Told you I'd eventually win you over."

"It took you a while."

"Even so," I reassure her, "you're more than worth the wait."

CHAPTER TWENTY-ONE

WITH A STRANGLED SCREAM, I throw yet another sweater onto the ground. It doesn't look any better on me than the last, or the one before that.

Cole told me to dress comfortably for our date, but my version of comfortable isn't fit for being seen out in public. So I don't know what to wear. A sweater and leggings? Sweatshirt and yoga pants? Bathrobe and slippers?

"Did you get stuck in a pair of pants?" Kennedy calls from my couch. "Cole's picking you up soon, and we're still waiting for a fashion show."

"Coming!" Frowning into my closet, I snag a navy blue sweater that Ava says is "kind of cute." She thinks most of my clothes are too baggy or boring, so that's the highest form of praise I can expect from her.

Kennedy and Sophie cheer as I walk into the living room, and though I roll my eyes at the theatrics, I appreciate the support. They stopped by to help me pick out an outfit. That somehow turned into them rummaging through my wine rack —carefully curated via the highly scientific method of label aesthetics—and picking one to uncork. Well, twist off.

"Cute! The sweater makes your eyes pop." Sophie scans me from head to toe over the rim of her glass.

"And it makes your titties look good," Kennedy adds with a wink. "I vote for this outfit."

"It's the only outfit we've seen," Sophie points out. "But I vote for it, too."

Wiping my clammy hands against my jeans, I exhale a deep breath. I've never worried so much about what to wear on a date, and I've never stressed about how a date might go. Either I like them or I don't.

But I already like Cole. A lot. And this is a big step. Agreeing to go out with him tonight means I'm officially opening myself up for a world of hurt. In the few months I've known him, he's made himself a steady presence in my life. One that makes me blush, and laugh, and get out of my comfort zone. And the farther I let myself fall, the harder it'll be to pick myself back up when it's over.

Kennedy offers me her drink. "You want a sip? You look like you could use it."

"I'm freaking out," I blurt out.

"There's no reason to be nervous." Sophie gives me a reassuring smile. "Cole's an amazing guy, and it's not like you haven't been on dates with him before."

"I haven't." Frowning, I plop onto the couch between them. "I made it clear I wanted to be friends."

My friends lean forward as if the move was choreographed and exchange a look. Huffing, Kennedy rolls her eyes. "Maya, I love you, but you and Cole have been dating since you met months ago. You just haven't been fucking."

Sophie nods. "She's right. The only difference is going to be the orgasms. Nothing to be nervous about."

I suck in a breath, readying an argument, but before I can

tell them all the reasons they're wrong, Cole knocks on my door, punctual as always.

Showtime.

I pull the door open, and his eyes light up in genuine happiness. "Hey, baby."

"We've graduated from bean to baby?" I tease with a small smile.

"I'll never retire bean, but now you can have a nickname and a pet name." He cradles my jaw and leans in for a kiss.

My breathing becomes unsteady as he dominates my mouth, his tongue tangling with mine in a sensual movement. Behind me, a round of whoops goes up, and when they reach a level too loud to ignore, he pulls back.

"We'll have to pick that back up later," he murmurs against my lips. "Didn't realize we had company."

"We were helping her pick out her lingerie," Kennedy shouts. "And making sure you got her pretty flowers."

Eyes closed, I take a calming breath so I don't do something completely warranted like strangle her.

Cole chuckles, bringing his mouth to my ear. "How drunk are they?"

I take a step back and straighten my shoulders. Sometime while I was trying on a multitude of outfits that I nixed before even showing my friends, they finished bottle number one and cracked open a second. "Very."

Inside my apartment, he shuts the door quietly and holds out a gorgeous bouquet. "These are for you."

I ignore the *oohs* and *aahs* from the couch and press my nose against the red roses. Their sweet smell brings a smile to my face. I've never gotten flowers from any man but my brother. Not even from Josh on Valentine's Day last year. Instead, he got me chocolates and a bottle of wine—which he proceeded to eat and drink—and then tried to convince me to have anal sex. Super romantic.

"Thank you. They're gorgeous."

"Gorgeous flowers for a gorgeous woman," he says, his eyes raking over me with a proprietary gleam that causes heat to creep through me.

I slip on a coat and rush Cole out of my apartment before Drunk and Drunker can embarrass me any further. "So what are we doing?"

"Well, I was looking at *PagePulse* and—"

I stop on the fourth-floor landing and hold up a hand. "I'm sorry, you what?"

"*PagePulse*," he repeats like it's a foreign word. "That site where you track the books you like."

"I know what *PagePulse* is. I just didn't know that you did. No offense."

The wicked tilt of his grin makes my knees wobble danger-ously as we continue down the stairs. "I looked up a few of your favorite rom-coms to get ideas for our date."

That in and of itself is worthy of a rom-com. *Swoon.* Grip-ping the railing to keep from tumbling, I peer over at him. "Were you inspired?"

At the bottom of the stairs, he hits me with his signature smile and rests his hand on my lower back. "Yep. In the books, they always do cute things like go to a museum, or the best ice cream shop in the city, or an arcade. But none of those are *you*, so I decided to think a little outside the box."

"Okay..." I truly have no idea where this is going. "So if we're not going to a museum, ice cream shop, or arcade, then what are we doing?"

He waggles his brows. "You're not afraid of heights, are you?"

———

I grip the taut muscle of Cole's thigh as the helicopter tilts and sways. Of all the scenarios I envisioned for tonight, enjoying a helicopter tour of Boston was most definitely not one of them.

"Is it supposed to be this rocky?" I yell over the choppy sound of the spinning blades. In the small space, Cole's scent—a mix of his woodsy cologne and *him*—surrounds me like a safety blanket. It calms me in ways that the weighted blanket Ava got me for Chanukah two years ago never has.

"I can hear you." Cole taps the mic attached to my headset. "And yes, we'll even out soon."

I nod and force myself to relax against my plush leather seat and take in the view. This experience? It's definitely set the bar for any future dates. Knowing Cole, that was probably his intention. He did tell me he plays to win.

"Oh." I tap my pointer finger against the panoramic window. "That's the Gardner Museum."

Cole peers around me to get a better view. "What kind of art do they have?"

"I have no idea," I admit with a shrug. "But I do know that the largest art theft in US history happened there. A hundred million dollars' worth of art was never recovered."

His laugh mixes with the steady thump of the blades and the whir of the engine. "Let me guess. You read about that in a book?"

"Yup."

He rests his chin on my shoulder, and we watch the skyline get farther and farther away as we cruise over the North Atlantic coastline. "You were right, you know."

A laugh bubbles out of me. "I'm always right, but could you specify?"

"That when you talk about books, I envision a very beautiful, sexy librarian."

I shoot him a dirty look, though I don't mind in the least that he'd use words like *beautiful* or *sexy* to describe me. I'd never attribute adjectives like that to myself, but the way Cole's looking at me makes it hard not to believe him.

"I said when men hear about my *job*," I huff, though there's no fire behind the words. "Not when I simply speak about books."

With a chuckle, he places a kiss on my temple. Then he settles back into his seat. For the rest of the ride, the helicopter maneuvers over and between buildings like it's an eagle while the captain points out historical landmarks. Overall, it's impressive, though I squeeze Cole's hand in panic every time we drop even the slightest bit.

I've known from the start that Cole is an affectionate person. But now that I've stamped his passport, allowing him to leave the friend zone, his attention has only amplified. The entire ride, he finds any excuse to touch me. Massaging my nape when I lean forward to get a better look, brushing hair away from my face, and toying with the silver rings on my fingers. It's intimate without being sexual. And by the time we land, every part of my body is attuned to his, desperately waiting for the next touch.

He helps me out of the helicopter, then rests a hand on my lower back as we crouch and scurry away, squinting against the gusts of air caused by the blades. I shiver in the cool night air and unabashedly use Cole's height and body to block me from the bulk of the wind. I don't feel bad in the slightest, considering he uses the cold as an excuse to keep my hand clasped with his.

"That was amazing," I remark as we enter the heated parking garage. "Thank you."

"Pretty cool, huh?"

"Very cool. You're going to have to think *way* outside the box for our next date if you want to top this."

"So there'll be another date?"

A smile plays on my lips as my heart thumps a little wildly against my breastbone. "I guess so."

Cole spins me around and slams his lips against mine. It's unexpected, since we're standing between two cars in the middle of the garage, but I sink into it, nonetheless. The intensity of his need overwhelms my senses and coaxes all the air out of my lungs. He backs me up until I'm pressed against a black sedan, his body molded against mine.

A car alarm blares in the relative quiet, jerking us apart. "We're going to be late for our dinner reservation if we keep this up," Cole pants, his breath hot against my neck.

"We should skip dinner," I suggest, my tone needy. "Head straight to dessert."

Cole snorts at my very lame come-on but tilts his head in consideration. "You're sure?"

His deep amber eyes search my face, looking for what? Hesitation? Uncertainty? The only thing he'll find is a deep longing to feel him everywhere. I can't get enough.

"I'm sure," I confirm, keeping my attention locked on him. "Of you. Us. I want this."

He groans as if the words themselves have been wrapped around his cock. I could most definitely get used to hearing that sound. With his hand tight around mine once more, he drags me behind him, weaving through vehicles, until we find his Porsche in the back row. Even in his frenzied state, he still opens the car door and waits for me to buckle before heading to the driver's seat.

The trip to his condo is fraught with tension, a match just waiting to be lit by the sparks between us. The radio is on, but the volume is low, making it possible to hear every uneven breath he takes. He speaks once, but only to say that Goose is at his sitter's because he wasn't sure how late we'd be out. I'm too turned on to tease him about how I know that's code for he didn't want his dog there in case he got lucky.

The drive to his condo is short, but it feels as though it takes hours. Unlike the last time I was here, I'm not focused on what's in his junk drawer or whether there's a secret sex doll in his closet. All I'm focused on is *him*. The way his eyes grow hungrier with each second that passes. The calloused hands gently gripping my waist. The rapid rise and fall of his chest.

But despite how clearly turned on he is, I need to be the one to initiate this. Cole's taken the lead in every aspect of our relationship so far, but this next step? It has to be my choice.

I place my hands on his chest and glide them upward until they're resting beneath his jaw. The tips of my fingers tangle with the hair brushing his nape as I pull his lips to mine. The kiss starts off gentle, but slowly, I lose myself to the softness of his mouth. I let my hands wander down the slope of his shoulders, then his arms. Then I trace the contours of his chest and abs.

I'm exploring lower, headed for his waistband, when, without warning, I'm scooped into his arms bridal style. This isn't the first time he's held me this way, though, unlike the last incident, I don't attempt to wiggle away.

He charges through the apartment like a man on a mission, but the moment we step into his room, his demeanor turns reverent. He peels each article of clothing off me like he's unwrapping a present, and by the time I'm fully naked, I'm too aroused to even consider being self-conscious. Especially when his eyes rake over my body like I'm a five-course meal.

"On the bed," he commands, his voice strained. "Let me look at you."

All I want to do is press my legs together to relieve the tension, but I follow his instructions, desperate to please him so he'll put me out of my misery and touch me. Splayed out, completely naked while he's still fully dressed, vulnerability finally creeps in. Even so, I can't help but feel sexy and wanton at the same time.

Finally, he joins me on the bed, stretching out beside me. "So fucking beautiful," he groans, tracing a single finger from my sternum straight down to my navel.

I screw my eyes shut in pleasure as he trails open-mouthed kisses down my body. His lips and hands are soon everywhere, caressing and teasing until I'm whimpering beneath him. Every inch of my body is on edge, begging for more of his touch.

"Spread your legs for me, baby," Cole murmurs against my thigh. "Need to taste you."

My cheeks flush at his command, but he's too busy gazing at my body like it's a rediscovered war treasure to notice.

His veneration gives me the courage to obey, and when I do, he rewards me with praise.

"Good girl."

I moan, needy and eager for his skin against mine.

He swipes his tongue against me, and all I can do is sink my fingers into his hair and hold on as he sucks and licks like a starved man.

And when he slips two fingers inside me, twisting and swirling and pumping like he's taken a crash course on every little way to please me, I cry out, my back arching of its own accord. Not even my vibrator can get me worked up so quickly. Cole lavishes my clit with steady swirls of his tongue, bringing me closer to orgasm with each circle and leaving me gasping for air.

I throw my head back against the pillow as the knot in my lower stomach unravels and I detonate with a loud moan. My pussy greedily clamps down around his fingers as wave after wave of euphoria rolls through me.

When my body goes lax, Cole stands and peels off his shirt. He struggles to undo his fly, which has grown impossibly tight against him, and when his cock finally springs out, I let out an audible gasp. The teaser I got when he strutted around in black joggers did *not* do him justice. His dick is long and thick, with a slight curve that's eerily reminiscent of the dildo in my nightstand drawer.

"Damn," I mutter to myself.

He chuckles as he pulls his socks off. "See something you like?"

"Yes." There's no point in lying. The man knows he's impressive.

I clamber off the bed, drunk on the need to touch him. He watches me, his irises blazing, the amber color molten, as I splay my hands over his chest and explore every inch of muscle.

God, he's gorgeous.

He lets out a deep groan as I snake my hand down to stroke him, reveling in the way he's impossibly soft yet hard. As much as I'd like to take the next few hours to explore his body, I'm far too needy for that.

I lower to my knees and tilt my head back. Then, holding his gaze, I run my tongue along the underside of his shaft. When I wrap my lips around his sensitive tip, his eyes flutter shut and he clenches his jaw. With one hand gripping his length, I gently toy with his balls using the other.

His responding curse emboldens me to swirl my tongue around and tease him. It's heady, holding this kind of power over him, despite being on my knees. Cole rests his hands on the back of my head, lightly pumping into my mouth yet not forcing my movements. I take him as deep as I can, setting a steady rhythm. When his thigh muscles have gone impossibly tense, he tugs on my hair until I release him. Then he leads me back to the bed. Only when I'm splayed out on my back again does he join me, easing his body over mine, giving me a fraction of his weight, and suck my lower lip into his mouth.

He has to release me to pluck a condom from his nightstand—that I may or may not have known was there from previous snooping—and slide it over his hardened cock. My body relaxes instinctively as he tosses my right leg over his shoulder and positions himself at my entrance. The delicious stretch as he enters me has me closing my eyes in pleasure.

"Eyes on me, baby." His thrusts are slow and leisurely to start, despite the hungry gleam in his eye.

Far less patient, I push my hips up to meet his, urging him to quicken his pace. The desperation riding my body is over-whelming and exciting all at once.

He chuckles at my attempt to top from the bottom and kisses me deeply with swollen lips. "Not rushing this, baby." With a moan, he nips at my collarbone. "I've waited too long to only last a minute."

I'm too far gone to even acknowledge his comment, and all rational thought leaves me when he brings my other leg into the crook of his arm, sinking deeper. Moans bubble up my throat as he rolls his hips against mine, hitting *that* spot perfectly, over and over again. Another orgasm builds deep within me but stays just out of reach. It's the purest, most plea-surable form of torture I've ever experienced. And as he snakes a hand between us and rubs leisurely circles against my clit, the words that escape me are incomprehensible. The man's a damn musician, playing my body to the tune of his choosing.

"So fucking beautiful," he murmurs, watching the way he slides in and out of me.

"Cole, I need to come," I beg as my pussy ripples around him. "Please."

Focus fixed on my face, he uses two fingers to gently tug on my clit, and like that, I come with a choked cry. Sparks of pleasure roar through my body as I tremble. A few more pumps of his hips, and he's following me into sated bliss, grunting my name as he comes undone.

We lie in a satisfied, sweaty pile of limbs, working to catch our breath, but when Cole's stomach grumbles, we burst into laughter.

"Clearly, I worked up an appetite," he says with a shameless smile. "How do you feel about Italian?"

"Works for me. I'm easy."

With an arched brow, he nuzzles into my neck. His body molds against mine like this is a practiced dance between the two of us. "Oh, are you? Good to know."

I roll my eyes, but there's no hiding my smile. "For the record, I don't usually put out on the first date."

"This wasn't our first date." Cole lifts his head, smirking. "It was about our thirtieth."

With that, he's on his feet, disposing of the condom and washing his hands, then placing an order for delivery.

"Should be here in an hour." He looms over me, capturing my mouth, nipping lightly at my bottom lip before leaning back and releasing it. "Wonder what we should do to fill the time..."

CHAPTER TWENTY-TWO

AS I LOOK DOWN at my watch again, I curse myself. Maya's not late; I'm just early and eager to see her. Having been on the road for the past five nights, I've had to survive on sporadic calls and texts. I'll take what I can get, but I've missed the feel of her hand in mine when she tells me about class and how her fingers lightly brush over the bruises I come home with pretty regularly. And I *really* miss the breathy moans she makes when I'm slowly moving inside her. The sharp intake of breath when I first enter her. The soft brush of her lips against mine when she comes undone around my cock.

Right on time, she steps out of the ivy-covered building where her class is held. She looks like an adorable marshmallow in her puffy white jacket. Not that I'd ever tell her that, since I value my life. Only as she takes the stairs do I notice the man next to her. He looks like a doctor on *Grey's Anatomy* with his cocoa-colored complexion, trendy wire glasses, and warm smile.

I immediately dislike him. And that feeling only doubles when he leans in close and makes Maya laugh.

Spotting my car, she waves goodbye to the fake doctor and

hurries my way. She clambers into the car and leans over the console, capturing my lips in a deep kiss. "Welcome back, Captain. Congrats on your back-to-back-to-back wins."

I chuckle and bask in the satisfaction her compliment brings. "Hey, baby. Thank you."

"How was the flight?"

"Good. Read a few chapters of *Alien Lovers of Planet Dexxar*. How was class?"

"Amazing," she says dreamily. "We focused on plot today, and in our workshop, we wrote short stories and had to include a plot twist at the beginning of each paragraph. It's supposed to help us really focus on why we choose each plot point and how it affects the story moving forward. Brian's feedback was super helpful. I feel like I'm finally hitting my stride."

"That's great." I keep my tone even, though the sound of another man's name on her lips has my hackles rising. "Who's Brian? Is he the guy you walked outside with?"

With a nod, she buckles her seat belt. "Mm-hmm. He was my critique partner for the exercise."

"Your partner?" Screw it, there's no way I can hide the potent jealousy consuming me.

"Mm-hmm. We offer critique and feedback during work-shops. Why are you being weird?" In my periphery, she assesses me, brows furrowed.

Once I've come to a stop at a red light, I turn to face her. She's still watching me, her head tilted expectantly. The fact that she can't put two and two together speaks volumes about how her exes have treated her.

"Because I'm jealous."

"Of *Brian*?" She throws her head back and laughs. The notion that a man could be jealous over her is so foreign that she doesn't even recognize it. "Cole, Brian's so focused on becoming the next James Patterson that I could show up to class in my birthday suit and he wouldn't notice. There's no need to be jealous, babe."

The pet name soothes the sharp edges of my insecurity, but I still frown as I ease off the brake and glide through the intersection. "But he knows about writing and books and all that shit. I don't."

"Does it bother you that I don't know that much about hockey?"

I scoff. "No, of course not."

"Same goes for me." She presses a brief kiss on my cheek. "I don't care that you don't love reading like I do. Opposites attract and all that."

I don't bother fighting the grin that creeps up on my lips. "Do you mind if we swing by Goldblatt's on the way to my place?"

"Oh! Goldblatt's is the *best*." She grins. "I'll pick up a babka to send to Ava. They're her favorite."

"My mom *loves* their profiteroles," I reveal, "so I like having them on hand when she visits."

As far as caveats go, that wasn't my smoothest, but I haven't found the nerve to outright tell Maya that my entire family will be here later this week, let alone broken the news that they're desperate to meet her. It took what felt like a lifetime to convince her to go on a date, so God knows how she'll react to this.

"That's sweet of you," she says, her expression serene. "She's visiting soon, I assume?"

"Yeah, my whole family's coming to town." *Christ, when was the last time my palms were this sweaty?* "Will you come to dinner with us on Friday?"

So much for easing into it.

Maya's eyebrows hit her hairline. "What?"

"Dinner. Friday. You. Me. And—"

"Your entire family," she finishes, hands clasped tightly in her lap. "Yeah, I got that. Are you sure? We only just started dating. I don't want to intrude. I've never done the whole 'meet the family' thing, so I can't promise that I won't completely fuck it up."

All I hear is that I get to experience another one of her firsts. "I'm positive. I want to be with you on my birthday."

Her eyes go wide. "Your birthday?"

"Yep," I confirm. "I turn thirty on Friday."

"Why didn't I know your birthday was coming up?" Maya squeaks out, her tone laced with panic.

She seems more concerned with this than meeting my family, which I suppose is a win.

I laugh. "Because you didn't stalk me on Wikipedia."

She smacks my arm, but there's no heat behind it. "This isn't funny. I don't have a gift for you."

"You don't need to get me anything."

"Of course I do." She rolls her eyes. "Aren't we supposed to get wiser, not dumber, as we age?"

"Harsh." I clamp my lips together to hide my grin. "You know, I'm fine with just a blow—"

"Do *not* finish that sentence, Nicholas Berrett," she says with an adorably grumpy pout.

"So you'll come to dinner? It'll be low key, I swear. And I made my mom promise not to bring up babies or marriage."

It's a miracle Maya doesn't unlock my car and tuck and roll her way right into the intersection. Her eyes, however, do widen, making her look like a deer in headlights.

Internally grimacing, I tell her I'm kidding. Although I most definitely am not. I did confirm with my mother that she had to be on her best behavior, which specifically involves no talk of new grandchildren or weddings.

Maya glances at me from the corner of her eye. "Only because it's your birthday."

———

Maya thrusts a neatly wrapped box into my hands. "I hope you like it, considering I only had a few days to choose."

"You're really harping on that, aren't you?" I rip into the gift like I'm three instead of thirty, and as I take in the thin, long box that houses a brand-new e-reader, a smile overtakes my features.

"I preloaded it with books I think you'd like." Maya motions to the box. "But if you don't think you'll use it or want something else, I swear I won't be offended. I got a gift receipt so—"

I shut her up with a lingering kiss. "I love it. Thank you."

She pulls away and blinks up at me. "Actually? Or are you just placating me?"

"It's perfect," I reassure her. "Now my teammates won't see the cover of my next read and give me shit. I saw on *PagePulse* that there are a ton of books in the *Alien Lovers of Planet Dexxar* series."

Maya groans into my chest. "Now I'm envisioning you as a sexy librarian. I totally get the hype now."

"Yeah?" I set the e-reader down and slide my hands to the globes of her ass, squeezing and shaping them until her breath stutters. "Maybe we should explore that fantasy of yours."

Before she went to work and I left for practice this morning, we had just enough time to sneak in a round of mind-blowing birthday sex. Even so, my cock jerks at the thought of her naked body splayed before mine.

Taking a step back, she shakes her head. "I am *not* meeting your parents with sex hair."

I imitate Goose's puppy dog eyes, but when Maya ignores my efforts, I grab my keys off the counter.

She's unusually quiet on the drive over, though she'd never outright admit to being nervous. Meeting my family a few short weeks into dating may be considered too soon for some, but if I went at Maya's pace for this, my nieces would be in college before they met her.

We're fifteen minutes from the restaurant when I ask, "You okay, baby?"

"I'm fine," she says, turning to face me. "Are *you*?"

I cock my head to the side. "Why wouldn't I be?"

She shuffles around in the seat, as if she can't get comfortable. "Because today is Nathan's birthday, too."

Ah. I like that she knows Nathan as just my brother. She admits hockey is "sort of entertaining," but she doesn't want to know about his scoring average or shot percentage. She wants to see photos of the cute matching outfits we wore as kids and hear about the time we switched places to take one another's tests in middle school. She wants me to be happy about the time I did spend with him rather than bitter about the time that was stolen from us.

"I'm okay," I reassure her. "We never made a big deal out of our birthday."

Her voice is hesitant. "What about your family?"

"They'll be okay." Not a lie, but definitely not the full story. "It's always tough on them, but they're more focused on meeting you than on my birthday. They're all excited. Especially Lily and Violet."

Excited may be an understatement. Mere seconds after we walk into the restaurant, they're running up to her with toothy smiles and a million questions. My mom's not much better. She throws her arms around Maya and squeezes her tight when my nieces finally take a breather.

Maya's not anti-affection, but she's not super tactile either, so it doesn't surprise me when she momentarily stiffens before returning the greeting. Emily and Darby welcome her with subdued hugs of their own, but my dad and Zach stick to polite handshakes.

"Everyone," I say with a grin, "this is my girlfriend, Maya."

"It's nice to meet you all." Maya steps close to my side, reaching for my hand as if seeking comfort, and I link our fingers together.

The maître d' appears to lead us to the table, but Maya tugs on my hand as the rest of the group follows.

I duck my head, surveying her apprehensive expression. "Everything okay?"

"You introduced me as your girlfriend," she accuses with a cute scowl that reminds me of a hissing kitten. "And we haven't actually defined our relationship."

"Yes, we have. I said 'Be my girlfriend,' and you said 'Oh, yes.'"

Her lips part and she barely stops herself from stomping her feet. "You asked me that during sex and I said 'Oh, yes' because I was *mid-orgasm.*"

Smirking, I pull her into my arms and run my tongue against the seam of her lips, begging for entrance. She makes a small noise that's somewhere between a moan and a gasp, but she returns the kiss without hesitation.

Pulling back, I tuck a strand of silky-smooth hair behind her ear. "Will you be my girlfriend, Maya? Pretty please?"

She sighs as if put out. "Fine. But only because you so nicely added *please* onto the end and you give me really good orgasms."

"While I have absolutely no qualms about using my best asset to get what I want, I am offended that it's my dick that convinced you and not my charming personality or wicked sense of humor."

"Don't make me rethink my answer," she warns with a wink.

I grin like an idiot as I place my hand on her lower back and usher her toward the table. As we order drinks and appetizers, my family asks Maya the typical get-to-know-you questions, but it's not until she's half a glass of wine deep and talking about her job that she really starts to relax.

"I can't read yet, but I like books," Violet announces. "Mommy says I'll learn next year when I'm in first grade. But I can sing the alphabet forward *and* backward."

"I like books, too," Lily adds. "My favorite's *If You Give a Mouse a Cookie.* Do you know that one? Or what about *Monster Math?* Grandpa bought it for me to help with my numbers."

"Oh, I love that one." Maya gives her a bright smile. Turning toward my dad, she asks, "You're a stockbroker, right? Cole mentioned it."

He smiles, always happy to talk about his job. "I am, indeed. Do you know what month is typically the worst in the stock market?"

Darby, Emily, and I groan in unison. His "fun facts" and "interesting tidbits" are quite literally the fastest way to put me to sleep. Nate and I spent every ride to hockey practices and games listening to him drone on. *Do you know how much of the stock market the United States represents? What does the Bull and Bear analogy represent? Did you know that someone used the stock market to understand the Hydrogen bomb?*

"Technically September," Maya responds without hesitation, "although October tends to see the biggest swings. Something called the October Effect, right?"

"You know the market?" I don't think I've ever seen my dad look so excited. Not when Nate signed with the Trailblazers, and not when I signed with the Bobcats. Not even the first time he held each of his granddaughters. His eyes alight with pure joy now that he's found someone who shows a sliver of interest in his job. God knows it's not any of his own kids.

"My brother's about to take his Series 79, so I know a little bit, but I read a thriller a few years back, and the main character was a financial analyst. That's where I learned about the worst months."

"You're amazing." Risking the chance that I'll get punched in the dick for extreme PDA, I wrap my hand around the base of Maya's neck and pull her toward me.

She gasps slightly against my lips as I claim her mouth.

Lily claps wildly. "Now you're going to have a baby!"

I burst out laughing and struggle to regain my composure thanks to the looks of horror on everyone's faces. Except for my mom, who looks interested in hearing about the likelihood of that possibility.

"Sweetie," Zach says, leaning toward his youngest daughter. "She's not having a baby."

"Is, too," Lily argues, arms crossed and pouting. "Mommy said that's how babies are made. When adults kiss."

"She also says that Uncle Coley likes to knock people up," Violet adds unhelpfully.

My heart lurches, and now I'm the one wearing a mask of horror.

Maya turns to me, her face flushed with amusement. "Anything you need to tell me, Cole? Because it's definitely too early in our relationship for me to be dealing with multiple baby mommas."

I shake my head and suck in a harsh breath. Only then can I chuckle at the situation. "Em, mind sharing exactly what you're teaching your children?"

"Girls, babies come from when two adults kiss and do a

special hug in private," Emily says, her face beet red. "And I said that your uncle knocks people *out* during hockey."

"Only sometimes"—Darby lifts her wineglass in a toasting gesture—"and only when they deserve it."

"Darby," Emily and my mom simultaneously scold.

Dinner continues in a blur of refilled wineglasses, overlapping laughter, and embarrassing childhood stories. It's the first birthday I've celebrated since Nate passed that's been even remotely lighthearted. My mom doesn't once excuse herself to the bathroom so she can cry in private. My dad isn't wasted on whiskey and lost in a rabbit hole of memories. My sisters aren't overcompensating with huge smiles and loud laughter.

It's normal. Nice. And I owe much of that to Maya.

CHAPTER TWENTY-THREE

COLE BERRETT

Have fun in class, baby. See you after the game.

MAYA SILVER

Good luck!!

WITH MY PHONE on silent and secured in my pocket once more, I push open the creaky door of auditorium 111. My classmates huddle in small groups, catching up on what their friends and acquaintances have been up to since our last class. I slide into an empty seat next to Brian, who's regaling a few other students with tales of his rec league's basketball game. The mood has changed dramatically since our first class, when we all sat in silence, rows away from each other. It didn't take long for us to find the people we clicked with and create bonds. There's something about reading someone's first draft that knocks any vulnerability or shyness away.

"Does anyone want to grab drinks after this?" Marie asks. She's a first-grade teacher interested in writing children's books. "I desperately need one. Or two. Who are we kidding? I need a pitcher of margaritas."

"Don't tell me someone mispronounced another word," I tease, taking my notebook out of my bag.

Her students are learning to read, and in the past two weeks, the same kid has mispronounced cook as *cock*, and, even more hilariously, dump truck as *dumb fuck*. I asked her for book recommendations for Violet and Lily—since I'm a little out of my element when it comes to children's books—and texted the list to Emily. Yup. I have his sister's number. Both of his sisters, in fact. His mother? She's already texted me, asking for book recommendations for her newly formed book club.

It should freak me out. But it doesn't. And *that* is what's freaking me out.

"Thankfully, no." Marie makes the sign of the cross like she's in church. "But it's parent-teacher conference season. My own personal hell."

"I'm down for a drink," Brian easily agrees. "There's a great dive bar near here. You in, Maya?"

I shake my head as I flip to the page I'm looking for. "I'm headed to the Bobcats game after class. Maybe next week?"

Marie nibbles on the edge of her pen, head tilted in consideration. "I never would have marked you as a sports girl."

"Sports romances, yes. Sports... not so much," I admit with a laugh. "But my boyfriend plays professionally, so I'm a hockey fan by proxy."

Brian and Marie stare at me, jaws gaping, before the rapid-fire questioning begins. As they talk over each other, I sink into my chair and hold up my hands. I sometimes forget that professional athletes are considered famous. I never think about Cole's popularity until we're out at dinner and a server or a person from a nearby table asks for an autograph or we're walking Goose and everyone we pass does a double take.

"Who are you dating?" Marie demands, her auburn corkscrew curls bouncing wildly. "And how are we just finding out about this?"

"I'd like to think there are a lot more interesting things about me than who—"

"I bet it's Cameron Davies," she cuts me off. "Am I right? He's got that whole growly thing going on. It's totally sexy."

I press a hand to my chest and laugh. Cole is going to *hate* that. "No, I'm not dating Cam. My boyfriend's Nicholas Berrett."

It feels weird calling him Nicholas, since I've only ever known him as Cole. It also feels weird calling him my boyfriend because he's transcended whatever the hell I thought a boyfriend should be. What I had with Josh and other men I've dated is laughable. Yes, part of that is my fault because I probably never gave them the chance to mean more to me, but even if I had, there's no way they could have ever made me feel the way Cole does. Like my name is a prayer and my smile can chase any storm cloud away.

"You're dating Nicholas Berrett." Marie blinks slowly and does the sign of the cross again. "Holy shit, Maya."

Brian whistles under his breath. "You have to take us to a game."

As he dreams up ways to turn a Bobcats game into a writing challenge or exercise, I take out my phone to update Cole.

MAYA SILVER

Brian and Marie want to come to a game!

COLE BERRETT

I might consider it. Though it depends. Does Brian know I'm your boyfriend?

MAYA SILVER

Marie thought Cameron was. LOL. But yes, he does. *insert eye roll here*

COLE BERRETT

Ignoring the first part. Does he also know that I'm the only one who gets to see you naked?

MAYA SILVER

Jealousy is kind of hot on you.

COLE BERRETT

Not as hot as you on your knees sucking my cock.

MAYA SILVER

Mind if I use that line in one of my writing prompts? I think it'll add some ~flavor~ to my story.

COLE BERRETT

How is it possible that you blatantly ignoring my sext is somehow sexier than if you had actually responded?

MAYA SILVER

Magic. See you later!

I'll be the one on my knees sucking your cock... in case that wasn't clear.

Just as I'm tucking my phone into my bag, Jaden waltzes into the room. Their skirt swishes against the floor as they make their way to the desk stationed in front of the old-school blackboard. Clapping once, they greet us. "My apologies for the tardiness. Let's jump right into things."

I scribble notes furiously as I follow the lesson on how effective writing involves making conscious choices about words, pausing only occasionally so my fingers don't cramp. It makes me jealous of Cole's ambidextrousness. I can attest he's just as talented with both hands, on and off the ice.

We split into small groups for a writing exercise during the second half of class. Marie's arguing with Brian over whether including "um" in dialogue can be beneficial when Jaden waves me over to their desk.

My stomach drops to my feet. While I don't think it's possible to be in trouble during a class I'm voluntarily attending—and I haven't done anything *to* get myself into trouble in the first place—that doesn't make me any less nervous. Marie calls it teacher's pet syndrome.

The skin around Jaden's lips crinkles as they smile at me. *They wouldn't smile if I was in trouble, right?* "Maya. I just finished reading your short story from last week and I have to say, I'm very impressed."

My cheeks heat and my heart thuds heavily. "Really?"

Our only parameters were that the story had to include a royal saying the word "fucking idiot" on national television. I truly have no idea where they come up with these plots, but it did kick my creative juices into gear. Once I put pen to paper—or, more aptly, my fingers to the keyboard—the story flowed from me. I've never finished an assignment so quickly.

"Yes. I think you should continue with it."

"It's a short story, though."

Way to state the obvious, dumbass.

"That doesn't mean it can't be something more. Seek out elements of your story that could benefit from embellishment or exploration," Jaden suggests. "Add new characters. It's your story, so you choose which direction it goes in. Think about it."

"I will," I agree with a smile.

As I return to my seat, Brian shoots me a questioning glance but is too focused on winning his argument to ask questions.

My mind wanders for the rest of the workshop, turning Jaden's words over and trying to make sense of the advice.

I wrote the story the day after meeting Cole's family. The genuine support and unconditional love they have for one another brought some of the lingering sadness related to my own upbringing to the surface. I needed an outlet for the despondence I thought I'd long ago buried, so I poured all my emotions into my writing assignment.

Apparently, it paid off.

The moment class ends, I call a rideshare and head to Airwave Arena. Only five months ago, I was attending my first hockey game, and now I weave my way through the crowds like an expert. Finding the suite is no longer a challenge, and Hank —a.k.a. Batman's Butler—greets me with a welcome smile. The one surprise is finding Kennedy in the plush seats with her legs kicked up like it's her personal office.

"Um, hi," I greet her as I slip off my coat. "I thought you weren't coming until the second period."

She hops from the seat like a damn kangaroo and wraps me in a hug. "My! I did the event drop-off earlier than expected, so here I am. Lucky you. God, it feels like I haven't seen you in forever."

"It's been five days," I remind her. "And we video-called yesterday."

"As I said, it's been *forever.*"

"Drama queen," I laugh, shaking out of her embrace. Her smoke detector went off twice during the thirty minutes we were on the phone. "You've been the one baking more cookies than *The Great British Bake Off* does in an entire season."

"I brought you some extras. You're welcome. They're in my purse."

I eye her oversized black bag. "You brought cookies to the game?"

"Oh, calm down." She waves a dismissive hand. "I said

cookies, not *cocaine*. And it's no worse than you bringing your e-reader."

"I didn't, thank you very much."

Never thought I'd prioritize a sport over my sports romances, but weirder things have happened. Maybe.

I wander to the buffet table and make myself a plate before joining Kennedy. Neither of us says a word as we ogle the players warming up. Honestly, it's very suggestive. One player rests on his knee pads, pushing his legs spread eagle and tilting his hips down to the ice. Another swivels and thrusts his hips to "open them up." I told Cole it looks like they're fucking air, and for a solid fifteen minutes, he couldn't decide whether he was offended or amused.

"Cole must be flexible," Kennedy comments with a slow clap. The man in question maneuvers his body into a stretch he calls the figure 4 twist.

"My sex life has definitely reaped the benefits of his workout routine," I admit. Considering I'm just over five feet and can barely touch my toes, Cole's flexibility is all the more impressive.

The fully clothed *Magic Mike* show doesn't go on for much longer. As the team takes their starting positions on the ice, my voice gets lost among the hundreds of fans yelling their support.

As Cole takes his spot on center ice for the face-off, my heart skips a beat. It's wild that this confident, crazy-talented hockey player is the guy who blessedly admitted *Alien Lovers of Planet Dexxar* was a "decent read once you get over the aliens having two cocks."

The first period is aggressively physical from the start. It's not unexpected, given the massive rivalry between the teams, but damn. Logan only lasts seven minutes before being penalized for tripping another player, giving our opponent a power play. Even though the Hellcats have the upper hand during these next two minutes, they only get one shot on goal, which is blocked by Cameron.

I whistle under my breath. "Cam's impressively nimble." He's got the height and muscle mass of an eighteenth-century Highlander but moves with the smoothness of an eel. Not that I'd ever tell Cole that. The last time I complimented one of his teammates, he got all growly. Although it was kind of sexy.

"He's an asshole."

"Cameron?" I frown at my best friend. He's the quietest of Cole's teammates, preferring to observe rather than participate in conversations, but I'd hardly call him an asshole for not being outspoken.

"He said my cake—the one I make with the raspberry whipped mascarpone—was dry." She tosses her dark blond hair over her shoulder. "My cakes are not too *dry*, Maya. They're perfect. He's clearly taken one too many pucks to the head."

My best friend can hold a grudge like no one I've ever met. She ran for class president in high school simply to beat out the girl who made fun of her for wearing her sister's hand-me-downs back in middle school. She shares a Netflix account with her family, and any time she's mad at her sisters, she fast-forwards the show they're watching so they never know where they left off. So Cameron calling her cake dry? Yeah, he's now forever in her burn book.

"When did he eat your cake?" I ask. "And yes, I realize how inappropriate that sounded."

"At some Bobcats Foundation event," she admits with a huff.

I smile at the mention of the Bobcats Foundation, knowing that it brought Goose and Cole together. "Maybe he just doesn't like cake."

"Well then he's not only an asshole, he's an idiotic asshole with no taste." She narrows her eyes at me. "Watch the game. Your boy's back on the ice."

I once told Cole that it's impossible to tell who's who out there. That they all look the same in their uniforms and helmets. And they skate too fast for me to read the names on the backs of their jerseys. Yet now I find him instantly. I always do, like he's a homing beacon. It's the way he's the first one back on the ice during a line shift and the way the other skaters defer to him. And yes, now that I'm overly familiar with every aspect of his muscular body, his frame is easily recognizable.

I don't take my attention off the action for the remainder of the second period. The Hellcats get a couple of shots off, especially when two Bobcats end up in the penalty box, but Cameron blocks them with ease. As I said: nimble as hell.

Cole crosses the blue line, passing the puck to Logan, and takes off. Logan bypasses the Hellcats' defense with a weird-ass turn that makes him look part-ballerina. He crosses the puck to Jake, who knifes it down low back to where Cole is now positioned. He takes the shot, and though their goalie blocks it, he corrals the rebound, turns, and buries it in the net, giving the Bobcats a one-point lead.

The crowd goes absolutely wild, and I join in, clapping and shrieking with the best of them. When I realize Kennedy is still sitting, I turn her way, only to see her holding her phone and pointing it at me instead of the ice.

I point toward the rink. "The game is that way."

"Oh, I know." She laughs. "But you're so cute. I couldn't help but capture the moment."

"Stop being creepy." I narrow my eyes, giving her the best glare I can. It's a struggle after the play I just witnessed. I'm still too excited. "And stop smiling at me like that."

She continues to grin at me like a lunatic but puts her phone down. "You're the one who can't stop smiling because you're *in love*."

"Remind me why I like you again?"

"You don't like me, you *love* me," she corrects. "Just like you *love* Cole."

I'm saved from responding when the crowd breaks into deafening cheers. I turn back to the ice just in time to see Cameron turn aside yet another shot by the Hellcats. He may not like Kennedy's cake, but not even she can dismiss his skill.

"Maybe it's not full love yet, but you're at least falling in love," she presses, once again drawing my attention away from the game.

My lips twitch despite my effort to keep a straight face. "I'll admit I now know why they call it falling in love and not something nice and sweet like sashaying into love."

Falling in love is uncontrollable and sudden, and there's no way to prepare for the landing. It's not a stumble; it's more of a leap. There's a weightlessness to the free fall. There's exhilaration and excitement and *hope*. It's a constant rush of adrenaline, and for the first time in my life, I'm embracing it rather than running in the opposite direction like I'm fleeing a horde of zombies.

Kennedy cheers loudly, causing the people a few rows in front of our executive suite to turn back and give us confused looks, since nothing exciting has happened on the ice since Cameron's save.

"I just love hockey," she shouts, throwing them a thumbs-up. Then, whipping around so fast her hair slaps her in the face, she says, "Now was that really so hard to admit? Because it's obvious he's in love with you."

My heart flutters at the idea, but my mind's too apprehensive to let me truly enjoy it. "You don't know that, Kenn."

"Anyone with semi-decent vision can see that he is. For

someone who reads so much romance, you're awfully jumpy when it comes to love."

"That's because in real life, we're not guaranteed a happily ever after," I point out.

But for the first time, I'm starting to think that maybe I've found mine.

CHAPTER TWENTY-FOUR

I PULL my car into an open spot on Maya's street, grateful to find one this close to her building's entrance. This way, she won't have to walk far to reach us. It's a relatively safe area, but her neighbors are questionable. Especially the guy who holds seances on every full moon.

Jake huffs under his breath. "I can't believe you're kicking me out."

"I'm not kicking you out of the car, Reid. I'm just asking you to sit in the back."

"But I always sit shotgun."

I fix him with an unblinking stare until he finally grumbles and unbuckles his seat belt. The huffing doesn't stop as he twists and turns his body, wiggling through the open space between our seats so he can climb into the back without having to leave the warmth of the car.

His dark blue eyes narrow on me in the rearview mirror. "Happy?"

"Impressed," I admit. I'm flexible, but there's no way I could imitate what he just did.

To add insult to his injury, a few minutes later, rather than opening the passenger door, Maya opens the back door on that side. "Oh! I can sit back here, Jake. I know you usually sit up front."

Ignoring his not so subtle *told you so* smirk, I peer back at Maya, who's staring at my friend uncertainly. She looks sexy as hell in a cream-colored sweater dress, and the black knee-high boots have my cock twitching. I can't wait to peel them off her later. "You're sitting up front, Maya. Now get your fine ass in the car before it freezes off."

The edges of her lips tilt up despite the eye roll she gives me.

Only when she's buckled do I lean over to steal a quick kiss. "Hey, beautiful."

"Hi. Guess what?" She hits me with a mega-watt smile. "My sister's coming to town. She has an interview for a summer internship with some marketing agency."

She pulls up her phone to recall the name of the place, and Jake lets out a low whistle. "That's impressive. I heard their internship program is super competitive."

"Fingers crossed she gets it. They usually only accept sophomores." Maya turns to me. "She wants to meet you when she's here. I know Logan's staying in Toronto after the game to visit family, but I hoped we could meet up when you're back on Friday."

"Do *you* want me to meet her?" The question is laced with a vulnerability I wish I could banish, but I need an answer. The distinction here is important. I met Elliott early on, so it was never a "step" in our relationship, but Maya wanting me to meet Ava? That's progress.

"Of course," she says without hesitation.

I press a kiss against her palm. "Good."

A dumb smile overtakes me and stays plastered to my face for the rest of the ride and as we enter Logan's "birthday banger." Yes, that is what the invitation said. Logan doesn't believe in small, intimate celebrations. He's more of a "group text my whole contact list" kind of guy. In addition to O'Leary's usual Saturday-night crowd, everyone from Logan's hairdresser to the owner of his favorite coffee shop to the Zamboni driver at Airwave Arena is in attendance.

Figuring that most of my teammates will be around the pool tables in the back, we head in that direction. Logan's nowhere to be seen—although I wouldn't be surprised if he's holding a procession somewhere—but Elliott's playing a tense game against a few defensemen, so we make a beeline for him.

The calculating crease in his brow melts away at the sight of his sister. Stepping away from the pool table, he encases her in a bear hug. "Yaya! I'm glad you came."

"I wouldn't dream of missing Logan's birthday."

"You also wouldn't hear the end of it," I mutter. It's honestly a miracle that his birthday isn't a national holiday in Canada.

With a chuckle, Elliott claps my back. Part of me was nervous that it'd be weird that Maya's brother is dating my best friend, but it's working in everyone's favor. I've gotten to know him as a friend rather than only as "my girlfriend's brother," and Maya never feels the need to sacrifice time with her family because of me—or vice versa.

"Congrats to you, man," he says, tipping his beer against his lips.

I bounce a curled knuckle against my thigh, my hackles raising in response to the casualness of his congratulations. There's no way he knows about the meeting next week. He can't. Only my agent and the general managers of the Bobcats and Devils do. But if not that, then what the hell would he be congratulating me for? Being out past eight p.m. on a Saturday when we have a game the following day?

I wrap my arm around Maya's waist, the simple act bringing me a sense of comfort. "For what?"

"I never thought the day would come when my sister chose a night out with her boyfriend over a night in with one of her many book boyfriends."

Maya swings her arm out to slug him in the shoulder, but he anticipates the move and easily sidesteps her.

I chuckle as she huffs. "It's because I'm special, right, baby?"

"Considering I hung out with you instead of reading what some people are claiming is the next breakout romantasy? Yeah, I'd say you're very special."

I press my lips against the top of her head. "You really know how to get a man all revved up."

Holding up his hands, Elliott backs away. "And that's my cue to get back to the game."

"All revved up, huh?" Maya pokes my stomach. "All those romance books I read must be rubbing off on you."

"I've said it once, and I'll say it again: a romance book about a bookstore manager falling for a hockey player would sell millions of copies."

"I can already see the opening line," Maya says, arching a sardonic brow raise. "Once upon a time, a hockey player made out with a bookstore manager and then ghosted her."

My heart stumbles a little at the easy way she threw that detail out. "And then realized he was being an idiot," I add. "Thankfully, the bookstore manager was so overcome by lust for said hockey player that she gave him another chance."

"Overcome by lust?" Maya laughs, her shoulders shaking. "I guess I'd read a story like that."

"You shouldn't read it. You should write it."

As a flush creeps up her neck, she ducks, like she's trying to hide it, and twists the material of my shirt between her fingers. "My teacher actually suggested turning a short story I wrote for class into a full story."

With pride filling my chest, I turn so we're face to face. "That's amazing, baby. When can I read it?"

"All I said is that they suggested it," she points out with a laugh. "Not that I'm going to do it. It'd be a while before you could potentially read it."

I frown at the word *potentially*. "As long as I get to read it before Brian," I tease with an eyebrow waggle.

"There's no need to be jealous, Cole. He's just my writing partner"—lowering her voice, she adds—"but you're the one whose cock I'll be coming on tonight."

Jesus have mercy. I love her romance books.

Throwing me a saccharine smile, as if she didn't just give me the world's biggest boner, she plants a kiss on my lips. "I'm going to find my friends and grab a drink."

For a moment, I stay where I am, reciting every Stanley Cup winner since 1990 to rein myself back in. When I'm confident that I'm not about to face my teammates with a massive hard-on, I grab a pool cue and corral a few of the guys into a new game.

I'm pulling back my arm to take a shot when I'm attacked from behind. A heavy weight hits me, like a jungle cat leaping onto my back. My cue skids off the side of my ball and accidentally knocks the other team's ball in.

I groan while my opponents high-five. "Logan, man, what the fuck?"

He clambers off me and tilts his head, pouting. "How'd you know it was me?"

"No other person I know would jump onto someone mid-game." Leaning against the table, I run a hand through my hair. "And I can't even be mad at you about it because it's your birthday."

He smiles at me, his eyes twinkling. "The rules are the rules."

Elliott storms over, his green eyes full of accusation. "What the hell are you doing over here, Berrett?"

I open my mouth to answer but think better of my smartass remark. I've never seen the guy look so pissed off, so I can't imagine he's alluding to the pool game. "Is there somewhere I'm supposed to be instead?"

"Considering my sister's asshole of an ex is attempting to buy her a drink, I'd say you definitely have other places to be."

Just the word "ex" makes my stomach harden. Obviously, Maya has a sexual history that predates meeting me, but fuck if I don't hate the thought of another man knowing what she sounds like when she comes.

Logan and I crane our necks, looking in the direction Elliott's pointing. When I find the asshole and see how close he's standing to Maya, I shove down the urge to charge over there and put my body between theirs. Despite my instincts, I don't want to be *that guy*. The one who's insecure in his relationship and doesn't trust his girlfriend enough to let her hold a conversation with someone from her past.

"That's her ex?" Logan whistles and slowly claps. "Damn. Nice work, Maya. He's fine as hell."

I roll my eyes. Objectively, yes, Josh—and I'm assuming this is Josh, since he's the only ex we've ever talked about—is a good-looking guy, but he's still the dumbass who cheated on her. And has seen her naked. And has most likely made her laugh. "Don't you think it's a little weird that you just called your boyfriend's sister's ex hot?"

"Not any weirder than Goose licking your toe while you fucked my boyfriend's sister." Logan waggles his brows.

"Once, dude. That happened *once*. And I regret ever mentioning it to you."

"I'm right here." Elliott grimaces. "So please stop."

"Why the fuck is he even here?"

Logan shrugs. "Maybe he knows my esthetician. Or goes to my gym. Who knows? This party's a free-for-all."

Across the bar, the fucker takes a step closer to Maya, despite the hand she's thrown up in warning.

I take it as my cue to step in. She doesn't need to be this close to her shithead ex for another moment. Plus, if I don't interfere in the next minute or so, there's a good chance Kennedy, who's standing on Maya's other side, will start a bar fight. I weave my way through the crowd toward the bar and snake my arms around Maya, tightening them until her back's pressed against my torso. "Hey, baby. Everything okay?"

She leans against me but doesn't take her eyes off Kennedy, as if she's certain a boxing match will break out if she glances away.

Kennedy jabs her finger into the interloper's chest. "This sorry excuse for a man doesn't understand the concept of *leave us the fuck alone.*"

Josh doesn't even register Kennedy's poke since he's staring, slack-jawed, at me. "You're Nicholas Berrett. Holy shit. Babe, do you know him?"

Babe? Hell no.

"Yes, Josh, I know him." Maya sighs and rests a hand over mine at her waist. "He's my boyfriend."

"He can also kick your ass if you touch her one more time." I zero in on where his hand is inching toward her arm. "So I'd be very careful if I were you."

He heeds my warning but ignores my presence otherwise. "Is *he* why you won't get back together with me?"

Maya rolls her eyes. "I won't get back together with you because you cheated on me."

"With someone who looks like the second coming of Cruella de Vil," Kennedy adds, crossing her arms over her chest.

Her ferocious protectiveness of Maya deserves a standing ovation.

"I was drunk," he argues, as if being under the influence excuses his behavior. "And—"

Maya rubs her temple. "I'm not arguing the finer points of you sleeping with someone else while we were together. I've moved on, and you really should, too."

"You think he's staying loyal?" Josh snorts, waving his hand in my general direction. He takes a swig of his drink. *Did he not hear the part where I said I could beat the ever-loving shit out of him?* "He's a professional hockey player, for fuck's sake, My. He probably has puck bunnies in every city."

"My relationship is none of your business," Maya snaps, eyes narrowing to daggers. "Nothing in my life is, because you're not a part of it any longer."

He shakes his head. "Was I ever, though?"

Maya goes rigid against me. "What's that supposed to mean?"

"You're *very* good at keeping people at arm's length. Don't try to deny it. You're like an iron vault who's determined to keep relationships from getting too serious." Josh's eyes shift to me. "Enjoy it while it lasts. I'm sure she'll dip out sooner rather than later."

I'm certain she'll either bitch slap him or bitch him out, but in the end, she simply shrugs. "This has been an absolute pleasure, but if you'll excuse me, I'd like to be anywhere but here."

Pushing away from the bar, Maya turns, and without looking back, she disappears into the crowd.

Josh twists his head to track her, but I hold up a hand to block him before he can take a step forward.

"Don't even think about it," I warn, my voice low. "You fucked up. Cut your losses, man. She's mine now, and I have no intention of letting her go."

His eyes go hard. "I—"

I shake my head. "I don't like you. At all. I sincerely suggest moving along before I have to show you just how much I don't like you. Understand?"

For a moment, I watch him, giving him time to think over his options. Luckily, he makes the right choice and leaves, although he does so with a scowl.

"Thank you for the backup," Kennedy sighs, leaning onto the bar. "He appeared next to us like a damn apparition. You want to go find her, or should I?"

"I got it."

I find Maya with Sophie, Jake, and Logan at a high top by the pool tables. A small frown plays at the corners of her lips as she listens to Jake, who's gesticulating wildly, clearly telling a story. She may claim she's fine, but I don't know how anyone would be after that. Makes me grateful that I've never been serious enough about a girl to have any real exes. Boston may be big, but it's not big enough for a lover scorned. Cameron's ex taught us all that the hard way.

Sophie greets me with a friendly smile and scoots over so I can stand next to Maya. How she and Cam share genetics is beyond me. Sophie's sunshine and sugar, while he's a rainy storm cloud.

"You okay?" I murmur into Maya's ear.

She shrugs off the question with a tight smile. "I'm fine."

"I've got two sisters, baby," I chuckle. "Fine never just means *fine*. Talk to me."

With a sigh, she glares at me. "This isn't the place, Cole. Drop it for now, okay? We can talk later."

Letting her think I'm letting the subject go, I turn to Logan. "Want me to go get the cake?"

Like he does every year, he feigns surprise when his favorite dessert is mentioned. As if he's not the one who sent Kennedy an entire "mood board" for his triple-tier chocolate cake with Oreo frosting. Instantly, he switches to party planner mode, debating where to set the cake so the gathered crowd can serenade him.

"Come get the cake with me." I grab Maya's hand before she has a chance to respond and pull her down the poorly lit hallway that leads to the stockroom. Once I've typed the four-digit passcode Logan gave me into the lock mechanism and am granted access, I tug Maya inside. Then I ensure the door locks behind us. The light flickers on, bringing into view the metal shelves filled with liquor bottles, mixers, and drink garnishes.

She takes in the cake box that's sitting next to oranges and lemons in the fridge and turns to me. "You really brought me here so I can help you carry that? I think you've got enough muscle to handle it, Cole."

"I brought you here to talk."

With a beleaguered sigh, she crosses her arms over her chest. "What part of we can talk *later* was not clear to you?"

I motion to the empty room around us. "Why talk later when we can talk now?"

"Why do you need to know *now*? Do you think he's right? That I'm keeping you at arm's length?" Her lips wobble a little before she reins in the emotion threatening to break through. "Because I'm trying not to. I really, really am. I meant it when I said we could talk about it later. I just didn't want to bring down the mood and ruin anyone's night."

"I know. That's not w—"

"And I'm not good at relationships, Cole. I never claimed to be. I've always dated just for fun, not because I was invested in an actual future with someone. Maybe I don't know how to do that. Maybe you should just cut your—"

Before she winds herself up even more, I firmly plant my lips on hers. And I keep them there until she sinks into the kiss.

"I was in the middle of talking," she mumbles against my mouth.

"No, you were in the middle of spouting bullshit, baby. And I won't let him, or you, convince you that you're not good at relationships."

She huffs out a sharp breath. "Objectively, I'm really not."

"Or you just weren't dating the right person." Wrapping my arms around her, I tug her tight against my body. "But now you are. And I'm not going to let you push me away. I'm just going to pull you closer. So stop fighting it. We'll figure this out together, okay?"

After what feels like an eternity but isn't more than about thirty seconds, the stress lines on her forehead disappear, and she rests her chin on my chest and nods. She goes lax against me, seemingly accepting what I've said. It's heady, knowing I have that kind of effect on her.

We stay like that for a minute, soaking in the feel of one another. Eventually, though, Maya lets out a long laugh. "How hugging me can get you hard is beyond me."

I hoped she wouldn't notice, but with her body pressed against mine, it's no wonder she does. "My dick always takes notice when you're close."

"Mm-hmm." She snakes a hand down my chest and over my abs until she reaches the body part in question. "You know... I once read a book where the main characters fuck in a supply closet at a party."

I school the surprise on my face, not wanting to appear too eager. "Sounds spicy."

With a light squeeze of my cock, she nibbles on her lower lip. "You have no idea."

Testing her resolve, I toy with the hem of her dress, gently guiding the fabric up her legs. I work it over her stomach and chest, and finally over her head and off completely, leaving her in just a lacy thong, bra, and those sexy-as-sin thigh-high leather boots. I've tasted and kissed every inch of her body, but it never fails to knock me breathless.

Neither of us says anything, not wanting to break the layer of anticipation the silence brings. I expertly unhook her bra, and when the heavy weight of her breasts spills into view, there's no stopping the moan that escapes me. *Goddamn.* My fingers trail against her soft skin, leaving goose bumps in their wake. Replacing my fingers with my mouth, I kiss my way down her collarbone to her cleavage, then lock my lips around a nipple. I take my time tweaking, squeezing, and sucking on them until she's rubbing her legs together.

Chuckling, I slip my hand between her thighs and drag my fingers over her clit in torturously slow circles. "Mmm. Already ready for me, baby?"

With her back arched like a goddamned vision, she nods. "God, yes."

I don't break eye contact as I lower to my knees, but once I'm in position, I drink her in. *Fucking hell, she's gorgeous.* "I think we can get you wetter, don't you?"

Without waiting for a response, I toss her leg over my shoulder, tug her thong to the side, and run my tongue along her pussy. I rhythmically flick at her clit, my movements quick but with the exact amount of pressure she loves. She grips the sides of my head as if she's worried I'll stop, and in return, I grasp her ass, tugging her tighter against my mouth, silently promising I'll do no such thing. Hips rolling against my face, she moans. The faster I lick, the louder she gets, until her arousal is coating my chin and lips as she comes with a strangled cry.

Maya's still catching her breath as I stand up, but I grip her hips and spin her around quickly. "Turn around and put your hands on the wall."

She shimmies out of her underwear, watching from over her shoulder as I unbutton my pants and take out my aching cock. Rubbing my thumb over the sensitive head, I take in the sight of her, wet and waiting for me. Her focus is fixed on my hands as I deftly roll on a condom. Thank fuck I had one stored in my wallet.

"This is gonna be fast and rough, baby." Kissing her shoulder, I line myself up at her entrance and slide home. The tight squeeze of her pussy never fails to pull a desperate groan from deep in my chest.

Maya pushes her ass back, taking me deeper, and I welcome the invitation. Every time with her feels like the first time, and there's no doubt in my mind I'll be just as feral for her at age eighty as I am now.

Gripping her hips for leverage, I punch forward, moaning at the way she takes me so well. "This pussy is mine, isn't it, baby? All fucking mine."

"Ye-yes," she chokes out, her core tightening around me.

"Good girl."

The moans slipping through her lips, sensual and full of need, are an addiction that no treatment can cure. With a hand between her legs, I rub her already sensitive clit, spurred on by her cries of pleasure. I get lost in the sound of her moans, in the warmth of her skin, and the feel of her surrounding me. As my thrusts become sharper, I place one hand on the wall for leverage. The slight shift lets me hit Maya's sweet spot, based on the way her jaw drops open and her walls clench tighter around me.

"Oh—" Her breath catches and her hips stutter, but I keep my pace steady as she explodes. She sinks her teeth into my forearm to muffle her shouts as she rides wave after wave of pleasure.

The way she grips me as she comes sets off my own release.

My hips falter as I climax, panting into her neck and diving into the blissful feeling.

Breaths sawing in and out of her, she drops her head back into the crook of my neck. "That was—"

"Hot."

"I was going to say a major health code violation," she laughs, "but hot works, too."

I brush my lips against hers. "You ready to go back to the party?"

She nods. "Thanks for making me talk."

"Thanks for making me happy."

THE BLOND WAVE of Ava's hair appears in my periphery as I help a customer choose between two thrillers. It takes a solid ten minutes and at least a dozen questions before she decides to just get both. After I ring her up and send her on her way, I hunt for Katrina to let her know I'm heading out a little early. Since she's always telling me to work less and live more, she claps and does a little jig when I relay the message.

I weave through the store, eventually finding Ava tucked into the oversized green and blue chair in the back corner. When I started working at the Book Nook, she would take the bus after school and do her homework in this exact spot. If Blythe thought it was odd that there was a sixth grader doing math problems in the historical fiction section, she never said a word.

As warmth floods me at the memory, I tug on the slicked-back ponytail she's rocking. "You ready to head out?"

She glances up at me through thick lashes, taking in my hat, gloves, and coat. "Ugh. I did not miss this cold weather."

A laugh bubbles out of me. My sister hates any weather that forces her to put on a coat and hide her outfit. I pull her out of the seat and link her arm through mine. "C'mon. Tell me all about the interview."

"They'd be absolute idiots not to hire me."

Her confidence and self-worth are enviable. "Obviously."

She launches into a play-by-play of her interview, going through what has to be *every detail*, including the nail color of the receptionist, the color palette of the room she was interviewed in, and her answer to every single question. She's still going by the time we make it to my apartment, and she's barely given me the space to ask follow-up questions.

Yawning, she sits on the couch and pulls up Netflix on my TV. "I'm exhausted. What time's Cole coming over? I need to be sedentary for at least an hour."

"You're exhausted?" I tease, plopping down beside her. "I'm the one who barely slept last night because *someone* kept rubbing her freezing cold feet against me."

"They were only cold because *you* stole the covers."

"Elliott has a very comfy pull-out couch," I remind her with a wide smile. "You could've had your own bed there."

"Yeah, but he's always at work or studying," she points out, waving the remote to accentuate her point. "Plus, this way we got to have a sisterly sleepover. You *did* change your sex sheets before I got here, though, right?"

"Gross." I shudder. "Can you not refer to my sheets as sex sheets?"

"I mean, they technically *are* sheets that you have sex in."

"We are not discussing my sex life."

In truth, Cole and I spend most of our nights together at his place. Not only does he have a bigger, comfier bed, but he can't leave Goose alone overnight. And while Goose is more than welcome to sleep at my apartment, he spends half the night howling at every unfamiliar sound. And he despises the violin player. Rightfully so.

Ava pouts, slumping against the cushions. "Oh, c'mon. You can spill at least one dirty deet."

Ignoring her, I circle back to the original question. "Cole will be here in an hour. He wants to shower after his flight and pick up some stuff for dinner first."

With a hum, she snuggles into my side like she's a kid again. "I can't believe he's cooking for us. That's so swoon-worthy."

"He is very swoony," I admit with a laugh.

"Swoonier than your book boyfriends?" She waggles her blond brows.

"Way swoonier than my book boyfriends."

Cole Berrett has turned me into a total fangirl. And I'm not mad about it.

Ava skyrockets off the couch and spins to face me, her cheeks flushed. "Oh my God. I can't believe I forgot to tell you. I've been so distracted by the interview."

"Forgot to tell me what?"

"Mom's coming to dinner tomorrow."

Though an icy sliver of dread instantly winds its way through me, I force a small smile. Trying to rein in my absolute and utter confusion, I merely mimic her words. "Mom's coming to dinner tomorrow."

"Yep. Exciting, right?"

That's one way to put it.

"Is she in town for something specific? Or just for fun?"

"To see us. Duh. I called her last week to tell her about the interview, and when she found out all three of us would be in Boston at the same time, she said she'd fly in to visit."

My heart pounds in my ears, making her words muffled. "So you've known about this for a week?"

"Oh, um, not exactly." She shrugs. "She booked her flight this morning because she wasn't sure if she'd make it back in time. You can change our dinner reservation since there will be four of us, right? I told her it wouldn't be a big deal. And if it is, we can always change restaurants," she goes on, her words flying from her at a rapid speed. "How amazing is this? It's been forever since we've all had dinner together."

"Yeah, it's been a while," I agree. *Almost a year, not that I'm counting.*

I talk to my mom on the phone now and then, though the conversations are rarely about me. Mostly, she fills me in on her life. Two weeks ago, she called me to tell me all about her newfound love for "the theatre." Pronounced "the-ate-er." *Gag.* I barely managed to squeeze in the news that I'm dating someone, and the topic only held her attention for about two minutes.

Ava rambles on about how nice it'll be when we're all together while I consider the possible reasons behind my mother's trip to Boston. Because I guarantee it has nothing to do with her kids all being here. We were all here for Thanksgiving, and where was she? Oh yeah. On a cruise with her boyfriend. And the time before that? For Elliott's graduation? She got food poisoning in St. Croix and missed her flight back. Food poisoning is code for sleeping through her alarm. She seems to have forgotten that a lie can't be used more than twice before it comes under suspicion.

I was planning to wait until Cole got here to open a bottle of wine, but desperate times call for desperate measures. While I pour myself a hefty glass of chardonnay, Ava turns on *Grey's Anatomy.*

"I can't believe you're choosing to rewatch this when I have so many amazing books you can read."

"One can never watch *Grey's Anatomy* too many times, sister dear," she singsongs, eyes glued to the screen.

I sigh and take a sip of my wine.

And then another.

Plus a few more.

By the time my boyfriend arrives, the wine's mildly tempered the dread that's churning in my stomach at the thought of seeing my mom. Still, when Cole wraps his arms around me in a hug, I bury my face in his chest as if it'll protect me from the emotional trauma I'm in for tomorrow.

I've just closed my eyes and exhaled when Ava coughs loudly, demanding an introduction. She immediately loves him because not only did he bring Goose, who automatically adds ten points, but he stopped at Goldblatt's and picked up babka. Yep. Swoon-worthy isn't a complimentary enough descriptor for Cole.

Taking a bag from his arm, I shuffle to the kitchen. "Ava, will you help put stuff in the fridge while I wash the vegetables?"

She glances up from the floor, where she's giving Goose a belly rub. "I could, but it would be rude to leave Goose halfway through his massage."

"You're not helping," Cole says, taking the bag out of my arms.

I immediately try to wrestle it back from him, to no avail. "Of course I am. You're not cooking dinner by yourself. Don't be—"

"You take care of everyone, baby," he argues, his tone soft but resolute. "Let me take care of you for a change. Yeah?"

Exhaling through my nose, I nod. Then I let him guide me toward a kitchen stool. With my elbows resting on the marble island counter, I watch as he gathers the ingredients for pesto pasta. A man taking control like this in the kitchen? It's hot.

"How was the game?"

He gasps and clutches a hand to his heart. "You didn't watch?"

"I did," I admit with heated cheeks. *Am I blushing?* "But I like when you give me your recaps, along with the inside scoop. Like who's secretly pissed at who for missing a shot or not being open. It's cute."

His eyes hold mine captive as he lifts a brow. "Cute, huh?"

"Very, very cute. Sophie wants to get season tickets. Not that the suite isn't amazing, because it is, but if we sit center ice, we'll be closer to the action, you know? I'd miss the free cheese fries and fancy little canapes—oh, and I'd definitely miss the private bathroom—but it could be fun. What do you think?"

"You're rambling." He tucks a piece of hair behind my ear. "You do know people who sit on center ice are more likely to get chosen for an intermission game, right?"

My stomach drops. "Never mind, then."

He drops a quick kiss on my forehead. "You really don't like attention, huh?"

"I really don't," I confirm with a shrug. "I've just never felt comfortable in the spotlight. I'm more of a behind-the-scenes kind of girl."

"You don't mind my attention, though, right?" He breaks into a crooked grin. "Because it's not going away anytime soon."

I give him a shy smile. "I don't mind it from you."

"Good."

He gets back to work, chopping a tomato while regaling me with stories from the game. He's complaining about the reaction time of one of his defensemen when Ava climbs into the seat next to me and interrupts him. "Before we get any further, what are your intentions with my sister?"

"What kind of question is that?" I sputter, my cheeks heating.

Cole chuckles as he pulls a pan out of a cabinet and sets it on the stove. "I like that question more than your brother point-blank threatening to saw off my balls with skates. And I'd prob-ably be arrested if I repeat what Kennedy said to me."

He turns to the stove, muttering something about a whisk and rolling pin.

"Oy," I mutter, resting my forehead on the counter. I didn't think it was possible to turn any redder, but I prove myself wrong. At least the marble cools my heated skin a bit.

"It's a fair question, though," Cole continues with an easy smile. "I have no nefarious intentions. All I want is to make her happy. Happily ever afters exist outside of books, you know."

It's a simple statement, but it has me melting in my seat, nonetheless.

"That's so sweet." Ava pouts, her lip stuck out and every-thing. "And you guys are being safe? Condoms and all of that fun stuff?"

The sip of wine I've just taken comes sputtering out. "*Ava.*"

"What?" She uses my shock to steal a sip of my wine. "I tried to talk to you about this earlier, but you shut down any reference to your sex sheets."

Cole throws his head back and laughs. "Sex sheets?"

"Don't ask." I shake my head. "I don't have enough wine for that."

Ava thankfully switches her line of questioning to one that doesn't make me homicidal, and within minutes, the two of them are debating which one of Ed Sheeran's albums deserves more hype and whether Nike or Adidas has the better running shoe.

Cole's boiling water for the pasta when Goose howls and butts his head into his owner's thighs. Ava jumps in her seat, scanning the room with a frown.

"It's how he politely requests to go outside," I clue her in. "Apparently."

She lifts a hand to her chest. "I really hope he doesn't do that in the middle of the night."

Cole chuckles. "Nah, he's a good sleeper. My, will you turn the water to low once it starts boiling? I'm going to take him out."

Ava nearly trips herself as she scrambles out of her chair. "I'll do it. I'll take him out."

"Are you sure?"

She nods with far too much excitement for a college student who's volunteering to do a chore. "Yep. It'll be good training for when I get my own dog."

I open my mouth to remind her that she barely knows how to feed herself, let alone another living thing, but decide it's not worth it. That may be a lesson she has to learn the hard way.

As the door clicks shut behind Ava and Goose, I blurt out, "My mom's coming to town tomorrow."

Cole snaps up straight, abandoning the garlic he's crushing. "Wow. Okay. Why's she coming?"

I swirl my wine, watching the liquid as it coats the side of the pristine glass. "I guess Ava called her last week, and when my mom found out she'd be in Boston, she decided to come in for a family dinner."

He leans against the counter, wiping his hands on a dish towel. "I didn't realize the two of them were close."

"I wouldn't necessarily say they're close," I explain. "But Ava looks up to my mom in a weird way. I think she sees her as more of a cool aunt. The one who shows up with amazing stories and gifts and showers her with affection but then leaves again for God knows how long. And I don't have it in me to ruin the illusion."

Head tipped back, I finish the rest of my wine in one go.

"She's not a bad person, even if she wasn't the best mom. She's just a trust fund baby who doesn't know the meaning of the word responsibility. Yeah, I spent more time with babysitters and teachers than I did with her, but at least she made sure I was supervised. And I had a roof over my head and good food on the table. That's more than a lot of kids can say."

Cole stalks over to me, his jaw clenched and eyes heated. And damn if it doesn't feel good to have someone else get riled up in my defense. He pulls me into his arms, and I rest my cheek on his chest, letting the steady beat of his heart soothe me.

"Providing the bare minimum doesn't excuse her being a shitty mom. She left you in a situation where you had no choice but to depend on yourself. And while it's not bad to be independent, you shouldn't feel like that's your only option."

"I know," I mumble into his shirt, allowing myself to be vulnerable in the safety of his arms. "I wish you didn't have that dinner meeting with your agent tomorrow."

He latches on to my arms, untangling himself from my hold. "You want me to come to dinner?"

I flush under the intensity of his stare. "Yeah, but you have your meeting. I get it."

"I'll reschedule it."

"You said it was important," I argue, searching his face for some indication that he's kidding. It's about details of his contract, which sounds like a big deal, although I'm only getting the hang of the actual game, so behind-the-scenes stuff is far above my pay grade. "I'll be fine. Promise. I'll just get really drunk and hope for the best."

My blasé act doesn't fool him. "Do you want me at dinner? Yes or no?"

"Well, yes. But that's not—"

"Then I'll be at dinner."

It's overwhelming how inherent it is for him to be there for me. To show up. To strive to make sure that when I say I'm okay, I actually mean it. It's overwhelming how much he cares.

For the first time in a long time, I don't feel like I have to deal with life on my own. And as strange as it is, simply looking at him is like coming up for fresh air after hours underwater.

I'm not sure if it was his throaty laugh or aggravatingly attractive smirk, or maybe his insistence on making himself a part of my life, but somewhere along the way, the spiky walls surrounding my heart opened up just enough to let him in.

Not trusting myself to speak, I simply wrap my arms around his neck and capture his lips in a long, drugging kiss.

We break apart at the sound of Ava cautiously opening my apartment door. "You guys aren't naked, are you? Because I don't want to be scarred for life when I walk inside."

Cole laughs into the crook of my neck. "Will you tell me what the hell sex sheets are later?"

I grin as his throaty chuckle vibrates through me. "Deal. And Cole?"

He lifts his head, his amber eyes locked on mine with an intensity that makes my heart skip a beat.

"Thank you," I breathe. "I know I could handle tomorrow on my own, but I'm really glad I don't have to."

CHAPTER TWENTY-SIX

MAYA TOLD me that both Elliott and Ava resemble their respective dads. What she failed to mention was that her looks weren't passed down from the guy marked "unknown" on her birth certificate. The fair skin, the dark hair that curls at the ends, and the sultry blue eyes? Yeah. All her mother. She's only just entered the restaurant, but even with a dining room separating us, their copy-and-paste genetics are as clear as day.

Maya digs an elbow into my side, snapping me out of my blatant surprise. "Would you stop checking out my mom?"

"I wasn't checking her out," I defend, averting my attention. "You just failed to mention that you look alike."

"Sorry, was that supposed to make me feel better?"

I place a hand on the back of her neck and squeeze lightly. To say she's on edge would be a gross understatement. "You're beautiful. She's a hag."

With a light snort, she settles back into the plush chair with a swirling blue design dancing across the fabric. The French restaurant is wildly ostentatious, with its white-clothed tables, massive chandeliers with crystal adornments, and oil paintings of castles in green fields. It's the kind of place that makes me afraid to touch anything.

"You just said we look alike."

I hum. "I take it back. While there are similarities, you, my dear, are the fairest of them all."

Sighing, she intertwines her fingers with mine under the table and rests her head against my arm. "I didn't mean to snap at you."

I brush my lips against her temple. The anticipation that's plagued her all day rubs at her frayed nerves in all the wrong ways. And the way her mom waltzed in five minutes ago and is still chatting up the hostess like they're long-lost friends despite already being fifteen minutes late isn't helping.

Ava returns from the bathroom and slides into the seat next to Maya, wearing a shell-shocked look. "There's a bidet in there," she whisper-yells, her eyes darting around. "Who the hell is cleaning their asshole at a restaurant?"

Her voice rises on the word *asshole*, causing Maya to close her eyes in mortification and me to choke on a laugh. Blessedly, we're saved from responding when a tinkling voice calls out, "My girls!"

Neither Ava nor Maya moves, because as their mother approaches the table, it dawns on us all that the extra seat wasn't a mistake on the hostess's part, but a seat for the man hovering behind Deirdre. A man I saw step into the restaurant but assumed was with the large party waiting to be seated.

While Maya doesn't act surprised by his presence, her hand tightens around mine. I rub my thumb soothingly against the back of it, a silent acknowledgment that I'm here.

"I didn't know he was coming," Ava murmurs. Face etched in hurt, she peers at Maya. It's easy to forget how young she is because she's so well-spoken and witty, but at only eighteen, she still has a lot of life lessons left to learn. Although if it were up to Maya—and me—being disappointed by their mother wouldn't be on that list.

Not letting a hint of annoyance show, Maya smiles at her sister. "The more the merrier. Right, Aves?"

Deirdre leans down to give each of her daughters a hug, then pauses, surveying me. "And who might you be, Mr. Tall, Dark, and Handsome?"

A spark of hurt flashes through me. Maya and her mom aren't close, but if she's never mentioned me to this woman, I can't help but feel like a dirty little secret.

Maya's jaw spasms, but she forces a polite smile. "Mom, this is my boyfriend, Cole. I told you about him on the phone. He's from San Diego, has a dog named Goose, plays for the Bobcats... ring a bell?"

"Hmm. Maybe." She taps her manicured finger against her cheek. "Anyway, it's lovely to meet you." She dismisses the topic and zeroes in on Maya. "Where's Elliott?"

Maya's muscles have once again bunched up with tension. "Stuck in traffic."

Deirdre huffs, rolling her eyes in a way a woman her age should be too old for. "He couldn't bother to leave early enough to be on time?"

"You changed locations on us an hour ago," Maya points out, her hand practically strangling mine. "We originally planned to meet at a restaurant near his office."

Rather than respond, Deirdre lifts her chin and moves on in her introductions. "Maya, Ava, you remember my partner, Keith, right?"

The man still hovering partially behind her holds out his hand. It's only then that I realize how young he is. With his slicked-back blond hair and light stubble, he looks like Brad Pitt circa the '90s. There's no way the guy's a day over thirty-five, making him far closer in age to Maya and me than to her mom. *Holy shit.* Deirdre Silver is a cougar.

I shake Keith's hand and introduce myself, all while shooting Maya subtle glances. As Deirdre and Keith take their seats, I whisper to Maya, "How did you fail to mention that your mom was in high school when her *partner* was born?"

She covers up her laugh by coughing into her arm, then leans in close, voice lowered, and answers, "I didn't think they'd last this long."

Once we've ordered a bottle of wine and a few appetizers, Ava dives into conversation, catching her mom up on things she should already know. She just aced an English assignment. *Well, duh. Maya helped her, so no surprise there.* Her roommate has a new boyfriend who stays at their dorm all the time. *Even I knew that; Maya filled me in on the drama weeks ago.* She wants to major in marketing but isn't sure whether she should minor in philosophy, too. *Maya thinks she should take a few more classes to see if it's interesting before deciding.*

"There's no money in philosophy," Deirdre advises. She flicks her hand as if shooing away the idea.

"There's nothing wrong with Ava taking the time to explore her options," Maya says. Her voice is even, if not a little strained. "She has time before she has to declare her major."

At Maya's urging, Ava made an appointment with a guidance counselor to discuss the possibilities. The counselor's helping her choose some elective courses that may better help her decide. Not that Deirdre would know this. Even *I'm* already caught up on the details, yet I've known Ava for less than twenty-four hours.

Deirdre gives her eldest daughter a blank stare for a beat too long before her lips curl into an imitation of an amused smile. "What's the saying, again? Mother knows best?"

The hair on the back of my neck rises, along with the rage simmering inside me.

As if she can sense it, Maya grips my thigh in a silent message to keep my mouth shut and takes a gulp of her wine. I have no idea how I'll make it through an entire dinner. I've heard enough about the woman across from me to know this behavior isn't new, but that doesn't lessen the anger I have toward her. A person who doesn't care enough to see how amazing her kids are? Who doesn't see how amazing Maya is? Who treats her as if she isn't the best goddamn thing in the world? She holds no esteem in my eyes.

The tension breaks as Elliott saunters up to the table. *Thank the Lord.* He shoots Maya a questioning glance but doesn't comment on the terse silence. "Hey, Mom."

Deirdre makes a big deal out of hugging her son, acting as if the reason they haven't seen each other has nothing to do with her gallivanting around the world, all but ignoring her children.

When Elliott slides into the open seat between Keith and me, I breathe a sigh of relief. I'm sure Keith's a fine guy, but the last thing I want is to spend all night answering his questions about the Bobcats' defense. There's a time and place for that, and dinner with my girlfriend's mother is neither of those.

If Maya thought my family dinner would even remotely resemble this, it's no wonder she was hesitant to come. Rather than reminisce about childhood memories or share inside jokes, the conversation is stilted and cold.

We make it through the main course without incident, but when Elliott asks the question Maya's been wondering all night, I have a feeling all bets are off.

"So, Mom," he says, wiping his mouth with his napkin, "what brings you to town?"

Deirdre gingerly sets her fork on her plate. "I need a reason? I can't just visit my kids?"

Maya raises a brow. "You *can*, but you definitely don't."

"Must you always have an attitude, Maya?" Deirdre slumps back in her seat and looks at Keith, lips turned down, as if this proves some sort of point. "I swear her goal in life is to give me grief."

Maya glares at her wineglass as if the alcohol is to blame for this.

Not wanting things to escalate, I turn toward Keith. "What do you do for work?"

Beside me, Elliott subtly nods, as if he's impressed with my ability to pivot. Being Logan's teammate has taught me how to skillfully de-escalate almost any disagreement.

"I'm a travel photographer," he replies with a small smile. "I was just on assignment with *National Geographic* in South Africa, actually. It was breathtaking."

I cringe internally. *Now I feel bad that I assumed he owned a gym or something.*

"Wow. That's impressive," I note. "I'm sure you've been to a lot of cool places, then."

With a chuckle, he sets his napkin on the table. "Jordan, Cambodia, Singapore, London. It's incredible, but it gets a bit lonely. That's why I feel very lucky to have met this lovely lady to share my travels with."

Deirdre lowers her head, blushing at the compliment. If I didn't dislike her, it'd be sweet.

"Do you do shows or display your work at galleries?"

"We're headed to one in Seaport after dinner tonight," he announces. "Sorry, I thought Deirdre mentioned it. You're all more than welcome to come, of course."

My gut twists painfully, and I can almost feel Maya's fury growing.

"So that's why you're here," Ava says, her usually bright voice dulled.

"It was a last-minute thing, sweetheart," Deirdre reassures her. "I would have visited anyway. Right, Keith?"

My phone rings loudly, startling us all and earning annoyed looks from nearby diners. I slip it out of my pocket to silence it. As Mark's name flashes on the screen, my heart thumps heavily against my sternum. *Deep breaths.* He told me he'd call when he had an update after the meeting.

"You can take the call if you need, babe," Maya says, nodding at my phone. "I know you had to cancel on him to be here."

I shake my head. "I'll find out what he needs after—"

The damn device vibrates again, this time in my hand.

Maya laughs softly. "It's fine. If he's calling you twice, it's got to be important."

With a quick kiss to her temple, I excuse myself from the table. The only benefit of this pretentious restaurant is that there are multiple private rooms in the back. I flag down a server, who confirms the last one is empty, and duck inside before calling Mark back.

It rings twice before he answers. "Devils want you. They're willing to trade the Bobcats Peter Knight and Lyle Cunningham plus two draft picks."

Lungs seizing, I fall into a chair. "Wow. Okay. You really waste no time, do you?"

"You don't pay me to shoot the shit," he replies with a chuckle. "Anyway, the Bobcats obviously wanted first-round draft, and..."

He launches into the nitty-gritty details of the meeting, each one making my head pound harder. Although the trade would be after the season is over, other moves happening around the trade deadline will factor into the way the final deal looks. Right now, thirty general managers are working to make the best moves and trades for their respective clubs. It's a bunch of grown men working on the same puzzle—yet not knowing what the puzzle looks like—and all the while, they think they're playing Monopoly. So it's hard to wrap one's head around. And considering I'm a large part of why the Bobcats consistently win, year after year, the Devils will have to come up with a *good* incentive in order to make it happen.

Angling forward with my elbow on my knee and the phone to my ear, I run my free hand through my hair. "So it'd be a three-way trade, pending the Bobcats acquiring the rights to a forward prospect from the Titans, who they can then trade to the Devils along with me."

"More or less," Mark confirms. "But things are looking good."

I shift on the surprisingly uncomfortable chair and force a deep breath. "Let me know if there are any other updates, okay?"

"Yep."

I end the call and, pressing the corner of my phone to my forehead, blow out a series of short breaths to gain control of my rapidly beating heart. Why is my body reacting like I've just received bad news instead of good? My home team, the team Nate and I grew up worshipping, wants me to play for them. Badly. I shouldn't have to convince myself that this is what I want. It *is* what I want.

Right?

A noise from the doorway has my head snapping up, and when the identity of the man leaning against the doorframe of the private dining room registers, my heart drops.

I sink into the seat, feeling completely fucked. "How much of that did you hear?"

Elliott, hands in his suit pocket, scrutinizes me, his gaze like an iron brand. "Enough to know you're being traded."

"Possibly," I correct him. "Nothing's confirmed."

He lifts a brow. "The trade deadline's in a few days, Cole. We'll know soon enough."

I sigh and rest my elbows on my thighs. "It'd be a post trade deadline; they want Rogers for the playoffs. After that, he'll retire. But regardless, there are still a lot of logistics to be worked out."

He nods and stares at a spot above my shoulder, as if he's processing the implications. "If moving teams is what you want, she wouldn't resent you for making the choice. She'd want you to be happy."

If I wasn't already sitting, that would've knocked me on my ass. Because it's the goddamn truth, and that makes it all the harder to leave.

"Maya and I are in a really good place. I don't want to ruin that by bringing up such a life-altering decision if it's not set in stone." A sharp pain lances my chest, forcing me to sit up and rub at the spot. "Given how hard she fought against us in the first place, I don't think bringing up the idea of a long-distance relationship will go over well."

Elliott crosses his arms over his chest. "Honesty is huge for Maya, and the trust she has for you? Don't take that lightly, man."

"I don't," I promise, praying he can see how earnest I am. "I never want to hurt her, which is why I'm asking you to not say anything to her yet. Give me some time to figure this out."

Elliott studies me for a long moment, his expression unyielding.

Heart in my throat, I tap my fingers against my thighs. It's a huge request. I'm asking him to keep a big secret from his sister, but he has to know my intentions aren't malicious.

Finally, he puffs out a deep breath. "You love her."

Relief floods me, pulling a chuckle from deep in my chest. "Is it that obvious?"

"To everyone but her," he says with the merest trace of a smile on his lips. "I'll keep my lips sealed for now. But figure out your shit sooner rather than later."

The plastic band choking my nerves snaps, every muscle relaxing a fraction. "I will. Promise."

"You're good for her. It's like she's finally living in one of her romance books. And she deserves that."

"She deserves the world."

With a light knock on the doorframe, he straightens. "I'm headed to my bathroom, which was my initial destination, just in case you thought I was stalking you." He gives me a wry smile. "I'll see you back at the table."

As I weave my way through the tightly packed tables in the main dining room, I'm relieved to discover no one shouting, screaming, or crying at ours. The instant I'm seated, my hand reaches toward Maya's back of its own accord. "What did I miss?"

"I asked the waiter whether they serve lobotomies, but he didn't catch on to my sarcasm, so he's asking the chef and getting back to me. How was the call? Everything good?"

Chuckling, I tilt closer and lightly press my lips against hers. "Everything's great, baby. It always is with you."

CHAPTER TWENTY-SEVEN

I'M USED to the noises in my apartment. Even the constant buzz of my fridge is part of the charm. I like to think of it as white noise as I lose myself in a new book. But the scratching on my door? That's a new one. One that makes my heart race as I set down the psychological thriller I've been lost in.

As I scan my apartment, my attention snags on the full moon outside the window, and panic surges through me.

Holy shit. Did the guy in 4D have a successful Ouija board night? Has the spirit he conjured come to get me? Or maybe a creepy girl with her head turned at an impossible angle? It goes silent, but only for a moment, and when the sound returns, it's with a vengeance. My fight-or-flight instincts kick in, and, to my absolute shock—because for twenty-eight years, I've strongly believed I'm a flight kind of girl—I pick up a kitchen knife without hesitation, head to my door, and swing it open.

Oh. At the sight in front of me, I deflate. Well, now I feel silly.

I hold the knife at my side—there's no need to point it at an innocent dog—and let out a relieved laugh. "You're not a creepy little girl, are you, Goosey Goose?"

Footsteps echo up the stairwell, and ten seconds later, an aggravated Cole appears on the landing. "Christ, Goose."

I lean against the doorframe. "Nice to see you, too, babe. You guys race up the stairs?"

Cole gives Goose a look of undisguised scorn. "The second I stepped into the building, he fucking sprinted upstairs and his leash slipped out of my hand. I've never seen him move so fast."

Beaming, I crouch and kiss the top of Goose's head. "He was excited to see me."

Cole's schedule has been overwhelming for the past few weeks, meaning Goose and I haven't had nearly enough quality time together. Neither have Cole and I, but I keep comments about that to myself. The last thing I want to do is cause him more stress. He's heading into playoff season soon, this time as a captain, and he's been training more than usual. Despite how tired he is, he still makes time for me, even if he falls asleep within an hour of showing up at my door.

"Sorry I'm so late. We sat on the runway for hours after landing, and then I was stuck in traffic because of a concert." He strides toward me like a man on a mission. "I tried calling, but I'm assuming you were reading and didn't—wait, is that a *knife* in your hand?"

I glance at the knife I use to cut apples. "Oh, um, yeah. I thought Goose was an intruder scratching at my door."

"So you opened the door for said intruder?" he asks, his voice rising with concern. "Wearing a sexy little pajama set?"

I look down. Okay, yeah, not my most well-thought-out plan, but I'd hardly call the matching cotton pajama set covered in daisies sexy. To each their own, I suppose. "Would you rather stand out there being a judgy Judy or come in?"

He grumbles in response, though he hustles into my apartment with more speed than should be possible for a man as exhausted as he is. The instant the door is shut behind me, I find myself pressed up against it.

He drags the tip of his nose along the column of my throat, the heat of his body soaking into me. "Mmm, I missed you. Your smile. Your laugh. Your naked legs wrapped around me."

A breath catches in my throat as he presses his broad chest against mine. His tongue traces my lower lip, the simple move causing the sensitive peaks of my nipples to harden.

"I'm going to take a shower," he says in that deep, rumbling voice of his. "Then I'm going to strip that outfit off you and make you come until the only word you remember is my name."

My knees wobble and my whole body heats. "Yes, please."

No point in being coy about how badly I want him.

I clean my kitchen to kill time while Cole showers. I'm unloading the dishwasher when the shower turns off, but once I'm finished, I practically skip to my bedroom. Though as I step inside, expecting to find him ready for sex, I instead find him ready for sleep. Scratch that. I find him *already* asleep, the overhead light still on and with one arm flung over his eyes, the other resting on his toned torso.

I could wake him up with a lovely little blowjob, but if the dark smudges under his eyes I noticed when he arrived are anything to go by, he needs the sleep.

Too wired from my potential run-in with a ghost, I snuggle up with Goose on the couch and read. Only when I can't keep my eyes open any longer do I curl up next to Cole in bed and fall into a peaceful sleep.

I wake up what feels like minutes later to a furry face nudging mine. My room's still bathed in darkness, but according to my phone, it's six a.m. Way too early for me to even consider waking up. I pet Goose on the head and then roll over, hoping he forgets all about me.

No such luck.

He presses his snout into my back and makes little growly noises that would be cute if it wasn't the literal ass crack of dawn.

Cole, who usually lets Goose out in the morning, is still dead to the world. I consider waking him, but just the thought makes me feel guilty. He's been in hotel beds for the past week, and my exhaustion comes from staying up too late reading. It's self-inflicted, and now I'll have to suffer the consequences.

With a deep sigh, I leave the cozy comfort of my bed. I find a pair of sweats and a long-sleeved shirt, then mutter obscenities the entire way down the stairs.

Outside, Goose doesn't want to just pee. No, no, no. He wants to explore. If I were Cole, I'd have the arm strength to pull the behemoth of a chocolate lab away from the trees lining my street, or the stray glove on the sidewalk, or the FedEx truck that drives by. But I have the muscle mass of a goddamn spaghetti noodle, so Goose drags me around like we've got all the time in the world.

I can't be mad at him about it, either. Not when he looks so happy with his tongue lolling out the side of his mouth.

Twenty minutes later, he finally decides he's done with the freezing outdoors. *God bless.* Even dressed in full winter gear, I'm racked with shivers as we enter my apartment. Not wanting to wake Cole by rooting around in my closet for a sweatshirt, I look through the clothes in the dryer—the ones I've been avoiding folding the past two days. I have to stick my entire top half into the drum to reach the sweatshirt stuck in the back— one of Cole's that I've gained ownership of, of course. Several socks and a few pairs of underwear tumble out as well, making me sincerely regret not dealing with this the other day.

Goose yaps eagerly as I pluck each item off the floor. Chuckling at him, I shove the clothing back into the dryer. It isn't until

I shut the door that I realize he wants to play. With my thong. It's on the floor, halfway between us, and Goose is ready to pounce, his body lowered to the ground, but his butt in the air, his tail wagging.

It's like a Western standoff. We zero in on the stray strawberry-printed thong before sizing up one another. I lunge for it, but Goose is way quicker than me and snatches it up with ease.

"Drop it," I demand, holding out my hand.

He wags his tail in response.

"Goose," I warn, putting on my stern face. "Drop the thong."

The speed of his tail wagging increases and he growls playfully.

"I'll tell your dad you were being a bad boy if you don't drop it." I wiggle my fingers. "I'm serious. I'll give you until the count of three. One... two..."

With another yip, he launches himself across my apartment like the Tasmanian Devil, sprinting laps around my kitchen table and couch, a wild gleam in his eyes. He changes directions a few times, miraculously managing not to break a kitchen chair or knock over a book pile when he spins around.

This goes on for a solid two minutes before he plops down at my feet, panting wildly, with the thong still in his mouth. Sighing, I head to the kitchen and turn on the Keurig. There's no way I'll get back to sleep after that sort of entertainment.

I'm adding milk to my freshly brewed coffee when Goose finally drops my underwear. Turns out the only incentive he needed was my lack of interest. *Go figure.* The thriller I was reading last night rests on my coffee table, the perfect way to spend an early morning. Instead, though, I can't help but peer over at my computer, sitting by its lonesome self on my tiny kitchen table that doubles as a desk.

Since Jaden suggested I expand my short story, I've spent

more time than I'd like to admit spacing out at work, letting the strands of the story weave themselves into a more fully formed plot in my head. But breathing life into that story? Giving the characters names and quirks and hobbies? Motivations, fears, goals? The enormousness of the idea is almost enough to make me swap out my coffee for a glass of wine.

I snag my thong off the floor—thank you very much, Goose —and head for the couch. Halfway there, though, I pivot and march to the kitchen table. I'm already up, so I may as well grab the bull by the horns and write a few of those ideas down… right?

Right.

By the time Cole saunters into the room in boxer briefs that showcase his impressive form perfectly, I've got a bare-bones outline typed up. And I don't hate it.

"Morning, sleepyhead," I greet him.

"Morning, baby." He yawns, stretching his arms above his head. "I'm surprised you were up before me."

I nod at Goose, who's curled up in a ball behind my sofa. "This dude woke me in the middle of the night to take him out." I pick up my mug and take a small sip. "And by the middle of the night, I mean, like, six o'clock, but that's very early for me."

"It is. Thanks for taking him out. I appreciate it." He kisses the top of my head. "Do I want to know why your underwear is on the kitchen table?"

I let out an amused chuckle. "They fell out of the dryer and Goose thought it would be fun to run around my apartment with them in his mouth like the devil possessed. I put them there when he finally dropped 'em."

"Dear God," he groans, running a hand through his hair. "You want to go back to bed? I know you hate mornings."

I hold up my mug, meeting his apologetic eyes. "One, I've

already had two cups of coffee. Two, I've had a very productive morning, as a matter of fact. Three, it's almost noon."

One would think I'd just told Cole that the world is flat and we're all figments of someone's imagination. His gasp is *that* dramatic. "Jesus. Why didn't you wake me, My?"

I stand and brush my lips against his. "You looked so precious all snuggled up in my bed."

"Precious?" He cocks a brow and chuckles. "Don't think anyone's called me that before."

"Well, it's true." Warmth filters through me at his proximity. "And you were exhausted last night, so I figured you could use the extra sleep."

He rubs a hand over his sleep-lined face. "Yeah, I haven't been sleeping well."

My chest tightens in sympathy. "Everything okay?"

He pulls me into his arms, and I tuck my head under his chin, reveling in his body heat. I swear the guy's a damn furnace. "Yeah. Just have a lot going on. And I missed you."

"I guess I sort of, kind of, maybe, definitely missed you, too."

The low laugh that escapes him vibrates through me. "Aw, thanks. Now, tell me about your productive morning."

I can't stop the smile that splits my face. "I'm tinkering with that short story. The one my teacher encouraged me to expand on."

"Tinkering?" He pulls back a fraction, assessing me, his sleepy eyes full of warmth.

"Mm-hmm. You know... toying with the idea, exploring my options, dabbling—"

Cole picks me off my feet and tosses me over his shoulder like a sack of sweet potatoes, and all the air is forced from my lungs. "I know what it means, smart-ass."

He digs his fingers into my side gently, and I squeal at the tickle attack, squirming as he strides for the couch.

"Cole!" I half laugh, half shout. "Put me down."

He hoists me off his shoulder, but instead of setting me on my feet, he drops onto the couch and maneuvers me so I'm straddling him with our chests pressed together. "There. Now you're down."

I rest my hands on his shoulders, catching my breath. "Was that necessary?"

"Yep. Now I can hear you better."

Though I roll my eyes at his bullshit excuse, a smile still plays on my lips. "As I was saying before I was rudely interrupted, I started mapping out story ideas."

The corners of his lips creep up. "When can I read it?"

I puff out a deep breath. "I told you it's not written yet. I literally *just* started really considering it this morning."

He shakes his head. "No, the short story. I want to read that."

"Oh." Heat floods my face.

Head tilted, he studies me. "Other people have read it, right?"

By "other people," he means Brian, whom he dislikes for no other reason than that the man exists. "People in my class have, yes."

"Then don't you think your own boyfriend should?"

Shoulders slumping, I sigh. "If you tell me you like it, I'm going to think you're saying that because you're my boyfriend. And if you tell me you don't like it, I'll pretend not to care but I'll secretly be super upset. See the predicament?"

Cole gazes at me until I start to squirm under the scrutiny. He's not going to let this go. *Shit.*

"You also don't read that much," I add.

He continues to stare just like Goose did this morning.

"And I don't know if I can trust your judgment, considering you don't like *New Girl*, an objectively funny show."

When he stays silent, I pull back, arms crossed, and frown. "You're being rude."

"I haven't said anything," he counters.

"Which is rude."

His mask finally cracks and he gives me a small grin. "You watch all of my hockey games even though you don't understand all the nuances and rules, right?"

"Yeah."

"That's no different from me reading your work." He squeezes my hips to emphasize his point. "And if I play poorly or have a bad game, that doesn't mean I'm a bad player, does it?" Without waiting for a response, he goes on. "So in the very unlikely event that your story isn't the best thing I've ever read —because honestly, I don't know if anything will top *Alien Lovers of Planet Dexxar*—that doesn't mean it's bad."

Tipping my head back, I let out a resounding groan. "Fine." I clamber out of his lap, barely dodging the smack he tries to land on my ass, and stomp to the kitchen table, where I find the story in my aptly titled Creative Writing Class folder. Once I've handed it over, I try to sit next to Cole on the couch, but he pulls me back into the same position. I can't say that I mind straddling my extremely sexy boyfriend, but it's not conducive to reading. Even so, he holds me in place with one hand while he dives in.

I study every micro-expression on his face as he pores over my words. The way the right side of his mouth twitches at certain parts or how his brows lift almost imperceptibly at others. He even chuckles a couple of times. The moment is uncomfortably intimate. Though I know Cole won't judge me based on what he's reading, it's hard not to feel as though that's exactly what will happen.

He finishes, and as he sets the papers to the side, my body tenses with anticipation.

"I really like it, My. And I'm not just saying that." His words are genuine, honest.

Even so, I chew on my lower lip. "So says every person who has ever lied."

He rests his hands on either side of my face, forcing me to meet his eyes. "I haven't lied to you yet, and I promise I never will." He moves in closer, his lips only an inch from mine. "So when I say I like it, I mean it."

Heart thrashing, I crash my lips against his. It's like striking a match, my body coming alive in an instant. Rather than question my reaction, Cole leans into it, one of his hands sliding into my hair and tilting my head back so he can control the kiss.

As our tongues tangle in a battle of dominance, I run my hands over his broad, muscled chest, lightly scratching my nails against his nipples. He hisses out a sharp breath, his hips jerking up, pressing his hardened cock against my clothed core. I grind against him slowly, enjoying each and every groan that slips through his lips.

He peels off my oh-so-sexy sweatpants and sweatshirt and explores each inch of skin he reveals, both with his hands and his mouth, until I'm shaking with need. His movements aren't the least bit rushed. He worships my body in a way that would have Eros and Aphrodite taking notes.

With agility only a professional athlete could possess, he slips off his briefs and rolls on a condom. All the while, he keeps me trapped against his body. Rather than move to my bedroom, he sits back down on the couch and settles me onto his lap with my thighs bracketing his. He places himself at my entrance, with one hand braced on my hip, and I slowly sink down on him. The stretch as he fills me has me moaning out his name.

"Fuck," he groans, wrapping his arm around my waist. "One

week without being inside you, and I forgot how tight your pussy is."

I roll my hips once, then again, building a deep rhythm, head tipped forward to rest on his shoulder. He splays a hand over my back, at the base of my spine, pressing me closer. Choppy breaths hit my neck as he nuzzles into the side of my throat. He follows the move up with soft kisses against the sensitive skin.

"So good for me, baby," he praises.

Before long, he pushes his hips up to meet mine, no longer content with letting me lead. As he grips my hips and tugs me down, driving into me, I gasp. And when he grinds his pelvic bone against my clit with each thrust, incoherent babble slips from my lips. The spark that'll light my orgasm flares to life as our bodies rock against one another.

"Feels so good," I moan.

"Like when I'm this deep, don't you, baby?" His tone is a low rumble that pushes me closer to the edge.

A deep line of concentration and pleasure graces the spot between his brows as he works me over. He looks gorgeous like this. Desperate and dedicated and delicious.

"God, yes."

He keeps up the pace, and in seconds, I explode into a thousand tiny pieces, clenching around his cock. I'm still shuddering around him when he groans, long and low, and stiffens as he releases himself.

Cheek pressed to his chest—which is now sticky with sweat—I close my eyes and relish the way he drags his calloused hands up and down my back. The steady sensation lulls me further into my post-orgasmic bliss. We stay pressed together, in comfortable silence, for several minutes, neither of us willing to pop the bubble we're in, neither of us ready to tumble back into the real world.

"*That's* what I was planning to do last night," Cole announces.

"Hmm," I mumble, my cheek sticking to his chest. "So you really liked the piece? Even though you'd probably never pick up a book about an ex-royal finding love on a reality TV show?"

His answering chuckle vibrates against my skin. "Before you, I probably wouldn't have set foot in a place that sells books, so I highly doubt I'm your target audience, but all those Bookstagram creators you follow? I'm sure they'd eat that shit right up."

"Maybe," I agree. "It's scary, you know? I'm excited to write, but I've never really done anything for myself before. I didn't do extracurriculars in school because I wanted to be home to help Elliott and Ava, and then in college, I worked as much as I could, so I had no time to join clubs. It feels like I'm fifteen steps behind my peers. They've all got it figured out, but I'm still discovering who I am."

"You can't compare yourself to anyone, baby," he softly reprimands. "We're all on our own journey, and it's never too late to start something."

Rubbing my brow, I sigh. God, I sound pathetic. "I guess."

He huffs. "Well, I know. *Hamilton* didn't debut until Lin-Manuel Miranda was thirty-five, so I'd say you're fine."

I lean back, studying his serene face. "I'm sorry, but how do you know that?"

"You told me Kennedy was a Broadway fanatic, but I didn't understand the extent of that until I accidentally told her the only show I'd seen was *Charlie and the Chocolate Factory*."

I cringe, because that's her least favorite musical.

"She's been texting me songs and facts about every show in existence, I think."

I snort and shake my head. "I told you so."

"When you become a famous author, I'll get to say I told *you* so. And then it'll be me asking for your autograph instead of the other way around."

"For the record, I've never technically asked for your autograph," I correct him. "You volunteered, and then I asked how much money I could make if I sold it."

Cole leans forward and claims my lips in a kiss that leaves me wiggling in his hold. "And look how far we've come."

cole

I'VE NEVER MINDED DOING interviews, which my publicist is forever grateful for, and now that I'm captain, the media requests have been nonstop. Especially as the regular season wraps up. Today's interview is for a podcast called *Coffee with Champions*. It's consistently ranked as one of the top comedy sports podcasts, and rumor is, the host, Ella Gold, is a force to be reckoned with.

This morning, one conference room at Airwave Arena has been converted into a recording studio, with wires running every which way. The giant oak table in the center is barely discernible under the heaps of equipment. And standing next to one of the microphones is a petite brunette wearing a Formula 1 shirt and a wide smile that showcases a dimple on her right cheek.

"Hey," I say, sticking out my hand. "Ella, right?"

She returns the gesture, her grip surprisingly firm. "Hi. It's so nice to meet you."

"You, too." I stuff my hands into my pockets. "Sorry I'm a bit late. I landed about an hour ago."

Ella waves off my apology. "I'm just happy we could make

this happen. I can only imagine how packed your schedule must be."

I swear I spend more time sleeping on planes and in hotel rooms than in my own bed during the season. But for the next week, the team will be in Boston. It's a fucking relief, though it's made me realize how fucking difficult it'll be to find time with Maya if Boston is no longer my home base.

Before I can spiral further, I shake the thought out of my head. Now is not the time.

Ella walks me through a breakdown of the show and then gets me situated with headphones and a microphone. She's professional but friendly, making it easy to see why so many big-name athletes appear on her show. There's nothing worse than an interview that feels more like an interrogation than a conversation.

She slips her own pair of headphones on. "You ready?"

Nodding, I give her a thumbs-up. "Let's do this."

She hits the record button, and with one more smile my way, she kicks off the show. "Hello, listeners. I'm Ella Gold, the host of *Coffee with Champions*, and we're in Boston today, chatting with the Bobcats' captain, Nicholas Berrett."

A hint of nervousness rises in me, but I tamp it down. A podcast is nothing compared to being the center of attention in a packed arena. "Thanks for having me."

"We have a lot to discuss, considering how damn impressive your career has been, so I'll jump right in," she says, her tone light. "Drafted into the NHL at nineteen, with two Stanley Cup rings to your name. Rumor is you're the good luck charm that earned the Bobcats their first Stanley Cup, breaking their eleven-year losing streak. How do you feel you've changed as a player over the years?"

She eases me into the conversation, asking questions about playing hockey as a kid and when I knew I wanted—and was good enough—to go pro. As instructed by my publicist, she doesn't ask explicit questions about Nathan. I'm fine with mentions of him here and there because he was and still is such an influential part of my life. But it's when interviewers start to get psychoanalytical and ask how his death affected my game that I lose my ever-loving shit.

We're talking about last night's game when Ella admits, "Don't hate me, but I rooted for the Trailblazers yesterday." She winces. "In my defense, I've been a fan since I was a kid. Curse of being from Chicago, I suppose."

"I didn't realize you were from Chicago." I shift in my seat. "I'm assuming you're a Desmond Rich fan?"

She nods. "He may as well have a shrine at my parents' house. When he was traded to the Devils, my dad acted like the world was coming to an end. He still laments about it to this day."

"The Devils definitely benefited from that trade," I admit. I was in high school when the four-time Stanley Cup winner came to San Diego. Nate and I snuck out and took a cab to the arena to watch his first game with the team. Got caught and ended up grounded for two weeks, but it was so worth it.

"I heard recently that you may be moving to the Devils next season. Any truth to that rumor?"

Fuck.

My heart lurches painfully, but I keep my face blank. If she's heard about the trade deal, then she's far more well-connected than I realized. Everyone involved has kept quiet about it, and any small rumblings that I was headed to San Diego died the moment the trade deadline passed. Cameron and Jake have been pressuring me to talk to Maya about the possibility, but the mere idea of upsetting her makes me nauseous. I can't lose her, but how can I ask her to move across the country with me, knowing she'll have to sacrifice the life she's built here? It's selfish, and she's the most selfless person I know.

"Rumors always fly around the trade deadline," I say, willing my voice not to shake. "If they were all to be believed, I'd be playing for about fifteen teams right now." I lift one shoulder. "You never know what changes the GMs will make to the team. We were halfway through this season when they traded one of our wingers and two of our defensemen."

Ella nods, but her brow crinkles with what I fear is doubt. "A lot of players agree that it's what they signed up for when becoming professional hockey players, but I can't imagine it's easy."

"It's not," I admit. "When I was drafted, I only played a season and a half with the Wildcats before I was traded to the Bruisers. You play with these guys day in and day out, build friendships and professional relationships, and just like that"— I snap my fingers—"you're living in a new city, wearing a new logo, playing *with* guys you've been playing against for weeks, months, even years."

"Sounds like you didn't like being traded very much," Ella teases with a raised brow. "I sure as hell wouldn't want to be."

"It's difficult, sure, but at the end of the day, this is a business. And when it comes down to making trades, in the end, it's about what's best for the franchise."

Lips pressed together, she regards me, her eyes narrowing. But rather than push the issue further, she asks, "How have you adjusted to being the team's captain this season?"

"I'd like to think I've adjusted pretty well." I chuckle, trying to rein in my relief at the subject change. "I've been here for a few years now, and in that time, the team has been through a lot of wins and a lot of losses. Knowing the team and management trust me to lead alongside the coaches is a huge honor."

"As one of the best teams in your division, the Bobcats will likely be headed to the playoffs. Do you have a strategy or a plan in place?"

"I wouldn't be a very good captain if I gave away team strategy, now, would I?"

Ella laughs and shoots me a good-natured smile. "No, but you'd be a very good podcast guest."

The rest of the interview goes off without a hitch, but by the end of it, I know I have to talk to Maya. Soon. If she hears about the trade talks from a podcast rather than from me, she'll be hurt. And when I tell her the truth behind said rumors? That'll be even worse.

It's a lose-lose situation.

I spend my drive home considering how to broach the subject. I'm in such a daze as I trudge up my front steps that I don't notice Maya bundled up in a jacket, leaning against my door, until I've made it to the top.

My steps falter, my heart stuttering. "Maya?"

She holds up a plastic bag, one with the classic smiley face and "Thank you!" printed across it. "I brought dinner."

I lunge forward and wrap my arms around her waist, peppering her face with kisses. Relief washes over me. *God, I'm happy to see her.*

Without my permission, my hands travel south and cup her ass.

She squeaks at first, though the sound is followed by an exasperated laugh. "Be careful of the food."

Oh, right. Releasing her, I take the bag and unlock my front door. "Not that I'm not thrilled you're here, but I thought you had drinks with your writing class friends." I guide her through the door, where Goose completely ignores me in favor of bumping into Maya's legs in greeting.

Well, then.

She massages a spot behind his ear until he's satisfied, and only then does he make his way toward me.

I crouch and give him the love he's looking for. "I'm second best now, huh?"

"It's the nails. They scratch better." Wiggling her fingers, she shows off her freshly painted nails. "And I did have drinks, but I decided to take a rain check."

"Why?" I grin. "Because you missed me so much?"

She nods, a flush of self-consciousness blooming across her cheeks. "Yes."

The honesty of her statement knocks the breath out of me. I cup her cheeks and run my thumb over her plush lower lip. "I've missed you, too. And I'm sorry."

Head tilted, she frowns. "For what?"

"That we haven't seen each other a ton lately. I didn't realize how heavily Coach Henderson would lean on me leading into the playoffs. Between the game plans, and—"

"I wasn't saying I missed you to make you feel bad." She brushes her own thumb along my jaw. "I'd never begrudge you for doing your job. And I know how important this season is to you."

I rest my forehead against hers. "You're too good for me."

"Probably," she agrees, rubbing her nose against mine.

We're still locked together like that when the familiar smell of garlic, basil, and tomato sauce floats around us, making my stomach rumble. I don't even have to look in the bags to know that Maya picked up eggplant parmesan, a house salad, and cheesy garlic bread from my favorite Italian restaurant—the same restaurant we got food from on our first date.

"Food first, talk later," Maya says, pulling away from me. She unpacks the bags and dishes out healthy servings for us both while I pour drinks. Water for me, wine for her.

For the better part of an hour, we talk about what we've

each been up to over the last few days. We alternate between taking bites of our food and commiserating over annoying customers and teammates with authority issues. After a week filled with action-packed games, long practices, and media interviews, the normalcy of a casual dinner with Maya brings me a sense of comfort greater than I thought possible.

"Damn, I needed this." I settle back in my chair, my stomach full and my heart happy. "Thank you, baby."

"You're welcome." She gives me a sweet smile. "How was the podcast, by the way?"

My heart stutters at the question.

This is it.

I have to tell her.

I can do this.

Taking a deep breath, I brace myself.

"It was good. There's actually something I've—"

A loud, obnoxious as hell robotic beeping startles me, cutting me off. It's the ringtone Maya assigned to Ava's number.

"Shit, sorry," she apologizes, silencing the device. "You were saying?"

I shouldn't have eaten so much pasta. Suddenly, I feel like I may empty my stomach onto the table. Needing a minute to collect my thoughts, I nod toward her phone. "See what she wants, bean. You'll be stressed if you don't."

And I need a breather.

She huffs out a breath, her shoulders dropping. "Are you sure?"

"Yep."

As she listens to Ava's voicemail, I steal a sip of wine from her glass. A shot of tequila would do a lot more to bolster my courage, but I'll make do.

"Holy shit," Maya squeals, her lips curling up like flames.

"Ava got the internship. She's going to be in Boston this summer."

Fuck. Fuck. Fuck.

How am I supposed to tell her now? She won't want to take time off and stay with me in San Diego if her sister's here. And I sure as hell can't ask her to move there with me if she's never even seen the city. If my ask was selfish before, it's just plain cruel now.

"That's amazing," I say, my throat thick.

Maya chatters about all the fun things they'll do while her sister is in town. "And after the playoffs, when you have down-time, you can join us, of course. Anyway, you were talking about the interview. There was something you wanted to tell me?"

Not anymore.

"Cole? Are you okay?"

I muster a weak smile, all the words I prepared disappearing into the ether. "Yeah, just tired. Do you want to watch a movie?"

She studies me for a moment, her brows pinched, but she doesn't push me to say more. "Sure. I'll pick something out."

By the time I've boxed up the leftovers and put the plates in the dishwasher, Maya's pulled up *New Girl* on Hulu.

"This isn't a movie," I grumble.

"You need to give it a chance," she demands, breaking into a wide smile. "The fact that you don't like it makes me very concerned about your sense of humor."

"Fine, fine, fine."

I lie on the couch, pulling Maya's body against mine so we're both facing the TV. I most definitely won't focus with her ass nestled against my cock like this, but I wouldn't want it any other way. With her body pressed against mine, I don't bother keeping my hands to myself. I slip my left hand under her shirt and trace small circles around the soft skin of her stomach.

Eventually, I move upward, cupping her breasts and lightly thumbing her nipples.

"Cole." Her breathy tone makes my name sound like a plea rather than an admonishment.

I smile against the top of her head. "Shh. Pay attention, baby."

"The same goes for you."

"I am."

Just not to the TV show. Satisfied with the shallowness of her breathing and the way her head keeps lolling back against my chest, I test my luck, shamelessly tucking my hand inside her leggings and running my middle finger through the slick heat of her. I toy with her, my movements slow, never changing pace and avoiding her clit.

She whimpers, and when she pushes her legs apart in an attempt for more, I finally dip inside her. She gyrates her hips in response, trying to get my fingers deeper, but instead, I settle them over her clit.

"Watch the show, baby," I whisper. "And I'll give you what you want."

Without a word, she nods, her body relaxing a fraction. As the credits of a new episode appear on the screen, I rub small, steady circles against her. Tuning out the noise from the show, I focus solely on Maya's breathy whimpers and quiet moans. When I sense she's close, I gently pinch the swollen bud. In response, she explodes, her orgasm washing over her like hot water, her hips writhing against me as she rides out the wild waves of pleasure.

Done with the pretense of watching TV, I scoop her up and head to my room. She's languid as I lay her out on my bed, sated and drunk on her release, and her eyes are hazy as she watches me pull off my clothes and grab a condom.

Running a finger over her smooth skin, I wonder how I got so lucky. "You're fucking art, Maya."

I push into her with a long, languid stroke, burying myself deep. Tilting my hips back, I slide out so just my tip rests at her entrance. Then I slowly push back into her. Each move lights me up inside. But despite how desperate I am for her, I keep my pace unhurried, gentle. A dangerous guilt roars to life inside me as I use my body to remind her of how fucking good we are together. How right we are for one another. I fight against it, tamping it down.

Maya wraps her legs around my waist, her heels digging lightly into my lower back, allowing me to drive deeper and graze that sweet spot that always makes her gasp.

She murmurs my name like a prayer, and I moan. The sound of my name on her lips is almost enough to send me over the edge. She breathes it out like it's the only thing keeping her steady.

I press an open-mouthed kiss against her neck and latch on to the sensitive skin with my teeth. And as I swirl my tongue around the mark to ease the sting, she sucks in a harsh breath, though she instinctively tips her head back to expose more of her neck.

Her choked plea for more spurs me on, my hips snapping with more force, allowing me to thrust harder and deeper. I press my thumb against her already sensitive clit as I ramp up my pace, relishing the sound of our combined moans. There's nothing but heavy breathing, slick skin colliding, and whispered words of praise as the pit of fire in my lower belly flares.

Needing Maya to come again before I do, I scrape my teeth against her nipple. When she detonates, squeezing my dick tightly like I knew she would, I latch on to her breast and let go. The tingling in my spine turns into an explosion, releasing an uninhibited moan of satisfaction.

Chest still heaving, breaths still coming fast, I roll onto my back, taking Maya with me.

Eyes heavy lidded, she rests her chin on my chest and murmurs a sound of acquiescence.

"I love you."

It's through my lips and hanging in the air before I can process what I've said. This wasn't how I planned to tell her. I'd hoped the confession would be accompanied by roses, and I had no intention of doing it naked. But now that it's out there, I sink weightlessly into the words. They're true. Truer than anything I've ever known. Maya's my constant in a crazy world, a shining star my body responds to like it's my true north. I love her.

Her lips part and she sucks in a surprised breath. "Cole, I..." She trails off, eyes moving to my chest rather than my face.

I know she loves me, too. It's in the way she says my name and smiles at my touches. But knowing she isn't confident enough or comfortable enough to return the sentiment? Yeah. It hurts a little.

I paste an understanding smile on my face despite the small pit that's opened in my stomach. "You don't have to say it yet, Maya. It's okay."

She looks back up at me through thick lashes, her eyes fathomless pools. "I just need a bit more time. I'm sorry."

"There's nothing to be sorry for."

If either one of us has a reason to apologize, it's me.

CHAPTER TWENTY-NINE

THE FOOD in the glass case that stretches across one side of the space makes my mouth water the second I step into the deli. It's filled with everything from pastrami to roast beef. There are several Jewish delis between my apartment and here, but Goldblatt's makes the best-corned beef sandwich in existence, so it's more than worth the drive. As a bonus, I was certain the incessant ding of the cash register and the whirring blade of the meat slicer would help distract me from Cole's demeanor these past few days. It hasn't. Instead, it's background noise as I rehash every one of our interactions over the last week.

"Should I get a corned beef sandwich with Russian dressing on rye bread," Kennedy asks with downturned lips, "or smoked turkey with Swiss cheese and spicy honey mustard on farmhouse bread?"

"They both sound good," Sophie muses. "I think I'll get a tuna sandwich on gluten-free bread."

"You're not gluten-free."

"Thanks, Captain Obvious," Sophie chuckles. "I'm not, but I've had the gluten-free bread here before because Cameron's celiac, and honestly, I like it more than their regular brioche bun."

"Cameron is celiac?" Kennedy's eyes practically bug out of her head. "But then he couldn't have eaten my cake," she sputters, throwing her hands in the air.

"Eaten your cake? Is that a euphemism?" Sophie scrunches her nose. "Oh my God. Are you hooking up with my brother?"

"No, but I am concerned at how excited you seem by that idea," Kennedy says, her cheeks turning a violent shade of pink. She turns to me, clearly desperate for a change in topic. "What are you getting, My?"

I tear my gaze away from the nearby jars of pickles. "Oh, I haven't decided yet."

"What's going on with you?" she asks, elbowing me in the side. "You've been zoning out all morning."

"Nothing, I'm—"

"So help me..." She levels me with a glare. "If you say you're fine, I'm going to start singing 'Tits and Ass' from *A Chorus Line* at the top of my lungs."

I shudder at the second-hand embarrassment that would cause.

She taps her foot against the worn vinyl floor, focus still fixed on me. "Well?"

"Cole told me he loved me," I blurt out, voice shaky. "And I literally just stammered the word 'I' and looked at him with dumb fucking Bambi eyes."

"Okay," Kennedy says, drawing out each syllable. "At least you didn't thank him. That would've been way worse."

I huff out a laugh, though nerves still riot in my belly. "True. But now he's acting sort of distant and preoccupied. He promises he's fine and we're good, but I can't help but think that's not the case."

Sophie plucks a bag of potato chips from a nearby rack as

we all shuffle a couple of feet forward in line. "It's probably because of the trade, not you. I wouldn't worry too much."

My heart stops as her words register. "Trade?"

Sophie looks from Kennedy to me, her eyes widening. "Wait, did he not tell you?"

"Tell me *what*?" I ask as the cashier hollers, "Next!"

Eyes now shining with sympathy, she bites on her lower lip. "He's being traded to the San Diego Devils."

The cashier shouts again, this time louder, but I don't move. I couldn't even if I wanted to. My mind spins like an out-of-control circus monkey and my face heats as I try to fend off tears. Happiness—for Cole, because the Devils are his dream team, his hometown team—wars with the hurt that comes with realizing he didn't deem me important enough to trust with this information. Because this move will undoubtedly affect our relationship.

A hand taps against my cheek. It's not a slap, but it's definitely not a gentle pat either. But it does the trick, knocking me out of my catatonic stupor. Kennedy waves the group behind us to the cashier, claiming we need a minute.

"Why wouldn't he tell me?" I whisper, rubbing the center of my chest as if that'll help ease the sudden tightness there. "Isn't that the sort of thing you tell the person you claim to love?"

The worry etched on Sophie's face dissolves into empathy. "I'm so sorry. I thought you knew. The deal hasn't been finalized, but with all the rumors floating around, I was sure he would've talked to you by now."

The weight in my chest strengthens, making it hard to breathe. I may like hockey, but I like it because of Cole. I'm not a die-hard fan who tracks trades and strategies. I don't debate about how some left-short defenseman compares to a second-tier prospect or whatever. I simply watch Cole's games, cheer for him, and call it a night. And he knows this. He *knows* I'm far enough removed from the sport that I wouldn't have heard the rumors. God, I'm such a fucking idiot.

Sophie shuffles from one foot to the other. "I only know because I overheard Logan and your brother talking about it when I stopped by Cam's to return the vacuum I borrowed. I'm really sorry."

A humorless laugh bubbles out of me. "So my brother knew, too."

And also didn't think it was necessary to tell me. *Great.*

"If Cole hasn't told you, it's probably because he's—"

"I don't care why he didn't tell me." I cut her off, my voice shaky. "The point is that he didn't."

The sinking sensation in my stomach only grows the longer I process the information. The indifference that usually settles over me like a long-lost friend who's been waiting in the shadows, ready to take center stage once again, is nowhere to be found. My mind and body seem determined to force me to feel every crack and fissure as my heart breaks. And it's *painful.*

How did I end up here once again? Opening up and trusting someone when I clearly had no business doing so. An old Mark Twain quote comes to mind: History doesn't repeat itself, but it often rhymes.

Kennedy places a supportive arm around my shoulders. "Let's order our sandwiches and brainstorm ways to make that grown man cry, okay? I have a rolling pin and lemon zester in my car, so we're off to a good start."

———

I push through the heavy doors of the Bobcats Community Ice Rink without a plan in mind. All I know is that I need to talk to Cole. Kennedy's suggestions would've ended with one of us in jail, and Sophie blames herself for my upset, so she wasn't much help. Though I'm a don't-kill-the-messenger kind of person, she faults herself for not telling me sooner. Kenn promised to smack some sense into her while I deal with *this*.

Today's practice is closed to the public, so the only noise besides my footsteps is the fast-moving blades of the players racing around the ink and a puck hitting the boards. Thankfully the security guard remembers me—probably from when I got knocked flat on my ass—and lets me through without issue.

I climb up the steps of the bleacher-style seating that faces the ice and sit on the cool, metal bench three rows up. Instantly, my attention is drawn to Cole, who's running practice shots with the team. Watching him is a punch to the gut, making my lungs constrict.

Does his team know? His coach? How many games does he have left with them before he leaves?

I close my eyes and focus on breathing, despite how painful it is. Breath in. Breath out. I'm not sure how many times I repeat this, but when my heart no longer feels like it's beating out of my chest, I open my eyes.

In that instant, as if choreographed, Cole notices me and slides to a perfect stop, a smile lighting up his face. He shouts to his coach, then hops out of the box and stalks toward me. All I want to do is curl up in a ball and cry, but I straighten my shoulders and walk back down the steps to meet him beside the plexiglass.

He grins at me, the signature tilt of his lips causing my knees to buckle. "Hey, baby. I didn't know you were coming to watch."

His cheeks are pink from exertion and the cool temperature inside the arena, making it so damn hard not to cup his face with my hands to warm him. "I'm not. I need to talk to you." I swallow past the lump in my throat. "Is there anything you want to tell me?"

Talk about ripping off the goddamn Band-Aid.

Frown lines bracket his mouth, concern flaring in his eyes as he takes in my defensive stance. He blinks, looking genuinely confused. "What do you mean?"

"Exactly what I said. Is there anything you want to tell me?"

He peers back at the ice, then focuses on me again, apprehension and confusion etched on his features. "Um, no. Not right now, anyway. Why? What's up?"

I nod, an ache settling deep in my bones. Why is it that no matter how hard I try, or how hard I love, I always end up getting hurt?

With a surprisingly steady voice, I say, "So you aren't being traded to the Devils?"

Panic flickers across his features, and he reaches for me.

With a shake of my head, I take a step back. Unless he wants to lose a hand, touching me is not in his best interest right now. Kennedy's waiting in the car with a pastry dough cutter, and she isn't afraid to use it.

"I was planning to tell you," he says, his face twisting into a grimace. He glances back at the ice, where a few of his teammates have stopped skating to watch us. "Can you stay until the end of practice? We need to talk about this, but I don't think now's the best time."

A brittle laugh escapes me. "When exactly is the best time, Cole? Clearly, it wasn't during the past few weeks, or even months. The conversation about season tickets didn't feel like the right time? How about when you told me you loved me?" My voice wobbles on those last words, but I keep my chin lifted. "Do you just need more time now so you can come up with an excuse about *why* you didn't tell me?"

"It wasn't like that, Maya. I tried to tell you—"

"I don't care that you tried. In the end, you had ample

opportunity, and you didn't. Even my own goddamn brother knew you were being traded before me."

He takes a step forward but doesn't attempt to touch me this time. "Don't be mad at Elliott. He overheard me on a call with my agent, and I asked him not to say anything to you until I figured out how to broach the subject."

"Oh my God." I shake my head, backing up another step. "And here I thought Logan had told him."

"Please trust me when I say I've wanted to tell you."

"Then why didn't you?"

"I was being selfish." He links his hands behind his head and paces two steps to my left, then turns and paces back. "I guess I just wanted things to stay how they were for as long as possible."

"And then what, Cole? You'd tell me the day before you packed up and moved across the country? Sounds like a great plan to me."

"No, I—fuck. I don't know."

I hug myself to ward off the chill of the rink. "Did you think I wouldn't be happy for you?"

His shoulders deflate. "No, that's not it at all, My."

"Because despite how fucking hurt I am"—I brush at a tear that's escaped down my cheek—"I'm still beyond happy for you. You're turning your dream into a reality. How can I not be happy for you?"

His face softens and he stops mid-stride. "I wasn't trying to keep this from you. I just didn't know how to tell you. I promise."

"It's been a matter of days since you promised you'd never lie to me, yet you were actively keeping this from me. So why should I believe you? I gave something to you that I haven't given anyone in a really long time." My heart is already in pieces, but forcing this truth out shreds it even further. "I gave you my trust. And you broke that. And what's worse? You clearly didn't trust me, either."

"I didn't lie," he says, his eyes imploring. "I just hadn't told you yet. There's a difference."

I break into a sardonic smile. "Do you know how often I heard that growing up? Do you know how many times my mom avoided telling me something so she could sidestep responsibility? It may not be the same as outright lying, but it sure as fuck feels the same in here." I splay a hand over my heart.

"I'm sorry, Maya." Cole moves toward me again, but this time I can't back up, my limbs too heavy to move. He wraps me in an all-encompassing hug. "Don't run away from this. From *us*. Please."

"There's no need for me to run." I blink in an effort to hold back more tears. "You're already gone."

"Berrett!" one of the assistant coaches yells. "Save the lovey-dovey shit for later. We're in the middle of practice."

A few of his teammates whistle catcalls and make kissing noises, completely oblivious to the true nature of our conversation.

He heaves out a sigh. "I'll come over later and we can finish talking, okay?"

I shake my head and back away from his embrace. "I need some time."

And by time, I mean a bottle of wine, a shoulder to cry on, and a fuck ton of Kennedy's homemade cinnamon rolls.

Cole opens his mouth to argue, but the shrill sound of his coach's whistle stops him. "Fine. I'll call you. I love you, Maya. Nothing will change that."

I wait until my back's turned before letting the tears clouding my vision fall down my cheeks.

CHAPTER THIRTY

Hi! You've reached Maya's voicemail. I'm sorry I can't come to the phone right now, but if you leave your name, number, and a short message, I'll get back to you as soon as I'm done reading my book. Thanks! Bye.

I DIDN'T EXPECT Maya to answer what feels like my hundredth call anyway, but a guy can dream. I can recite every word of her voicemail greeting backward at this point. I get it. I fucked up. Rather than trusting her with news about the trade —trusting in *us*, believing that we could figure it out—I kept her in the dark.

Every time it was on the tip of my tongue, something would happen that would make me want to keep things as they were for a moment longer. Because I'm not just leaving her, but a city I've grown to love, a team that was there for me and kept me going when my brother passed, and a new role as their captain.

Goose cuts into the silence, barking sharply. Though he doesn't leave his spot by the window, he looks over his shoulder to ensure I've heard him. I'm sure the whole neighborhood has.

My dog's got a set of pipes on him. He throws his head back and yowls again, then finally runs to the front door.

"Goose." With a sigh, I heave myself off the couch. "C'mon, buddy. It's just a squirrel."

It's a miracle I hear the doorbell over his howling. Hunched forward, I check the peephole, and when I see my baby sister standing there with a suitcase, I stumble back a step.

"Darby?" I mutter as I yank the door open. "What the fuck?"

Goose runs in tight circles around her until she squats to pet him. "A simple hello would've sufficed, but a 'what the fuck?' works, too, I suppose."

"Hello," I chuckle, looping my arms around her. "Did you just get in? What are you doing here?"

"Seriously?" She drags her suitcase over the threshold, smacking my hand away when I attempt to help. "I texted you a reminder two days ago."

I rack my brain for a minute before I recall the memory. *Darby. Annual Northeast Dental Conference. Staying with me for a night.* "Shit. It's been a week from hell, and it completely slipped my mind. I'm sorry. The guest room's clean, though, so you're good to sleep in there."

She gives me an exasperated laugh. "Isn't it the middle child who's usually forgotten about, not the youngest? Such bullshit."

I tug Goose to my side so he stops head-butting Darby's thighs. "Want me to order dinner?"

"Nah." She shakes her head. "But I would like a glass of that 2006 zinfandel you keep for special occasions after I shower."

With that, she's gone. I'm not sure whether it's a younger sister thing or just a Darby trait, but she doesn't take no for an answer. I swear she could talk her way onto an international flight without a passport if she put her mind to it. I have no doubt she'll convince me to have a glass with her, even though I have to be at practice early tomorrow, so I cut straight to the punchline, take out a bottle of wine, and pour two glasses.

While I wait for her to return, I join Goose on the couch, sinking into the soft, leathery seat. This wine cost more than I'd ever admit, but rather than savor the taste, I take a large mouthful like it's Gatorade. With nothing better to do since Maya won't speak to me, and because I've ignored them for the past two days, I scroll through the messages the guys sent in our group chat after Maya showed up at practice. Cameron and Jake's texts are sympathetic, but Logan's contain emojis that get increasingly more aggressive. The last one he sent includes an eggplant, a knife, and an upside-down smiley face.

Darby, now wearing pajamas and a relaxed smile, grabs the other glass of wine from the coffee table and joins me on the couch. "Mmm. Thank you."

"That was the quickest shower in history. Did you even use soap?"

She gives me a dirty look over the rim of her drink. "When you grow up with three older siblings who monopolize the bathroom, you get into the habit of showering quickly."

A small smile ghosts over my lips. "Funny."

"You've made some changes to the place," she comments, cozying up next to Goose. "It looks nice."

I survey the space. My bookcase now boasts a few current titles in addition to the aesthetically pleasing books I've never read. A Polaroid photo of Goose lying on Maya's lap hangs on the fridge, and an extra e-reader charger is draped along the counter next to the blender. "Yeah, I guess so."

She takes a sip of wine and studies me, wearing an all-knowing expression that's frighteningly similar to our mom's. "What's going on?"

I'm tempted to pretend nothing's going on, but I don't have the energy. "The Bobcats are trading me to the Devils."

Darby's dark brows hit her hairline and she heaves herself forward. "Oh shit. Wait, why? You're their best player."

"They didn't initially want to, but the Devils approached them, and if they accept, it'd clear up cap space for some new prospects."

"It's not a done deal?"

I shake my head and pick at an imaginary piece of lint on my sweats. "The plan was a three-way trade, but it didn't pan out. Mark says the Devils are close to securing something else, but he doesn't know the details."

"Damn. I had dinner with Mom and Dad last week and they didn't tell me any of this."

I twirl the stem of the glass between my pointer finger and thumb. "Probably because I haven't told them yet."

She sucks in a breath. "Back that ass up. You haven't told Mom and Dad that you're moving *home*? You didn't, I don't know, think that was something they'd want to know?"

Head lowered, I rough a hand over my jaw. "Maya didn't even know until two days ago."

"How'd she take it?"

"Considering it wasn't me she heard it from?" I lock eyes with my sister. "Not too well."

Her mouth compresses into a tight line. "You didn't tell your *girlfriend* you were traded? To a team across the country? That's —well, fuck—that's about the stupidest thing you could do. Or not do, I guess. Why are you keeping this so hush-hush?"

Avoiding her gaze, I focus on the framed photo of Maya and me on the end table. She gave it to me on Valentine's Day. It's the one that the helicopter company insisted we take after our skyline tour. In it, we're both wearing ridiculously wide smiles. "I guess because telling people makes it more real."

"And that's a bad thing because..." She trails off, head tilted like she's trying to read my mood.

"It's not. It's just—fuck. I don't know, okay? I don't know what I want."

It's the first time I've admitted it aloud, and it feels like a weight's been lifted off my chest. But alongside that comes the grief and guilt.

Goose rests his chin on my thigh as if he knows I need the comfort. Scratching behind his ear, I take a swig of wine. "Do you remember when Mom and Dad got Nate and me skates for our birthday?"

"Oh, I remember." She rolls her eyes. "I stole Nathan's and turned them into houses for my Barbies. He told me if I ever touched his skates again, he'd hide all my dolls."

I can't help but laugh. Nate was always territorial about his gear. At some point, he wouldn't even let Mom wash his jerseys. "Sounds like him. I have those skates, you know, if you want them. Make a dollhouse for your own kids one day or something."

A smile springs to her lips. "Thanks, Cole. That'd be nice."

I nod, coughing to get rid of the knot in my throat. "Anyway, we made a pact that we'd make it pro and play for the Devils one day. And then, as we got older, we figured we had our whole careers to make it happen. But then he passed, and now there's only me."

Darby leans over and gives my arm a squeeze. "You're not alone, Cole. You have us, and your teammates and friends, and—"

"I know, Darbs. What I mean is that it's only me to see our dream through. And suddenly, I'm being given the opportunity, but rather than shout from the rooftops with joy, I'm confused."

"Take Nathan out of the picture. Do you *want* to play for the Devils?" She rests her elbows on her thighs and leans forward. "I thought you realized this, but Nathan's no longer around to hold you to your end of the deal."

I sputter, causing wine to drip down my chin and onto my shirt. "Christ, Darby. Way to be callous."

She sticks her wine-stained tongue out at me. "My therapist says that using humor to deal with loss is healthy. And considering how much I pay her, I'll take her word for it." She settles into the cushion again. "What I'm trying to say is that Nathan wouldn't hold it against you if you made the best decision for *you*. You may be twins, but you were still two completely different people. There are plenty of ways to honor him that don't involve playing for the team you worshipped as kids."

I stroke the top of Goose's snout. "I'm not tattooing his name onto my ass."

"I drunkenly suggested that *once*," she huffs. "And I mean that you can honor him by living your life the way *you* want to. Play for the Bobcats, or the Penguins, or the Stormhawks, or whoever. But play for them because *you* want to. Not because once upon a time, you and Nathan wanted to. People grow up, Cole. They're allowed to grow out of dreams, too."

My hand falls still on Goose's head as her words hit me. They hit me harder and faster than any opponent on the ice ever has. And I've broken quite a lot of bones. "When'd you get so smart, kid?"

"I'm telling you, man. My therapist knows her shit. If you do end up moving to San Diego, I'm more than happy to send you her number, but I don't think you'll move."

"Why not?"

"Because San Diego hasn't felt like home to you for a long time." She eases the truth of her words with a lopsided smile. "Which I'm okay with, because if you move back, you'll cockblock me until I die alone with all my cats."

I only planned to have a small glass of wine, but on second thought, maybe I need one more.

CHAPTER THIRTY-ONE

"GO AWAY. I'M NOT HOME."

My raw throat protests as I shout at the door, but that's what happens after crying on and off for a day. I'm not typically a crier, but once I got started, it was like Niagara Falls and a water park coalesced in my tear ducts. Sophie gave me a couple of packages of under-eye patches that contain hyaluronic acid and caffeine to "depuff my marshmallow eyes," but I'm still a splotchy, red-hot mess with a scratchy voice.

Despite my demand, the knocking persists. Knocking is a generous description, considering it's Elliott. On a normal day, the way he pounds on the door sounds like someone's launching cannonballs at my apartment.

"What part of *go away* was not clear to you, Elliott?" I call out. "I'm mad at you. That means I'm allowed to ignore you."

I hate arguing with my siblings, but Elliott keeping Cole's secret from me? What the hell happened to sisters—and brothers—over misters?

Elliott lets out a long breath and knocks again. "Maya, answer the door. If I don't give Ava proof that you're okay, she's going to jump on a plane and fly here herself. And as much as we'd both love to see her, she's got a midterm in a few days, so—"

I stomp to the door and throw it open. "What do you want —Oh."

Kennedy flashes me one of her signature smiles. The kind that makes it difficult to be annoyed by the intrusion. *And* she's holding a Tupperware filled with something chocolatey, which definitely tempers my ire.

I lean against the doorframe in a sad attempt to block them from coming in. "Is this an intervention?"

"No, but based on the state of your apartment, I'm wondering if it should be." She peers around me, eyeing my space. The once neat piles of books divided by genre and trope are now scattered across the floor in a haphazard manner.

Did I kick a pile of books in frustration? Maybe. Did that pile then knock over another pile, which caused a domino effect? Most likely. Did it make me feel better? Absolutely.

As I tie my hair back into a ponytail, I glare at them. "What are you doing here?"

"Making sure you're not so deeply enmeshed in a book that you've forgotten to shower or sleep." Kennedy shrugs. "And your brother wasn't sure you'd let him in, so I came as backup."

She walks right past me and into my kitchen, with Elliott hot on her heels.

Sighing, I close the door behind me. Apparently being left alone to process my feelings is too much to ask for. At least Cole's graduated from calling and is now sticking to texts. I finally gave in and responded, but only to say that we'd talk after his game this weekend. He replied by sending me romantic quotes from my favorite books.

I shuffle into my kitchen wearing a frown despite being overwhelmed by the scent of fresh brownies. "Seriously. What are you doing here?"

Elliott answers by locking me in a bear hug that's impossible to wiggle out of. Trust me, I try. After ten seconds of squirming, I begrudgingly relax into the embrace.

"I hate it when you're mad at me, Yaya."

"Then don't do things that make me mad," I grumble against his chest.

Snorting, he tugs at the end of my ponytail. "I didn't touch alcohol or smoke weed until college because I was scared of making you mad."

Kennedy huffs a laugh from where she's sitting on my counter, her long legs dangling over the edge. "Being on the receiving end of your death glare sucks."

It takes a lot to make me mad—truly, deeply mad—but when a person does, I don't half-ass it. I go full passive-aggressive, with the accompanying side-eye and bitchy tone. I'm not proud of it, but we all have our flaws.

Elliott loosens his hold on me, and I take a step back, ensuring I'm out of random hug-attack range. Kennedy dips into the Tupperware and holds a brownie out to me, but I shake my head.

"Are you here to apologize?" I ask my brother, arching a brow at him.

He sighs heavily. "No, I'm here to explain myself."

That takes the wind out of my sails. "So you're *not* sorry?"

"Sounds like a line from a Taylor Swift song," Kennedy giggles, licking chocolate from her fingers. "But I digress."

"Am I sorry that keeping the information to myself inadvertently hurt you? Yes, of course. You're my big sister and I hate seeing you upset. But not telling you was in your best interest."

I throw my hands up. "How the hell can you say that not telling me my boyfriend's being traded and moving across the country is what's best for me?"

"If I'd told you without giving Cole a chance to talk to you himself, you would've cut your losses and run." His eyes soften in a way that has always made it hard to be upset with him. "You'd swear it couldn't work, citing every excuse in the book, when really, you're scared. You hate change, Ya. I'm not blaming you, because God knows you have every reason to, but sometimes change is good."

Too caught off guard by the depth of what he's saying to come up with a snarky response, I merely say, "Well, Cole didn't tell me himself, so…"

Real fucking mature, Maya.

Elliott shrugs. "He fucked up on that account, but I genuinely think it was because he didn't know how to tell you. His reasons for hiding it from you weren't malicious. It's no different from when you failed to mention to anyone that you got a scholarship to Northwestern."

Kennedy sputters, sending brownie debris flying.

I'm too shocked by my brother, once again, to protest at how gross that is. The *only* person who knew I got a full ride to Northwestern was Kennedy, and I made her swear on her love for the original cast of *Wicked* that she'd never tell anyone.

"What?" I stammer, my chest tightening, making it hard to breathe. "I don't—I mean—that has nothing to do with this."

"Oh, yes, it does." Elliott crosses his arms over his chest. "You kept that admissions letter tucked away in a drawer because you *knew* Ava and I would feel guilty that you turned it down so you could stay close to us. And you were right. It kills me that you gave up your dream because there was no one else to look after us. But you did what you thought was best, and I don't blame you for that. I hate you a little for it, sure, but your intentions were pure."

"So this was you doing what you thought was best for me?"

He shrugs, suddenly looking more like a sheepish kid than my adult brother. "I guess, yeah."

I exhale through my nose and give a slow nod. It'd be hypocritical of me to stay upset with him, given all I've hidden over the years in an attempt to make his life easier. That doesn't necessarily make it *right*, but I made a judgment call, the same as he did.

"When did you grow up and get so—"

"Intelligent? Thoughtful? Remarkable?"

It takes effort to keep my eyes narrowed when the urge to chuckle is so strong. "I was going to say frustratingly logical."

With a grin, he swipes a brownie from Kennedy and pops the entire thing into his mouth. "You have to talk to him, Yaya. You can't stay holed up in your book cave forever."

My body sags. "I don't even know what to say to him at this point," I admit, rubbing my brow. "I didn't even know a trade was on the table, let alone a very real possibility. He blindsided me."

"I'd like to preface this by saying I'm not choosing sides," Kennedy says. "I'm just playing devil's advocate... no pun intended." She eyes me, silently making sure I'm listening. "Imagine you meet this amazing guy. The two of you fall in love, and then you find out that your favorite author wants to co-write a book with you. But in order to do so, you have to move to Los Angeles for an unknown amount of time. Maybe one year, maybe five. You have no idea."

She pops another piece of brownie into her mouth and wipes the crumbs off the front of her shirt.

"How would you tell your boyfriend that? Especially when his whole life—his family, his friends, the job he loves—are all *here*? And on top of that, he's skittish about relationships and change in general."

God, empathy's a fickle bitch.

Because when she puts it that way? Yeah. I understand

where Cole's coming from. But that doesn't make it hurt any less.

Kennedy studies my face for a thoughtful moment. "*Do* you love him?"

"Yes."

There's no hesitation in my answer. I wholeheartedly love Cole. Even though he didn't tell me about his trade, and even though he's moving to San Diego.

I love his dedication and his drive. The way he cares. The crinkles next to his eyes when he laughs. The soft smile he wears when I talk about a book. I love how passionate he is about hockey and how earnestly he supports my quest to find my own passion. There's no world, fictional or real, in which I'm not enamored by Cole Berrett. I think about him more times in a day than I'd ever care to admit.

He's better than any book boyfriend I've ever had.

But unlike the fictional men who live between the pages of my favorite romances, Cole's real. And he's mine.

Kennedy tilts her head back and drops the last piece of her brownie into her mouth. "Okay, cool."

I rear back. "That's it? *Okay, cool?* You're not going to ask any follow-up questions?"

She has the audacity to frown at me, as if she's offended that I'd expect her to do that, even though we both know she totally would. "I've been friends with you for over twenty years, Maya. You take things at your own pace, but once you're in, you're all in. Now you just have to figure out how to tell him that."

As I survey the pile of romance books that now decorate the floor behind my couch, a slow grin pulls at my lips. Because I have the perfect idea. "How would you feel about me getting back on the ice?"

CHAPTER THIRTY-TWO

PLEXIGLASS SHUDDERS as I'm slammed into it for the third time in as many minutes. At the sound of a whistle, I whirl around, taking my gloves off and tossing them onto the ice. We've been playing 3-v-3 games during practice, but based on Logan's behavior, the rules have changed, and it's now 5-v-me.

"What the hell is your problem?" I shove him in the chest. "Why the fuck are you cross-checking me? I'm on your team."

"You won't be on my team for much longer, though, will you?" He smiles, but there's no warmth behind it. "And you hurt Maya, which upset Elliott, which, in turn, upsets me. Get it?"

I level him with an unamused look. "One, I turned down the trade. Two, I—"

He tackles me like we're playing fucking football, taking me down to the ice, where my arm is quickly pinned beneath my side. *Christ.* It's been a while since someone knocked me on my ass outside of a fight during a game. It takes a second to regain my senses, and only when Coach Henderson blows his whistle repeatedly does Logan back off a fraction.

"Ten-minute break," Coach yells. "Clark! Control yourself, God dammit. This isn't a fucking gymnastics floor routine."

Logan grins down at me, his blond hair flopping against his forehead. "You mean it? You're really staying?"

"Dude," I groan. "Get off me. You weigh a fuck ton."

A crease appears between his brows. "I *knew* you were lying to me when you said my jersey didn't make me look fat."

Using my one free arm, I shove him with all my strength. As he rolls onto his back, he lets out a whoop that reverberates around the rink. I push back onto my skates and wipe off the ice shavings scattered across my gear.

The rest of the team cools down with water or stretches, but Cameron and Jake skate to where Logan's still sprawled on the ice and haul him to his feet.

"What the hell is going on?" Cameron asks, lifting his goalie's mask.

"Captain Cole is staying." Logan breaks into a triumphant grin. "He says he'd miss me too much to ever leave and—"

I toss my glove at his face. "Not true."

Jake takes off his helmet, shaking his sweaty hair out. "You waived your no-movement clause for the trade?"

"No, I'm staying," I amend, the heavy weight on my chest for the past few weeks completely lifted. "But the reason has nothing to do with Logan."

"Maya?" he guesses with a smug smile.

I shake my head. "Not her either."

If I factored Maya into my decision, I worried that there could be a chance I'd eventually resent her because of it. And that wouldn't be fair to either of us. Rather than live with that kind of what-if hanging over me, I made this choice for me and me alone. Not for Maya or Nathan or anyone else.

Cameron's lips twitch into an almost smile. "Happy you're not leaving us. How pissed is your agent?"

I cringe at the memory of that conversation. "He respects my decision, but I can't say he's happy to have spent the past few weeks working on a trade that's now irrelevant."

"He gets what? Five percent of your salary?" Cameron snorts. "He'll be fine."

"Plus, you give great holiday gifts," Logan adds.

With a grunt, Jake hits his stick against the ice to focus our attention. "What was the deciding factor?"

"My contract's up in two years. Maybe I'll feel differently then, but I'm happy where I am now. The team still has a lot of work to do, and I want to be part of our success story."

"Can you work on Logan's anger management first?" Cameron asks, poking the Canadian bear.

Jake nods. "Or work on his speed? He's been slow as hell with the puck during face-off."

"Oh, fuck you both," Logan whines. "Jake, you spend more time checking out my ass than checking on the opposition. And Cameron? You're a little *too* good on your knees, if you know what I mean. You getting extra practice?"

With a sharp breath in, I wait for the arguing to ensue. As much as their bickering fuels my daily headaches, I'd miss it if I played for another team.

"Berrett!" Coach Henderson shouts. "Stop lollygagging and get your ass over here."

Grateful for the excuse to bow out of playing referee, I skate toward the bench, where Coach is poring over a page on his clipboard. "What's up?" I ask, arms resting against the boards.

"Rockwell called me this morning," he says. If he spoke to the Bobcats general manager, then the implication is clear.

Internally, I wince. I'm not sure how in the loop he was about a possible trade with the Devils, but surely management gave him a heads-up.

He looks up from the clipboard, his expression impossible to read. "How are you feeling?"

"I'm feeling really good," I admit with a nod. "It was the right decision for me. I'm not saying I'll never be up for a trade. That's just how hockey is. But I want to finish out the rest of my contract with the Bobcats. Maybe more. You and the team believe in me enough to let me wear the captain's *C*, and I know there's a lot more I can offer the team."

He finally looks up from his clipboard. "While I appreciate the explanation, I meant how are you feeling about the game tomorrow? Rockwell and the other higher-ups are confident, but I wanted to check in with you."

"Oh." My face heats. *Well, now I feel fucking stupid.* "We're ready."

"The team feels confident about our new breakout tactic?"

My lips tip up at the words *our*. "Mm-hmm."

Coach Henderson tilts his clipboard so I can see the simplified tactic we'll be employing in the game tomorrow, then finishes our conversation by blowing his whistle, nearly piercing my eardrum in the process.

The team gathers on the ice where we go through drill after drill until our bodies scream for reprieve. I've never been a fan of ice baths—what kind of monster enjoys having their balls curl up into their abdomen?—but by the time we're done, I crave the way it'll soothe my muscles.

Logan swings his arm around me as we head into the locker room. "Do you have a firework guy?"

I shrug him off. "Do I have a firework guy?"

"Yeah." He rolls his eyes. "A guy who does fireworks. You know? Those things that go *kaboom* in the sky and send pretty, sparkly lights raining down?"

"I know what fireworks are. I just don't understand why

you'd think I, of all people, would ever have a fucking firework guy on call."

"No need to be snappy about it," he huffs as we head into the tunnel. "It was just a question."

I take a long swig of my water and wipe my face with my sleeve. "Well, the answer is no, I don't have a firework guy."

He swears under his breath. "Okay. Then do you have a plan for how we're going to win Maya back?"

I arch a brow, even as my heart rate ticks up. "We?"

He wiggles his eyebrows. "We're teammates, aren't we?"

CHAPTER THIRTY-THREE

MY BODY VIBRATES against the plastic stadium seating as the first game of the playoff season begins. My nerves have nothing to do with how the Bobcats will play. I have no doubt they'll kick ass. It's because, in eighteen minutes and thirty-four seconds, it'll be me on that ice instead of the players.

"Are you sure this is a good idea?" Kennedy asks for the tenth time since she showed up at my apartment to ride with me to the arena. "You have the coordination of a baby with vertigo and bruise like a ripe banana."

My head spins just a little. "I'm absolutely not sure that this is a good idea."

"Is it too late to back out? I feel like a sloppy blowjob could be just as effective. And possibly even more appreciated."

The older couple in front of us turns around in abject horror, and I cover my face with my hands. But rather than sink into her seat with embarrassment, Kennedy tosses a handful of popcorn into her mouth and smiles daringly at them.

"You'll be fine," Sophie reassures me with a broad smile. "The ice won't be as slippery after it gets chewed up by skates. Just walk like a penguin."

Kennedy, who's already focused on the game again, turns our way. "Isn't the phrase *walk like an Egyptian?*"

Sophie sits straighter, making her plastic chair creak. "You don't know the penguin song?"

Kennedy and I exchange a confused look. *The penguin song?* "Definitely not."

"When things look kind of icy, and the path ahead is dicey," she sings, "walk like a penguin. Keep your toes pointed straight, and short steps for your gait. Walk like a penguin." Shaking out her arms, she goes on. "Make sure your limbs are loose, so you don't fall on your caboose... and walk like a penguin."

For a moment, Kennedy and I look at her in stunned silence, but in perfect synchronicity, we burst into laughter. And not simple "ha ha, funny" laughter. No, it's shoulder-shaking, uncontrollable, thigh-slapping laughter that continues until tears stream down our faces.

"Oh God, Sophie," Kennedy gasps, swiping at her eyes. "Who taught you that?"

"I took skating lessons as a kid," she huffs. "You'll be thanking me when it stops you from falling on your butt."

I bump my shoulder against hers. "You mean my caboose, right?"

She narrows her eyes at me, but when the crowd breaks into cheers, she whips around and scans the ice.

The Jumbotron lights up, and *Berrett Scores* flashes in capital letters. All around us, fans yell like their lives depend on it. I don't know how athletes can play in such a noisy setting. My stage fright could never.

I force my body to face the ice so I don't miss anything else and let myself get lost in the excitement of the game. As expected, the Bobcats dominate the first period. Whatever they ate for breakfast was clearly packed with a serving of kick-ass-and-take-names, because *damn.* Even Logan is on his best behavior. Could be a tactic, and if so, it's working. Since the first puck drop, the opposing team has seemed confused by his lack of asinine comments and fighting.

A few minutes before the period ends, Sophie and Kennedy walk with me to the area behind the Bobcats' goal. A group of young teenage boys are gathered nearby, roughhousing and laughing.

As I take them in, it dawns on me that they're likely the other game contestants. "I think I'm the only one—"

"With tits?" Kennedy snorts. "I was thinking the same thing."

I scan the space, desperately searching for an elderly lady or middle-aged man. "Are we in the right spot?"

"This is where Cameron said the intermission game contestants are supposed to gather." Sophie takes in our surroundings and points at a woman wearing a Bobcats polo standing nearby. "But maybe we should ask someone."

Awkwardly, I approach the woman, noting her clipboard and walkie-talkie. "Um, hi. Is this the right spot for the intermission game contestants? I wanted to make sure, because it looks like it's just me and—"

"The Cubs."

"The Cubs," I repeat dumbly. "Uh…" I scratch at my jaw and glance back at my friends. "Who are the Cubs?"

Her lips stretch into a sympathetic smile. "A midget team in the Bobcats' youth league. You must be Maya. We don't usually pair individual fans with junior league players, but Cameron Davies specifically requested that you participate in the first game."

Only because my dumb ass requested that so I wouldn't have to wait two full periods before getting out on the ice. The anticipation alone would've killed me.

"A midget team?" Kennedy mumbles behind me.

"Registered teams play in different classifications," Sophie explains, fighting back a laugh. "Sixteen years old and younger are considered midgets."

"You've got to be fucking kidding me," I mumble. I'm facing my biggest fear by playing a game against baby hockey players. *Lovely.* Talk about setting myself up for success.

The period ends with the Bobcats up by one, and the moment they leave the ice to do their team pep talks or whatever, the announcer's voice booms over the loudspeaker.

"Ladies and gentlemen," he calls, making the whole arena rumble. "While the players cool off, we're going to let things heat up out here on the ice with a game of *musical chairs*!"

My stomach drops. *Oh, you've got to be motherfucking kidding me.*

"Showtime, baby," Kennedy sings as she rubs her hands together. "Break a leg."

I shoot her a glare as a Bobcats employee herds me and the five Cubs onto the ice. Though I'll never admit it to her, Sophie's catchy penguin song runs through my head, helping me stay on my feet. I clench and unclench my fists as I go, my breaths quick and shallow. The announcer's voice fades into white noise as I focus on taking small stomp-like steps to the center of the rink.

The Bobcats' mascot high-fives us as we form a circle around the chairs, the force of the greeting almost enough to send me toppling. Somehow, I stay upright and once again focus on breathing. *Deep breath in, deep breath out.*

As I chant the reminder, I scan the stands, taking in the *thousands* of people with their attention glued to the game. Why the hell could anyone think that imagining a crowd of people in their underwear will help with stage fright? The idea alone makes me feel awkward and uncomfortable, and with the fear already lodged in my chest, I don't need another emotion to battle right now.

A rock song flows through the speakers to start the game, our cue to move, so with a steadying breath, I take a step forward. *Here goes nothing.* Shoulders pulled back, I walk around the perimeter of the chair circle. Scratch that; the other players walk. What I do is similar to how I'd walk if my tampon was at risk of falling out. It's a half-waddle-half-hop situation.

With very careful, controlled steps, I make it a quarter of the way around before the Cubs player behind me power walks right on past. It's a circle, so it's not like he's going to get to the finish line any quicker, but whatever. To keep from being distracted, I focus on pacing myself, but just as I've found a rhythm, the music cuts off.

Naturally, I get nowhere close to finding an empty chair. Instead, I get knocked over by two Cubs as they wrestle for the seat closest to me. No penguin can help me as one of the boys throws his arm back and elbows me in the boob, knocking me off balance and straight onto my ass.

Okay. Fucking ow.

The plus side? I didn't smack my head this time. Though I can't say this is any less embarrassing than my last fall on a frozen surface. Flat on my back, I close my eyes and pray the ice will crack open and swallow me whole. My face is so red I'm sure I look like fucking Elmo. I think I'm officially done attempting to set foot on a hockey rink. From now on, no matter what, I remain on non-icy surfaces.

I haven't even considered how I might find my way to my feet when a comforting voice reassures me that he's got me and hands slip under my arms and haul me up. On instinct, I sink into the familiarity of Cole's touch, focusing on that rather than the thousands of eyes no doubt trained on the spectacle.

Popcorn sales are going to skyrocket after that theatrical performance.

Cole's hands lightly roam over my neck and arms, as if he's looking for injuries. The joke's on him, since the only thing hurt is my pride. When he's satisfied I'm not about to bleed out, he rests his hands on my waist to steady me.

I clutch the front of his jersey with both hands, the material cool against my skin. "Hi."

He grasps my shoulders and shakes me gently. "Christ, My. What are you doing? Trying to give me a heart attack?"

"Trying to be romantic," I admit, nibbling on my lower lip. With him in skates, I have to tip my head way, way back to make eye contact. "Did it work?"

He rubs at the stubble on his chin, his dark eyes warm despite the cool air. "Baby, help me out here. I'm not sure what part of being knocked over by a tween during musical chairs is supposed to be romantic."

Well, when he puts it that way...

Though the tween in question is wearing a jersey with his name on it, Cole hits him with a dangerous scowl. The kid's eyes widen, and he takes a step back, as if realizing beating me to the chair may not have been in his best interest.

I tug on his jersey, forcing his attention back to me. When his eyes meet mine, it hits me square in the chest like Cupid's arrow.

"I was taking a page out of one of my romance books," I admit, ducking to hide behind the collar of my jacket. "The whole grand gesture thing. I'm sure you saw it when you were stalking my *PagePulse*."

He chuckles, his eyes dancing. "This was definitely a grand gesture."

Once I've confirmed that he's got a good hold on me, I pop

up on my toes and loop my arms around his neck, then tug his body tight against mine. "Remember when we were at O'Leary's and you were teasing me about not liking attention?" I ask, my voice shaky and low. "And I said that the day I admit I'm in love with you is the same—"

"The same day you play one of the intermission games," he finishes, his features softening at the memory. "Wait." His grip on my hips tightens. "Does this mean..."

"I love you," I blurt out. "I'm sorry I didn't say it earlier. I think I've loved you since you bought that alien book. I was just scared. And honestly, I think I'll always be scared because you're the best thing that's ever happened to me, and the thought of losing you physically hurts."

With a long exhale, he brushes his thumb against my cheek. "You won't lose me, baby. I'm right here."

At any other time, a statement like that would make me melt into his arms. But I need to finish before I lose my nerve. "I need you to know that I meant it when I told you how happy I am for you. The Devils have always been your dream, and I fully support you. If that means..." I clear my throat. This part is tricky, because I'm working under the assumption that he'd want this, too. "If it means moving to San Diego so I can be there for you, then that's what I'll do." My breath leaves me in a rush. "I don't like the beach," I add, "or the mountains, or, honestly, the outdoors in general. But surely there are good coffee shops and less active activities in the area. I can find a job in another bookstore and write from wherever. I have every intention of taking advantage of your miles, though, so that my family can visit. But—"

In a classic Cole move, he shuts me up with a kiss. His lips are warm and familiar and comforting as he softly licks at the seam of my mouth.

Without hesitation, I grant him access, and as our tongues

glide against one another, a small moan from deep in his chest escapes.

I don't know how long we kiss, but eventually, the raucous cheering from the crowd pops the bubble we've found ourselves in.

Cole places his hands on my cheeks and smiles against my mouth. "As honored as I am to know you'd move to San Diego with me, there's no need. I turned down the trade. And before you panic, I made this decision for myself. It's what I want."

I open my mouth, ready to protest, but snap it shut again. Finally, I say, "But the Devils are your dream."

"They were the dream Nathan and I shared." He breaks into an earnest smile, tucking a stray piece of hair behind my ear. "But he's not here anymore, and my dreams have shifted. There are all kinds of ways to honor him that don't involve uprooting my life when my heart's not in it."

My body lights up with excitement, making me feel like I'm standing an inch off the ground. "Yeah?"

He gives a bashful shrug. "Yeah. Like falling in love, getting married, and eventually having a few kids who grow up begging to hear stories about how amazing their Uncle Nathan was."

I know I've made the right decision when the word *marriage* doesn't make me want to book the first flight to Spain and change my name.

I rake my fingers through the hair at his nape. "I like that idea."

"You have no idea what you do to me, Maya," he murmurs against my lips. "How consumed I am by you. How *desperately* in love with you I am."

"If you think I don't feel the same way about you, then you took a few too many hits to the head last period." I laugh, leaning against him. "For the first time in my life, I don't want to disappear into my books so I can live another person's love story. Because you're not only who I want, but who I *need*."

Cole picks me up by the waist and twirls me around. "You're stuck with me now, baby. I'm your happily ever after."

Face heating in the best way, I can't help but smile. He's only partially right. "You're my happily ever always."

COLE

Maya pops her head into the bathroom and rakes her eyes over my naked body. My cock perks up under her gaze, despite having been buried inside her less than an hour ago. It's a good thing my stamina on the ice extends to the bedroom as well.

"Something you need?" I tease from the shower as I rinse the soap from my body. "Or are you just here for the free show?"

Her head snaps up and a flush creeps over her cheeks, as if she's embarrassed that she's been caught ogling me. "Oh, um. Yeah. Sorry. It's safe for Goose to drink water out of the Stanley Cup, right? Google said that I could clean it with soap and water, so I did, but I wanted to make sure—"

The noise that comes out of my mouth sounds inhuman, and the way it echoes off the tile walls could easily burst an eardrum. "Please, tell me you're kidding, baby."

Her eyes widen and she takes a cautious step back. "Is that a no?"

I nearly fall on my ass scrambling out of the shower. *Jesus Christ.* Players have done weird shit with the Cup after winning —everything from using it as a cereal bowl to baptizing their babies in it—but I'm not one of those guys. It's a *trophy,* meaning it should be treated with the reverence and respect of one.

Letting my fucking dog use it as a water bowl? I'm never going to win a game again.

I'm wrapping a towel around my waist, stumbling all over myself, when Maya bursts into a fit of giggles. "It's not funny," I grit out. "You may not be a die-hard hockey fan, but—"

"Babe, chill. I'm just fucking with you," she says with a candy-sweet smile. "I'm staying a strict ten feet away from that thing."

My shoulders sag with relief. "You just wanted an excuse to check out my naked ass, didn't you?"

"No, but I do have something to show you." She gives me a secretive smile. "Come to the kitchen when you're done, okay?"

She disappears before I interrogate her about what she's got planned, so I dry off quickly and slip into a t-shirt and a pair of gym shorts, then head into the kitchen.

When I find Maya, she's at the table with Goose, who has somehow fit his large body between the legs of her chair. If he had to save one of us in a fire, it most definitely wouldn't be me. I swear I'm the third wheel, though I can't bring myself to be resentful. If anyone understands his affection for her, it's me.

As I shuffle closer, I glance into the entryway, where the Cup is on display. Reassured that it's untouched and unbothered, I sit beside Maya and give her my full attention. "What's up, baby?"

She beams at me. "I finished."

"Finished what?" I take her in, trying to decipher her comment, only now noticing the thick stack of papers piled in front of her. "Holy shit. You finished your book?"

She nods shyly, a pink hue flirting with the soft lines of her face. "It's only a first draft. I'm sure there's a ton of work to be done... but, yeah. I finished."

I plant a firm kiss against her lips. "That's amazing, bean. Congrats."

"And you get to read it before Brian," she adds with a teasing wink.

I don't bother to hide my satisfied grin. Brian may be her writing partner, but I'm the partner who truly matters. I slide the papers across the table, then straighten them in front of me and flip to the second page.

The first two words, centered near the middle of the page, make my throat go tight and heat prick at the backs of my eyes.

To Nathan.

"You're dedicating it to Nathan?" I choke out. Gratitude warms my heart until it's nearly beating out of my chest.

"Yeah... is that weird?" She peers at me from the corner of her eye. "I thought, well, this is my own way of honoring him. Without your brother, you wouldn't be the man I'm in love with, so I wanted to thank him somehow, even if it's only—"

I press my lips against hers. It's the only way I can express how damn much this means to me. My brother would've loved her.

"If I didn't know any better," she says when I finally release her, "I'd think you don't like how much I talk. You always seem to be hushing me up with a kiss."

"Maybe I just enjoy kissing you," I chuckle. "Thank you for showing me this, baby. We may have met on accident, but loving you? That's a choice I'll make every day for the rest of my life."

"I love you, too." She smiles against my lips. "And I'm totally using that line in my next novel because it's absolutely adorable."

Thank you for reading ICE ICE BABY! If you enjoyed Maya and Cole's story, please consider leaving a review or sharing it with your friends.

Want more Maya & Cole? Scan the QR code below for a bonus epilogue!

Stay up-to-date on all of my future releases by subscribing to my newsletter (www.carlyrobynauthor.com/newsletter) and following me on social media (@carlyrobynauthor).

acknowledgments

I can't start these acknowledgements without thanking the reason this book exists: you, the reader.

When I wrote my debut back in 2022, it was just a challenge to myself and I had no plans outside proving to myself that I could do it. I never expected what would come next. But I took a leap, hit publish, and because of you, I'm still here—years later—writing the stories and characters we've come to love.

Thank you for showing up, for reading, for believing. You've made it possible for me to live my dream every single day.

To Rachel and Mollie. One of the best parts of becoming an author has been making friends like you. There's no one else I'd rather leave rambling voice notes for or text unhinged thoughts to. Thank you for your friendship. I'm forever grateful for you.

To Valentine, my agent & publicist (or as I lovingly call you, my "momager"). You're a voice of reason when I'm spiraling and a vote of confidence when I'm faltering. Thank you for all that you do!

To Beth, my amazing editor. I genuinely don't know what I'd do without you. You help bring my words to life, my use of the word "fuck" at a minimum, and keep me at a socially acceptable amount of em-dashes and "well."

To Sahara, my hockey queen. Thank you for your endless support, hockey knowledge, and sharing a brain with me. I truly couldn't have done this without you, and I'm so glad I didn't have to.

Finally, to my parents. You may not fully understand this author world, but you're there for every step of it, supporting me endlessly, and I love you.

Drive Me Crazy

Drive Me Wild

Drive Me Home

Carly Robyn writes contemporary romances with heat, heart, and humor. When she's not writing or reading, you can find her spending time with her family, scrolling through TikTok, exploring Chicago's restaurant scene with friends, taking a million pictures of her dogs Quincy and Owen, or binge-watching anything true crime related while drinking a Diet Coke.

Follow her on social media for updates: @carlyrobynauthor.